KILLER

KUNG PAO

VIVIEN CHIEN

St. Martin's Paperbacks

This is a work of fiction. All of the characters, organizations, and events portrayed in this novel are either products of the author's imagination or are used fictitiously.

First published in the United States by St. Martin's Paperbacks, an imprint of St. Martin's Publishing Group.

KILLER KUNG PAO

Copyright © 2020 by Vivien Chien.

All rights reserved.

For information, address St. Martin's Publishing Group, 120 Broadway, New York, NY 10271.

www.stmartins.com

ISBN: 978-1-250-22830-7

Our books may be purchased in bulk for promotional, educational, or business use. Please contact your local bookseller or the Macmillan Corporate and Premium Sales Department at 1-800-221-7945, ext. 5442, or by email at MacmillanSpecialMarkets@macmillan.com.

Printed in the United States of America

10 9 8 7 6 5 4 3

For Lisa,
Thank you—to the moon and back.

ACKNOWLEDGMENTS

Thank you always to the following people:

My terrific agent, Gail Fortune, without whom I'd be lost; my amazing editor, Nettie Finn, who is invested in this journey as much as I am. I am so looking forward to the adventures ahead of us. To the fabulous Kayla Janas, Allison Ziegler, and Mary Ann Lasher, who make this series continue to shine; and to my publisher, St. Martin's Paperbacks, for having continual faith in my writing abilities. Your support and dedication to this series have been paramount. I am beyond fortunate to have such a wonderful team.

To Sisters in Crime, both locally and nationally, for all you provide to women in the mystery genre. And to the Crime Writers of Color for helping so many who felt misplaced finally feel like they have a home and a voice.

To my dad, Paul Corrao, who never stops believing in me; my mother, Chin Mei Chien, and my sister, Shu-Hui Wills. To the late Effie Corrao who I continue to miss on a daily basis. They have all in their own

ways guided me through this wacky thing called life. I wouldn't be the person I am today without their influence and guidance.

To my amazing friends and family who keep the cheerleading and positivity flowing. I can't thank you enough.

To my readers, whose enthusiasm and encouragement to keep this series going mean more to me than words can express.

And lastly, but certainly never least, to Hannah Braaten. It was my great privilege to work with you as we watched this series develop and grow from those first shaky pages to completed manuscripts. Not only do I thank you, but Lana thanks you as well. You will be missed among the plaza of Asia Village and all its crazy characters.

CHAPTER
1

"Lana Lee, you're the only person in this world who would *choose* to dye their hair gray," my sister, Anna May said, scrutinizing the photo of a sassy model with the hair color I wanted for myself. I had been carrying the picture around in my purse for inspiration. "Are you sure this is a good idea?"

"First of all, it's not just any gray," I replied, grabbing the photo out of her hand. "It's gunmetal gray. And second, of course it's a good idea. It's gonna be my best hair yet." I ran a hand through my pink peekaboo highlights. The color was beginning to fade, and I was tired of keeping up with one of the weakest colors in the rainbow.

"I don't know why you can't just leave your hair alone. You've been on this bizarre hair-dyeing kick for a while now. Don't you want to give it a rest before you damage your follicles any further?" Anna May, who was slightly older and much more reserved than me, tucked a lock of smooth, glossy black hair behind her ear, exposing a dainty pearl-drop earring. Her typical

hair length was always just a little past her shoulders, except on the rare occasions when she broke out a curling iron.

Everything about Anna May was classic. Her makeup was forever neutral and appeared almost nonexistent. Her nails were either cherry red or French manicured—never anything besides the traditional white tip. And her style of dress often reminded me of things you might find in Jackie O's closet. But it worked for her, and I would begrudgingly agree that my sister was a beautiful woman.

I, however, was the total opposite and staunchly refused to look anything like her. As previously mentioned, I like to mix up my hair color, and lately have been experimenting with more unnatural hues. My nails are whatever shade I feel fits my mood or the season, and my makeup . . . well, I own every color of eye shadow that exists. As they say, variety is the spice of life, and I like a vibrant life.

I waved her concern away with the folded-up photo before stuffing it back into my purse. I wasn't going to let her sensibilities rain on my parade. After all, it was my favorite time of day: five p.m. on a Friday, and I was getting ready to leave work, where I'm the manager of my family's Chinese restaurant, Ho-Lee Noodle House.

Was it my lifelong dream to end up working for my parents and to leave work smelling like sweet and sour sauce on a daily basis? No. But it was actually working out pretty well despite my original protests. Turns out that I like to be in charge of things. Even better, I was good at it.

But it was now the end of the workweek, and after a long five days of managing the daily functions of the

noodle shop and dealing with the public I was thrilled for the weekend to begin. The next morning, I would be pampering myself at the salon, Asian Accents, and my stylist, Jasmine Ming, was as excited as I was to be dyeing my hair this stunning shade of gray.

So even though I wouldn't be on the clock tomorrow, I would still be headed to Asia Village, since both Asian Accents and the Ho-Lee Noodle House are under the same Asian-inspired roof. Located in the quaint suburb of Fairview Park, the Asian shopping center is about twenty-five minutes away from Downtown Cleveland. If it's me driving though, I can make it in about seventeen. But don't tell my boyfriend—he's a cop.

The enclosed plaza has everything you could think of under its sky-lit roof. In one fell swoop, you can get your hair done, purchase books by your favorite authors, grocery shop, have dinner, update your cosmetic collection, enjoy a doughnut or three, and even sing some karaoke, if it tickled your fancy. I haven't even mentioned the fact that you can also stock up on tea cakes, or find the perfect supplements and herbs to compliment your new healthy lifestyle. After all, you might need something to counter all the doughy goodness you purchased from Shanghai Donuts.

Our family's noodle shop has been at the plaza since before I was born, and I'd spent more time within those four walls than I'd care to admit.

Anna May had in recent months taken an internship at a prominent law firm in Cleveland—Andrews, Filbert, Childs & Associates—so her ability to lend a hand at the restaurant had become extremely limited. But since our evening helper and resident teenage thorn in my side, Vanessa Wen, was currently out with

the stomach flu, Anna May had agreed to give up her Friday evening to help out. There's nothing worse than a twelve-hour workday in my book.

"Seriously, Lana, how long are you going to maintain this lifestyle? You're twenty-eight years old now—and before you know it, you're going to be thirty—and you don't take care of yourself at all. Things don't get easier as you age, trust me. You eat horribly, you don't work out, and you're not even trying to look like an adult."

I swear that I tried to withhold my eye roll, but sometimes it just happens without me realizing it. This is what my sister is best at. Lecturing me. Even though she is a measly three years older than me, she acts like she's about ten. And she has all this "worldly" wisdom to pass down to her incapable younger sister. Lucky me. "I don't see what my hair has to do with any of this."

"It's a gateway, Lana. You're not taking life seriously, and it's showing in your hair."

I gaped. "That is the most ridiculous statement I have ever heard in my life."

"You refuse to grow up." She folded her arms over her chest and lifted her chin. "I think this new rebellion says it all."

"New rebellion?" I snorted. "Me dyeing my hair is not a rebellion. And I think I'm doing pretty well considering. I mean, after all, I am running this restaurant. And doing a bang-up job, I might add."

"Henry says—"

I held up a hand. "Henry says? So, is your new love interest the reason why you're giving me this lecture? Unbelievable."

Anna May had recently started "casually dating" one of the partners at her fancy law firm, which I was

pretty sure wasn't the best idea, but did that stop her? Of course not. My sister often found justification in her own actions because she considered herself to be the most level-headed person on the planet.

She held her head even higher. "Henry says that personal presentation is everything. You are your own representative, Lana. Do you want people to view you as this immature, young woman who constantly chooses to go against the grain of society?"

I started to dig in my purse for my car keys. She was just getting on top of her soap box, and I had plans to meet Adam for happy hour at the Zodiac, a local bar where my best friend and roommate, Megan Riley, bartended. I didn't want to give up any more of my personal time listening to this drivel.

Anna May continued spouting at the mouth while I tuned her out. I heard something about how I would have never fit into the lifestyle I had previously hoped to have for myself. And maybe she was right. A year ago, I'd daydreamed of being a glamorous businesswoman with a corner office and enough high-powered suits to overflow a walk-in closet. But that fantasy had died the minute I walked out of my previous job. After all, you can take your boss flinging papers in your face only so many times before you have to say enough is enough.

"I'm going now," I said, talking over her rant. "Adam is waiting for me at the Zodiac."

"Oh, don't even get me started on how you're always wasting your time at that stupid bar." Anna May uncrossed her arms, and put her hands on her hips, mimicking our mother's lecturing stance. "I hope you don't have a drinking problem on top of everything else."

I let out a deep groan and flung my purse over my shoulder. "Thanks for helping out tonight," I said, unwilling to dignify her statement with a response—much less a justification. "I'll talk to you later. Call me if there's an emergency."

I started to walk out of the restaurant, dropping my usual shuffling steps and taking the long strides that I normally reserved for high heels. I'd manage to keep my cool and not engage in a screaming match with my sister as I'd been well known to do. And she said I wasn't mature. Ha.

But my swagger was quickly ruined because just as I was about to exit the restaurant, Ian Sung, property manager to Asia Village, was walking in and blocked my exit. Damn. So close to freedom.

"Lana." Ian, who was impeccably dressed in a navy blue Italian suit and polished light brown dress shoes, gave me a once-over. "Are you on your way out for the day? There's something I wanted to discuss with you."

"Can we walk and talk?" I asked him. "I'm running late for an appointment."

Anna May snorted behind me.

Ian's eyes shifted to my sister, and he regarded her with a stiff smile.

He didn't seem to like Anna May very much, but I had no idea why. I wish I could say the same for myself, but unfortunately Ian held a torch for a relationship between us that was never going to happen. It wasn't that Ian's a bad guy or anything, but there was something about him that I couldn't quite put my finger on that rubbed me the wrong way. Despite my mother's extreme interest in making him my boyfriend, I couldn't view him in that light.

Ian nodded in agreement and held out his hand, signaling for me to lead the way.

I turned to glare at my sister one final time before leaving. So long, maturity.

Once we were outside the restaurant, Ian cleared his throat, loosening the tie at his neck. "So, I was hoping to discuss the end of summer sidewalk sale with you. Of course, it will be a longer discussion than what we can have on the way to the plaza exit, so maybe we could get together on Monday morning to have a real conversation. Perhaps we could grab some coffee and breakfast at Shanghai Donuts?"

I watched him from the corner of my eye, as I kept making my way toward the exit. Clever move, asking to meet up at one of my favorite Asia Village establishments. The only thing better he could have said was for me to meet him at the Modern Scroll, the plaza's bookshop.

"I suppose I could ask Nancy to come in an hour early on Monday morning. I couldn't meet you until ten o'clock though." Nancy Huang was our only full-time waitress, and Peter's mom. Peter was the head chef at our restaurant and fell into the guy best-friend category.

"That will work out perfectly." Ian replied. "I'll see you then."

"But why me?" I asked.

"What do you mean?"

"I mean, why me? Aren't the particulars of the sidewalk sale something you should discuss with the entire board of directors for the plaza and not just me?" Okay, I was part of that board, but still, I was only one member. Why did he always have to single me out?

"Lana, I think you know the answer to that."

I cringed. I could guess, that's for sure.

"You're the only person on the entire committee that I trust implicitly. I know that you want to get things done just as much as I do, and I don't have to worry when I know you're involved with something."

"Wait, involved?" I blanched slightly, suddenly worried that this sidewalk sale might be taking up more of my time than I'd planned for. "What do you mean *involved*?"

"Well, we can discuss all of that at our meeting on Monday morning," he said, suddenly in a rush to get out of our conversation. As we had reached the main entrance, he stepped in front of me. "Allow me to get the door."

As he opened the door with a big smile, we turned just in time to see a dark gray Nissan abruptly back out of one of the employee parking spots and slam into a brand-new, white Cadillac sedan. I jerked back as the two vehicles collided and the sounds of metal scraping against metal caused my teeth to clench.

Ian stepped out on to the sidewalk in front of me, and I followed quickly behind him.

"Hey, doesn't that Nissan belong to June Yi?" I asked, pointing to the gray car.

He held a hand up to his head and massaged his temple with his thumb. "Ugh, of course it does."

CHAPTER 2

June Yi, co-owner of Yi's Tea and Bakery, is known for her unshakeable ability to be difficult at all times. And as Ian and I neared the car accident, both of us knew without exchanging a word that this wasn't going to go well.

As we approached, the door to the Cadillac whipped open, and Mildred—Millie—Mao stumbled out of the sedan. She held a hand to the side of her neck and cringed in pain.

Had there been a debonair way to gasp, I'm sure that Ian wouldn't have been able to help himself. Instead, his hand shot up to loosen his tie again—it seemed to be a nervous habit of his.

If there was anybody who could equal how horrid June Yi was to deal with, it was Millie Mao. Millie was a mahjong player who frequently participated in tournaments against the plaza's four cherished widows, the Mahjong Matrons. Though she could be hard to handle at times, she brought a lot of business to

the plaza and spent just as much herself, so naturally Ian treated her like royalty.

June swung the door to her Nissan open and launched herself out of the driver's seat to inspect the damage to the back end of her car. "Are you crazy?" she yelled to Millie. "Did you not see me backing out of my parking space?"

Mille hobbled around the open driver-side door of her luxury car and rubbed the side of her neck. "Backing out? Who backs out with the gas pedal all the way to the floor? You are the crazy one, June Yi! Besides, I have the right of way. You hit me on purpose!"

"Ha!" June wagged a finger at Millie. "You are always blaming people for your carelessness! You should have been watching where you were going."

Ian stepped up to the women, his tie almost completely undone at this point. "Ladies, ladies, let's calm down, shall we? Is everyone okay? That's our main priority."

I stayed a few feet behind Ian. None of this was really my business, but Millie's Cadillac was blocking in my car so it wasn't like I could exactly leave at the moment.

"I am fine," June spat out. "But look at my bumper!"

"Your bumper?" Millie shouted. "*Your* bumper? Look at the front of my car! It's ruined. And my neck hurts. I think I have whiplash. Did you slam on the gas to get out of your parking spot or what?"

My eyes were struggling not to roll into the back of my head.

Ian held up his hands, gesturing for the women to calm down. "The damage doesn't appear to be too bad. Perhaps you should swap insurance information so both of you can be on your way."

Millie had already pulled her cell phone out of her

purse and began dialing. "I'm calling the police. We are filing a report. No one is moving from this spot until a policeman shows up."

"Good, then it will be on record that it's your fault," June replied, her lips twisting in a satisfied grin. "They can see for themselves what a reckless driver you are."

Millie narrowed her eyes before turning her back to all of us.

June realized I was standing behind Ian and turned to acknowledge me. "Lana Lee, what are you doing here? Snooping about as usual?"

My jaw instantly clenched. June and I didn't have the best track record. Not that she was ever that pleasant of a person, but she had been especially nasty to me since I began working at the noodle shop. Some of her hostility was partially due to the fact that when the original property manager, Thomas Feng, was murdered, she automatically assumed that my family and I were up to no good. She'd also had it out for Peter at the time, believing we'd all been in on it together. Never mind that none of us had anything to do with Thomas's death whatsoever.

On top of that, she despised the fact that Ian valued my opinion most of anyone's on Asia Village's board of directors committee. Any time that I had an idea or a suggestion, she would immediately poo-poo it— sometimes before I could even finish my pitch.

Without even bothering to give her an obligatory smile, I pointed to my car. "Millie's car is blocking me in. Trust me, I'm not happy about being stuck here. I have places I need to be."

June scowled. "That doesn't mean you need to stand over here. This isn't any of your business, young lady. Why don't you wait somewhere else?"

Ian took a step closer to June, offering her a gentle pat on the arm. "Ms. Yi, I'm sure you're just shaken up from the accident. There's no reason to take that out on Lana."

June jerked her arm away from his hand. "Of course you would stick up for her. It's disgusting how you coo over her. And what business is this of yours anyway?"

His hand again went to his tie, his fingers fumbling with the realization that there was no longer a knot in place. "As property manager, I've come to assess the damage and make sure that everything and everyone is okay. I'm sure you can understand that, Ms. Yi."

Millie turned around, now off the phone and appearing more than satisfied with herself. "The police and an ambulance are both on their way. I'm not sure I can turn my head." She held on to her neck, putting on her most pitiful facial expression.

There are many times I've wanted to give out Academy Awards for best dramatic performances around this place, but today's production really took the cake. There was a small chance that she wasn't faking it, but knowing Millie Mao's sue-happy personality, I doubted the likelihood of her actually being hurt by what seemed to be a pretty minor accident.

I went over and sat on one of the wrought-iron benches that lined Asia Village's outdoor sidewalk and pulled out my cell phone to let Megan and Adam know that I was running late. I thought about heading back inside to Shanghai Donuts to grab a doughnut or two, but I'd been pushing the limits lately and the button on my pants was already threatening to pop.

* * *

I'd forgotten my book at home, so while I waited for something entertaining to happen, I continued to lounge on my bench, scrolling through Pinterest and checking my social media. June paced the length of her car, mumbling under her breath and glaring at Millie every chance she got.

Millie, on the other hand, was seated gingerly on a bench about ten feet away from me, talking in harsh whispers on her phone. She seemed to be calling everyone she knew. I tried to eavesdrop as best I could, but she proved to be quite talented at keeping her voice low.

Twenty minutes later, an ambulance arrived followed by two police cruisers that came to assess the damage and begin filing an accident report. As soon as the officers stepped out of their vehicles, both women approached them at lightning speed and began talking over each other, trying to tell their side of the story. The two men raised their eyebrows at each other before ushering Millie and June to opposite sides of the parking row.

I waited as patiently as possible on my little bench hoping that this would all be taken care of soon, and I could be on my way. I didn't even have the opportunity to listen in on what either party was saying because they were all out of earshot.

A tow truck arrived shortly after to take away Millie's Cadillac, and I watched her hobble to the ambulance with the policeman she'd been talking with. He offered his arm in assistance as she continued holding her neck as if her head might fall off if she let go. June seemed to be lecturing the policeman who was taking her statement, and I could tell by his facial expressions that he was more than annoyed with the situation.

I had immersed myself with pinning dog memes when I noticed some movement in my peripheral. The officer who'd been talking to June was now walking away, chattering into the radio attached to his shoulder. He greeted the other cop with a head nod as they met in between their cruisers. A few words were exchanged, another head nod, and then both of them got into their respective cars and took off.

June stormed back over to her vehicle appearing rather displeased, her eyes jerked toward the ambulance. The doors were shut, and Millie was still inside. By the look on her face, I could tell June wanted to go another round in a screaming match, but the paramedics were ruining her chances.

Ian, who had been rushing around strategically setting up hazard cones, came strolling over to me. "What a way to end the workweek." His brows furrowed; his forehead was slick with sweat. "Sorry you got held up in all this."

"It's fine," I said, not really meaning it. "What's going on with Millie?"

He turned to glance at the ambulance. "She's going with them to the hospital. She told me she called her brother and he's going to meet her there. I guess the car wasn't drivable and she's claiming she can't turn her head to either side, so she wouldn't have been able to drive anyway."

My eyes shifted away from the ambulance in time to see June glaring at Ian and me before she started her car and sped away. I groaned. "She probably thinks we're talking about her."

His attention turned away from the ambulance and followed June's car as it left the lot, her trunk badly dented, and her bumper threatening to fall off at the

first sign of a Cleveland pothole. He let out a sigh that I even found impressive. "It doesn't really matter. By tomorrow, the whole plaza will be talking about it."

Finally, free of the plaza, I headed over to the Zodiac, where Adam and Megan were waiting for me.

Megan Riley has been my best friend since the moment we met. It's not every day the universe conspires to bring you face-to-face with someone who makes you think, *Yes, you are my human.*

We met in college, bonding over a business class-syllabus that was about twenty-five pages too long. I hated that class, but it brought me my best friend, so how much could I really complain?

Since then we'd been inseparable, and a few short months after we met, we decided it would be a good idea to move in together. Both of us had been straining to keep our bills paid and up to date, so sharing rent seemed like a great option. And far from becoming one of those cautionary tales about why best friends should never live together, we'd become closer than ever.

Detective Adam Trudeau, on the other hand, was a newer addition to my life—but the way he melded into my every day, I could hardly believe that we'd only been seeing each other for a little more than six months. He'd been the lead detective investigating the murder of Thomas Feng, and again, even though I'd hated the whole situation, I was thankful that Adam had been brought into my life.

That's me, always trying to find the positive in the weirdest and worst situations. Although after my run-in with the two meanest women in Asia Village, staying positive was more of a challenge than usual.

I stepped into the astrologically themed bar, its walls covered with murals depicting the twelve signs of the zodiac. I paused to deeply inhale the wonderful scent of fried food and smiled as I spotted Adam sitting at his usual stool, beer in hand. Megan was behind the bar rinsing glasses and singing along to the Black Keys blaring from the bar's speaker system.

The muscles in my upper back relaxed. I felt at home. In a way, the Zodiac was kind of like my version of *Cheers*, though I was still working on getting everyone to yell "Lana!" when I walked in. Unfortunately, it seemed like the only person amused by that joke was me.

I hopped up onto the stool next to Adam and planted a kiss on his scruffy cheek. His reddish-brown hair was tousled and getting a little on the long side. He'd been working a case that was stressing him out, and it showed a little in his appearance. When he wasn't elbow deep in a case, he was always clean-shaven with a fresh haircut and eye-bag free.

"Hey, dollface." He leaned over and returned the gesture, his day-old scruff tickling my cheek. "How'd it end with the accident?"

I groaned. "Millie and June wouldn't stop bickering until the police showed up. Finally, they separated them at opposite ends of the parking aisle."

Megan noticed that I'd arrived, gave me a wink, and started pouring various liquors into a shaker.

"I bet you it was Wakefield and Clark who had to deal with those two. Poor SOBs." Adam chuckled as he took a swig of beer. "Any time we get a call from Asia Village, they do a coin toss."

"Shut up," I said, unable to withhold a laugh. I en-

visioned cops sitting in their squad cars flipping coins and announcing their results over the radio.

"Half the time we bet on whether or not *you're* involved."

"Stop it." I pinched his arm playfully. "If you're betting and winning, you better share the proceeds with me."

"How do you think I paid for all those fancy dinners last month?"

I gave him another pinch as Megan sauntered over with a brownish-orange drink. "What the heck is that?" I asked, turned off by the color.

"It's a Scorpio Sizzle," she replied. "It's also on the house, so drink up. I'm trying some new mixtures for the upcoming season and I need a guinea pig. This one has a little apple cider in it . . . you know, to make it fall-ish."

I took a cautious sip. Megan was without a doubt a great bartender. But she did have a few misses here and there, and unfortunately, I was usually the one to find out the hard way.

"Not bad," I said. "What kind of liquor did you use?"

"Spiced rum. Good, right?"

"Yeah, I think this will go over well. Too bad the coloring resembles vomit."

Megan had recently been promoted to manager after an attempt to quit because of the owner's complete lack of ability to find new help when one of the other bartenders walked out. She had been incredibly patient during the entire process, filling in when needed and working extra-long shifts. But eventually she'd had her fill of being underappreciated for her efforts

and tried putting in her two weeks. That got the owner to straighten up right away. He hired two new bartenders and promoted Megan to manager, which gave her the ability to create her own schedule and work better hours. Though she still worked a crazy amount, she was much happier now, and in turn, so was I.

A few customers strolled in for happy hour, and Megan zipped away to greet them.

"So, how was work aside from the drama just before you left?" Adam asked, wrapping an arm around the back of my stool.

I shrugged. "Same ol' stuff. Although, Anna May and I got into *another* argument right before I left . . . and then I ran into Ian . . ."

"Uh-oh." Adam groaned. "What does he want now?"

"Not entirely sure, we have a meeting on Monday morning. It has something to do with the end of the summer sidewalk sale thingy."

"Is that the professional term?" he smirked.

"Har-har."

"Why would just the two of you need to meet for that? He annoys me."

"No clue, but I have a feeling I'm not going to be happy about it."

"And Anna May?" Adam asked. "What's *her* deal?"

"The usual—getting on my case about my hair, my lifestyle, the way I inhale oxygen."

"What are you doing to your hair?"

I pulled the picture out of my purse. "I'm getting this done tomorrow morning."

He took the photo from my hand and assessed it, then looked up at me and back at the photo. "I like it. What's the problem?"

I repeated what my sister said, mimicking her facial

expressions of disgust for dramatic effect. June and Millie's performance must have inspired me.

Adam handed the picture back to me. "Don't worry about what your sister says. You know she does this all the time trying to get a rise out of you."

"True," I replied, shoving the picture back in my purse. "Plus, if this is my biggest problem, then what do I really have to complain about, right?"

"Exactly." He rubbed my shoulder. "Let's just enjoy a nice, relaxing weekend and be thankful your sister is the biggest thorn in our side."

CHAPTER
3

I woke up extra early on Saturday morning for my hair appointment. I didn't have to be there until nine o'clock, but I wanted to make sure there was enough time for me to lounge with a cup of coffee and fully wake up.

Kikkoman, my black pug, stirred from under the blankets near my feet as I attempted to shimmy my way out of bed without waking Adam. He actually had a Saturday to himself for once and I didn't want him to unnecessarily get up when he could enjoy the benefits of sleeping in.

Kikko poked her head out from under the blanket and her tongue flopped out of her mouth as she seemingly smiled at me.

"Let's go outside," I whispered.

The two of us snuck out of my bedroom, and I shut the door behind me. Shuffling into the kitchen, still half asleep, I prepped a pot of coffee before taking Kikko out for her morning tinkle. It was a quiet morning at

our apartment complex, and we took our time stopping at all of her favorite trees and bushes.

It was a little muggy for this early in the day and I knew it would end up being a scorcher. In Cleveland, you hate to whine about the high summer temps since there are so few months that are actually warm. But after a week or so of ninety-degree days, you can't really help yourself. Despite my ability to sweat like a man—while other Asians are stereotypically known simply to "glisten"—I wasn't looking forward to autumn like so many other people do. The highlight of the fall months for me are the limited-edition cereals like Boo Berry and Franken Berry. Oh, and hoodies. Can't forget those.

But deep down, I was a spring kind of gal. I enjoyed my blooming flowers and April showers. Not to be cliché, I really do love when things blossom back to life. It's almost as if you can smell the promise of hope and new beginnings in the air.

We finished our walk and returned to my apartment, where I found Adam slumped back on the couch, holding onto a coffee mug as if it were a lifeline.

When I managed to get her leash off, Kikko waggled her tail and scuttled over to him.

"What are you doing awake?" I asked, hanging up the leash and my house keys.

He held up his cup without lifting his head. "I smelled the coffee."

I went into the kitchen and grabbed myself a mug, adding cream and sugar. "So, what are your plans for the day? Anything exciting?"

"Lounging until you're done with your hair, and then I thought maybe we'd go do something summery . . .

go to the beach, or maybe putt-putting and ice cream after?"

"Sounds like a plan to me," I said, joining him on the couch. "It's so exciting that we get to actually spend almost a full Saturday together. It's been a while."

"Well, this damn case has been sucking up all my time. But we wrapped up for the most part yesterday. Now I'm hoping for a lull in crime. Try not to cause any trouble, okay?" He rested a hand on my leg and squeezed my knee playfully.

"Trust me, there's nothing I want more than some peace and quiet."

After I downed three cups of coffee, I got dressed and headed over to Asia Village. Adam went home, and the plan was for me to meet up with him at his place as soon as I was done with my hair. Then it was off to Edgewater Park.

I knew I'd be at the salon for about two hours between all the dyeing and cutting, so I made sure to bring a book with me. I didn't much care for the old issues of *People* magazine they had lying around the salon. Unless, of course, it was the Sexiest Man Alive issue. That always kept my attention.

I pulled into the Asia Village parking lot, passing through the dragon-wrapped archway at the entrance, and found a decent spot near the main doors. There weren't many cars in the lot, which was pretty much par for the course during the summer months. The real action around here started up in the fall and petered out in the late spring months.

That's why Ian came up with the idea to have an

end-of-summer sidewalk sale. He thought it would help drum up some business and make up for some of the slow time we'd had in July. I hated to admit that it was a great idea, but it was . . . I only wished I would have come up with it first.

Grabbing my book and purse off the passenger seat, I got out of the car and made my way into the enclosed shopping center. The air-conditioning blasted me with a wave of cold air as I opened the doors and sent goose bumps up my arms.

The salon was right by the entrance to the plaza and I could hear the Chinese pop music coming through their closed glass doors. They liked to keep things lively on Saturday mornings. Probably to help keep people awake while they were waiting for their dyes to set in.

Yuna, Asian Accent's receptionist, was standing at the front desk bopping her head up and down. Her multi-colored hair, which I could only describe as unicorn inspired, was held up in a high ponytail and swung back and forth as she moved. Giant, metallic silver earrings shaped like rain clouds danced against her cheeks.

She flashed me an enormous smile, her lips covered in cherry-tinted gloss. "Good morning, Lana!"

"Hi, Yuna, how are you?" Despite all the coffee I'd had, my response was not as peppy as hers.

"Amazing! It's a beautiful day out and we're packed with appointments, so lots of business and lots of gorgeous hair to be done!"

I smiled in return. If I had only half her enthusiasm for life, I'd be a happy gal.

"Would you like any tea, coffee, or spring water?"

"Sure, I'll take some coffee." After all, what could another cup hurt?

She bounced away and I took a seat on one of the plastic chairs lined up against the wall. It was about ten minutes to nine, so I had a little time to kill. I decided to get started on my book.

Before I could even get through the first sentence, June Yi walked in. Her eyes landed on me as she stepped through the door, and she pursed her lips, looking down at me with dissatisfaction. Apparently, my mere presence was upsetting to her.

Same as yesterday, I didn't bother with the obligatory smile. I had given up on niceties with her a while ago. I turned my attention back to my book, but I couldn't help peek out of the corner of my eye at her. She wasn't unattractive—it was clearly her personality that made her so difficult to look at for long. If memory serves me correctly, I don't think I'd ever seen her smile.

With her hands folded in front of her, she waited at the receptionist desk for Yuna.

A minute later, Yuna returned with my coffee, whizzing around to where I was seated and handing me a bright pink mug that had their salon's logo on the side. "Careful, it's freshly made and super hot."

"Thanks, Yuna." I took the cup gingerly from her hands and blew at the wafting steam.

She spun on her heel and went to welcome June with the same exuberance she greeted me with. I had to give her credit. I could never be that excited to see June Yi. Not even if I was trapped in a ditch with no way out but her. Okay, maybe if the ditch was filled with poisonous spiders. Then I suppose she'd be a sight for sore eyes.

June mumbled her appointment information as if inconvenienced by the simple act of speech. Yuna

nodded emphatically. "Yes, you'll be with Lisa today. Can I get you something to drink while you wait?"

"Green tea would be fine, please," June replied.

"Right away, Ms. Yi!" Yuna disappeared toward the back of the salon again.

June turned to the available chairs and made a production of picking the one farthest away from me then crossing her legs in the opposite direction.

I didn't know if she thought I would be insulted by her rigid body language, but instead of letting her know that I'd noticed—and since I definitely didn't care—I kept my focus on the book in front of me.

Thankfully, a few minutes later the only woman I trusted with my hair, Jasmine Ming, came to the rescue.

Her apple cheeks were highlighted with shimmery bronzer, and when she smiled, they lifted, crinkling her almond-shaped eyes, which were expertly smudged with smoky charcoal shadows. "Hey, Lana, so good to see you!" She came around the receptionist counter and hugged me as I stood. "I'm so excited to get started on your hair. We're going to do some experiments with this new metallic dye I have. It's going to be fantastic."

Experiments?

I heard June chortle behind me, and it took everything I had not to turn around and glare at her. "Do you think it'll turn out all right? I feel like this pink isn't going to fully come out." Even though the pink had faded considerably, I worried that it would leave a trace of brassiness to the end result.

"Not to worry, my love, I have just the thing for that." Jasmine grabbed my free hand and pulled me to her styling station. "Sorry to leave you with that

curmudgeon. Hope you weren't waiting too long," she said, once we were out of earshot.

"Nah, it's okay. I have my book anyways." I held it up for her to see.

"You and your books," she laughed. "What are you reading now?"

"It's called *Gone to Dust*," I replied as I sat down. "By this guy named Matt Goldman."

"Matt Goldman . . . where have I heard that name before?" Jasmine tapped her chin with the tip of her comb.

"Maybe you heard it from—"

"I know! The Blue Man Group."

I twisted in my chair to gawk at her. "The Blue Man Group? No, I was going to say *Seinfeld*."

"Oh, so he was in *Seinfeld*?"

"No, but he was a writer for the show. He worked on some other sitcoms too, plus Ellen."

"Huh, but definitely not one of the Blue Man Group then?"

I laughed. "No . . . different guy."

"Well, what's the story about? Is it any good?"

"It is. It's about this impossible case that the police can't figure out, so they call in a P.I. in order to help solve it."

"Figures." She wrapped a cape around the front of my body, clasping it snugly around my neck. "You've been on a P.I. kick ever since you started hanging out with that Lydia Shepard woman."

"I liked P.I. stuff way before then, I read a lot of Sue Grafton too, you know. And besides, me and Lydia don't *hang* out."

"Well, you'll have plenty of time to read while your

dye is setting. But let's hurry up and get our gab on before this place gets too crowded."

I knew she was going to talk about the accident that happened with June and Millie. Aside from the fact that June was currently in the salon, I had known from the moment it happened that it would be a topic of conversation around the plaza. June, who basically got along with no one but her twin sister Shirley—though Shirley wasn't quite as bad—always made for good gossip. There was hardly a day that went by without her offending someone, somewhere.

"I heard that Millie plans to sue June for an absurd amount of money. The Mahjong Matrons stopped in yesterday to report that Millie had a concussion and whiplash, and that something was wrong with her shoulder from where the seat belt was holding her back."

I rolled my eyes. "It couldn't have been that bad. The airbag didn't even deploy."

Jasmine began separating sections of my hair, isolating the faded pink strands. "Well, you know Millie. I bet she's just been waiting to sue someone at Asia Village with as much as she comes here. I heard she sued someone over on the East Side in Asia Town. Big surprise, another car accident."

"Doesn't anyone catch on to her antics?" I asked. I couldn't believe people got away with that sort of stuff.

Jasmine shrugged, looking at me from the mirror. "Who knows? People get away with so much these days, it's unreal."

"Well, I don't feel that bad for June to tell you the truth. I mean, she's not exactly the nicest person in the world."

It was as if she heard me. In the reflection of the

mirror, I watched her walk by and scowl at me. Oops. Maybe she *had* heard me. Walking behind her were two of the Mahjong Matrons, Pearl and Opal. They didn't notice me sitting there, and I decided to keep quiet for the time being. Getting my hair done was supposed to be a relaxing experience. I didn't feel like being surrounded by a crowd—or overly social— while my hair was being bleached.

Jasmine started to apply the bleach, and the conversation moved for a while to what was going on in my personal life. We talked about Adam and Megan, and then she caught me up on *her* life. She'd been dating a new guy and things were starting to get serious between them.

Once she finished foiling my hair and the bleach was working its magic, she patted me on the shoulder and told me she'd be back in twenty minutes. I pulled my book out and was just about to pick up from where I left off when I caught Millie Mao's reflection in the mirror.

I think it was safe to say "Uh-oh."

CHAPTER
4

My eyes darted around the salon checking for June's position, and I wondered how long it would take the two women to realize they were both at the salon. I couldn't see much from where I was, but I knew that June's stylist, Lisa, had a workstation near the back by the shampoo sinks on the opposite side of where I was sitting.

I observed Yuna through the mirror's reflection talking casually with Millie, who was making gestures to her own neck, and I figured she must be inquiring about her injuries. Millie was outfitted with a neck brace and an arm sling.

Yuna was a future Mahjong Matron in the making. She and Ho-Lee's teenage waitress, Vanessa, were quite the budding gossipers. After all, you needed someone to "spread the juice" amongst the younger generation.

No one else seemed to notice that Millie had arrived, and I waited for the tension to thicken in the entire salon. I knew it was going to happen. There was no avoiding it. And just my luck, this would have to happen while I

was trying to have a nice, low-key morning getting my hair done.

I tried to shake away the feeling of impending doom and honed back in on my book. But all I was doing was reading the same sentence over and over again. I checked the time on my cell phone—only five minutes had passed since Jasmine disappeared to do whatever it was that she did while my hair set. I tapped my shoe on the footrest and scanned the room.

When I checked back to see what was going on up front, I saw a salon worker who I didn't know by name greeting Millie. The girl had fire-engine red hair and a full sleeve of tattoos on her left arm. I would have to ask Jasmine who that was, and I found myself a little caught off guard that I didn't already know. Was I completely in la-la land these last couple of weeks that I didn't notice a new employee in the plaza?

The girl turned and held out her arm for Millie to grab onto. Millie linked her free arm with the girl's and hobbled slowly alongside her as they made their way to the back.

"A nice pedicure is exactly what I need," I heard Millie say.

"We'll set you up with a soothing foot soak first," the girl replied in a syrupy sweet voice. "I have these amazing eucalyptus tablets that I add to the water, and they work absolute wonders."

"Oh, that does sound wonderful," Millie cooed. "It's been one heck of a week, and I'm not the spring chicken I used to be. I don't heal from these things as easily as I used to."

I wanted to gag. Man, was she laying it on thick.

The two women passed me, and my blood pressure rose just a smidge as I saw the direction they were

eaded in. The foot spa chairs were near the shampoo sinks, and so there was no chance that June and Millie wouldn't see each other. My free hand gripped the arm of the chair. A siren went off in my head: *brace for impact.*

If I had convinced myself for even one minute that it would take more time for either woman to notice the other one, I was wrong. Because right away I heard June yell, "What are *you* doing here?!"

I cringed at the bass in her voice.

"Me?" Millie shouted back. "What does it look like I'm doing here? Trying to relax after you nearly killed me yesterday!"

"Ha! You missed your calling to be in the opera, Mildred. You are so dramatic. I barely hit you and you know it."

I swiveled in my chair, but all I could see was Millie with her hand on her hip, staring at what appeared to be nothing. I imagined June on the edge of her seat with her finger pointed fiercely at her accuser.

The girl with the red hair put an arm around Millie and tried to guide her away. "Let's get you to that foot spa."

Millie struggled to hold her position. "You probably hit me on purpose, knowing you and your wild temper! Everyone here knows that you're an angry woman. That's why your only friend is your sister!"

"At least I can trust my sister. I can't say the same for you, you old witch."

Gasps filled the salon.

"Absurd!" I heard a familiar woman's voice yell from the other side of my mirror. "We are trying to pamper ourselves, not listen to this incessant bickering. Can you please shut up?"

June replied to the mystery woman I couldn't quite place. "Why don't *you* shut your mouth?"

Jasmine appeared from out of nowhere and clapped her hands together. The music volume was lowered, and she addressed the salon with an authoritative voice. "Ladies, please. Let's all try to be respectful of one another. We like to make everyone's experiences at Asian Accents as enjoyable as possible."

There were mumbles heard around the salon, and Jasmine shouted a "thank you" to everyone before scuttling back over to me. "We need to get this bleach out of your hair. . . . I can't believe this," she hissed. "Is there no end to these women and their pettiness with one another?"

"I hate to say I saw it coming," I told her. "The minute Millie walked into the salon, I knew it was only a matter of time before one of them exploded."

Jasmine lifted a piece of the foil to check the coloring, then tapped my shoulder. "You're definitely ready. Let's go."

I shuffled in my cape to the shampooing station and immediately felt the tension I'd been anticipating. I finally saw June, and the expression on her face told me everything I needed to know. She was one hundred percent not a happy camper. The scowl she wore seemed so natural, you'd think that was her permanent face—and maybe it was. But there was something more sinister in her eyes today. She kept her attention focused in Millie's direction while Millie pretended as if June wasn't even in the room.

I tried to settle back in my chair, letting my neck rest on the lip of the shampoo sink. Taking a deep breath, I closed my eyes and did my best to unwind. Getting my hair washed was one of my favorite things.

Especially since Jasmine always included a gentle head massage.

My hair washing went without incident, and I began to loosen up a little, hoping the worst outburst was behind us. Jasmine wrapped my freshly washed hair into a fluffy white towel, and we made our way back to her workstation.

Jasmine began to comb the knots out of my hair. "So, I heard that Ian is putting you in charge of the end-of-summer sidewalk sale."

My eyebrows shot up. "What?"

"Yeah, he didn't tell you?" She glanced at my reflection. "I heard you're going to be in charge of all the coordinating—"

"Ugh, I hate him," I said, squirming in my seat, my agitation levels rising back up. "I talked to him yesterday before the accident and he said something about me being 'involved.' I should have known that's what he meant."

"Try and act like you're hearing it for the first time when he officially tells you. I don't want to be outed for beating him to it."

"He actually told you?"

"Well, no, he told Cindy Kwan at the Modern Scroll, and she told Kimmy Tran, and then Kimmy was in here last night getting her nails done and she told my manicurist Tracy, and Tracy told Yuna, and *then* it got to me."

I shook my head in disappointment. "I'm surprised the Mahjong Matrons didn't help spread the news."

"Spread the news about what, my dear?" a voice from behind me asked.

I glanced up into the mirror and saw that Pearl, Opal's older sister, was smiling back at me. Her graying

hair, which she left naturally colored, was twisted up in pink foam curlers, and a fuzzy pink pillow was wrapped around her slender neck.

Blushing, I said, "Oh nothing important, we were just talking about the upcoming sidewalk sale."

"Oh yes, I heard that you'll be in charge of the event," she replied, bowing her head. "I'm sure you will do an excellent job."

I groaned.

Opal, the softest spoken of the Matrons, came up from behind Pearl. It appeared that both of them were getting their hair curled and set this morning. Opal gave my reflection a delicate smile. She was a tiny woman, at least a half foot shorter than her sister. They had the same almond shape to their eyes and the same thin lips that they tried to accentuate with matching lipstick—a matte toasted almond that they no doubt purchased from the plaza's cosmetic shop. Aside from their height, the only major difference between the sisters was their noses. Opal had a small nose that turned up slightly, and Pearl's nose had a stronger bridge and was straight as an arrow.

"I am always excited to see what hair color you will choose next, Lana," Opal commented barely above a whisper.

"Maybe I'll see you before we all leave and you can tell me what you think," I said.

"Perhaps, we shall," Pearl replied for the two of them.

Then both women went on their way to put their heads under those big bulky dryers that I hate so much.

Jasmine had a dye bowl ready with a mixture that appeared to be a very metallic silver. It reminded me of liquid mercury.

"Are we sure this color is going to take?" I asked. "It looks awfully light. Maybe you should add some black to it or something?"

"Don't worry, girlfriend. This is totally going to work. Have I ever steered you wrong?" She swirled the mixture one last time before taking the tinting brush to my hair.

"No, I suppose you haven't." Underneath the cape, I had my fingers crossed in hopes that I wouldn't have to take that statement back.

Not even fifteen minutes later, Jasmine was just about done adding the color to one side of my head, when we heard something splash, a startling shout, then a pop, a whiz, and boom, and then the room blackened as the power fizzled out. The women in the salon gasped, including me.

"What's happening?" a woman asked. "Did the power go out?"

"Hold on, ladies," Jasmine said from behind me. "We might have blown a fuse with all these beauty appliances going at once."

I saw a phone flashlight turn on and realized that Jasmine was navigating her way to the back room where the fuse box must have been. The salon was almost completely dark except for some dim light coming from the entrance.

About a minute later, the fluorescent lights flickered back on, and beeps and rings sounded as the salon equipment returned to life.

My eyes took a moment to readjust, and before I could fully focus my vision on any one thing, there was a blood-curdling scream from the back of the salon.

I whipped around and saw that it was the red-haired

girl I didn't know. She yelled, "Yuna, call nine-one-one!"

I rose from my chair to see what was going on. A breath caught in my throat. It was Millie Mao in her foot spa chair, and from the look of things, it appeared she'd been electrocuted.

I sank back into my chair, and covered my face with my hands, squeezing my eyelids shut tight. Unfortunately, the image was not going away.

CHAPTER 5

The salon turned into chaos central. Jasmine and the other Asian Accent employees corralled all the customers to the waiting area up front. Women half into their beauty processes huddled together. Some were crying; others were rambling to each other, and some to themselves. I stood off to the side near the front door, staring out into the plaza, wishing I had picked another day to get my hair done.

Jasmine had locked the doors, and a crowd was forming outside of the salon. People gathered together speculating what could have happened inside the plaza's beauty shop.

I could see my friends Kimmy Tran and Rina Su standing together near the edge of the crowd. Kimmy made eye contact with me, and I returned her questionable gaze with a shoulder shrug. I turned away from the interior of the plaza, so I didn't have to meet eyes with anyone else. The only safe place to focus on was the floor.

Jasmine stood behind the receptionist desk and

clapped her hands together, this time more quietly. "The police are on their way," she announced somberly. "They've asked that everyone stay put for the time being. I know some of you have dye in your hair that might need to come out. If that's you, please stand over to the left, so we can assess what stage of the process you're in. I don't want anyone's hair to fall out or get severely damaged. There's a utility sink in the back room, and I think that would be the most appropriate to use. Of course, none of you will have to pay for your services today. I thank all of you for your patience while we get things under control."

We all shuffled around one another. I went to stand with the other women who still had dye in their hair. That's when I realized that the woman's voice I had recognized earlier but had been unable to place was Ms. Evelyn Chang—an extremely wealthy socialite, and one of Donna Feng's good friends. The five of us exchanged awkward glances.

Most likely because I was the only person she knew in our little group, Ms. Chang came to stand next to me. Her hair along with the skin near her temples was covered in dark brown dye. She was a slender woman, a bit taller than myself, and in her late forties. "Isn't this just an awful mess? Terrible shame," she said with a tsk.

Without her having to say so, I knew that she was thinking about how this would affect Donna, who was the owner and silent partner of Asia Village. In the past year, Donna had been through quite a bit of her own drama, including the loss of her husband, Thomas. I knew the last thing she needed to hear about was a tragedy befalling the beloved plaza.

Jasmine joined our huddle of women and acknowl-

edged the others before turning to me. "Are you okay?" She put her hand on my arm.

I nodded, raising my eyes to meet hers. "Yeah . . . how are you holding up?" I realized that her hand was shaking. "I know that's a stupid question."

"I've never . . ." She squeezed her eyes shut. "I'm okay. The police will be here soon." Her eyes shifted to my hair. "I'm so sorry we didn't get to finish. We're going to have to leave it like this until tomorrow. I'll make a special house call to make it up to you."

"Don't worry about my hair," I whispered. "There are more important things going on right now. I'll survive."

Tears began to form in her eyes. "I know, but I'd rather think about your hair. It's less upsetting."

I put my hand over hers and squeezed.

There was a rough knock at the salon's glass entrance, and I saw a uniformed policeman wave for someone to unlock the door. Another officer stood slightly behind him and was addressing the crowd. By the motions he made with his hand, I assumed he was telling them to disperse.

Jasmine removed her hand from my arm and rushed over to the door. "Thank you for coming so quickly. Please, come in."

"No problem, ma'am," he nodded. "The coroner's office is on their way. There are also two detectives coming as well. Make sure this door stays locked until they get there. Can someone take us to the crime scene?"

"I'll take you," Jasmine said. "Yuna, please handle the door situation. No one in or out."

Yuna sped over without saying anything and locked the doors again. People in the plaza craned their necks

to see what was going on. The policeman's warning hadn't had much of an effect.

I noticed that Ian had shown up and was at the salon entrance gesturing for Yuna to let him in.

"No, I'm sorry, Mr. Sung," Yuna shouted. "This is a crime scene. No one can come in or out right now."

She said it so loudly that all the people standing in the front of the group heard, and as soon as the news made it to the back of the crowd, chatter could be heard through the salon's glass walls.

I groaned inaudibly.

Out of the corner of my eye, I saw Kimmy turn around and rush to Ho-Lee Noodle House, no doubt to tell my sister about what was happening.

A few minutes went by, and Jasmine returned. "Lana, I think we should wash your hair out now . . . follow me."

I stepped through the group of other women and followed Jasmine to the back. We went the long way around the opposite side of her workstation where a duplicate row of cutting stations were lined up. As I walked, I felt as if I were tiptoeing, not wanting to make any loud or heavy sounds as I moved. When it dawned on me that I was also holding my breath, I let out all the air I'd been trapping in my lungs.

We neared the door of the back room, and my peripheral vision caught sight of the crime-scene tape the policeman had hung up around the designated area. I kept my head straight, refusing to see anything more than necessary. I read the sign on the door instead, which said SALON EMPLOYEES ONLY.

Jasmine opened the door, and we both scooted into the back room. She closed the door carefully so it

wouldn't slam, and I stood behind her, unsure of where to go. I'd never been back here before.

"I can't believe this is happening," she said, her voice a little shaky. "I don't even know what to think or feel right now."

"It's okay," I replied. "That's perfectly natural. It's all a little overwhelming at first. But the worst part is over now, and we're going to be all right."

"Is it though?" Jasmine asked. "The body . . . Millie is still there . . ." She pointed to another door off to the side. "The sink is in there."

I followed after her. "I know, but—"

"And what about all these people here? Will any of them ever step foot in this salon again? I mean, what an awful experience. If this isn't a reason for therapy, then I don't know what is."

I remembered Penny Cho's reaction when a dead body had been found at the Bamboo Lounge. It was quite close to Jasmine's, but when Penny's thoughts had taken a turn in the direction of what I perceived as selfishness, I had been a little surprised at her reaction. Now, though, I could understand a bit better the thought process behind two women I considered friends thinking of their own businesses in these tragic situations. Turns out it's easier to think about how things affect you personally rather than the reality of a dead body.

"Do you know what exactly happened?" I asked, unsure of what to say. The last thing I wanted to do was upset her further.

Jasmine shook her head and turned the faucet on, holding a finger under the running water to gauge the temperature. "My only guess is that she was

electrocuted. I could swear it was a nail lamp floating in the foot bath."

"A nail lamp?" I asked. My mind's eye attempted to recreate the compact, rectangular light box used to dry gel manicures being knocked off the side of the nail station and hitting the water with a plunk. The imagery of electrical currents sparking and illuminating the water sent shivers down my spine.

"I tried not to look too hard at anything. Samantha and I unplugged everything and then she checked Millie's pulse. There wasn't one . . ." Jasmine stared off into oblivion and I couldn't imagine what that initial moment had been like for her. I had come close to finding a dead body myself, but I'd never touched one. I shuddered at the thought.

"Who is this Samantha person anyway? Is that the new girl I saw with the red hair?"

Jasmine nodded. "She just started last week." She tapped the side of the utility sink. "Can you lean over this all the way?

I nodded and bent over the edge of the basin, holding on to the sides to steady myself.

She attached a showerhead to the faucet and turned it to the lowest setting. I felt the cool water trickle down the back of my head, and watched the metallic dye fill the sink and go down the drain. It was kind of hypnotic watching the run-off swirl through the small holes of the drain guard, but then the water started to drip down my face, so I had to close my eyes.

"Thankfully you have these peekaboo highlights, Lana. It won't be as noticeable that you're half blonde under there. I promise I'll be over first thing tomorrow to finish it up."

"It's really no problem. You can come by anytime,"

I said. Then I remembered that the next day was Sunday and I had dim sum plans with my family. "Actually, if it's not too much trouble, do you think you could come by in the morning?"

"Not a problem. You're one of my best customers, so I'll do whatever I can to keep you."

"Jasmine, you don't have to worry about that at all. There's nothing that would make me stop coming here."

"You're such a sweetheart for saying so." She finished rinsing the dye out and wrapped a fresh towel around my wet hair. "I hope you're okay without a blow dry?"

"Oh yeah, totally fine. It's so warm out, it's not like I'll catch cold or anything."

"We'll head back up front. I think the police want to get a statement from everyone before they let people leave."

"Sadly, I know the procedure," I sighed.

"Did you see anything?" Jasmine whispered.

I had a feeling she wouldn't really want to know if I had. But I shook my head. "No, I could hardly see toward the back, and I was facing the other way. I didn't even catch anything odd in the mirror.

She sighed relief. "Well, that's good."

My brain froze for a moment. *"Well, that's good?" Did she mean it as "that's good I didn't see anything so I wouldn't be traumatizedit?" Or, "that's good because then I didn't see who did it?" Lana!* I scolded myself. *What are you thinking? This is Jasmine we're talking about. You've known her forever.*

"Lana?" Jasmine studied my face. "Is everything okay?"

"Yeah, uh, I was wondering to myself if anyone did see anything. And if they did . . . what did they see?"

"If you think about it, we don't even know for sure, really," Jasmine said. She started to walk back toward the door to the salon. "I mean for all we know, it was an accident. Maybe someone tripped over a cord or something."

I followed behind her, curious of both our thought patterns. *Had it been an accident? Had I just assumed that she was murdered? How else would the nail lamp fall into the water?* I found myself a little more confused than I would have liked.

When we stepped out into the salon, I noticed that more officials had arrived. I was unhappy to see that one of the two detectives was Adam. He had his back to me, and his head was bent down as he talked to one of the salon patrons. It appeared that he was writing something in the notebook he always carried with him.

Jasmine squeezed my arm. "I'm going to take care of another client; I'll talk to you later."

I nodded and gave her an apologetic smile. Part of that apology—though unspoken—was for my crazy brain and for considering for even a moment that she might be trying to hide something.

I meandered up toward the front, where Jasmine was prepping to take another woman into the back room for a rinse.

It was only a few minutes before Adam came over to talk to me.

"Well, dollface, it doesn't look like there's going to be any beach for us this afternoon." He gave me a polite smile but kept his hands to himself. Adam was always professional when he was in detective mode.

"Do you think this was a murder?" I whispered to him. I checked over my shoulder to see if anyone was standing nearby.

"You know I can't tell you that," he replied.

"Although, I suppose you wouldn't be here taking statements from everyone if there wasn't something suspicious, right?" I asked, trying to get even an ounce of a clue from him. "Or would you, just to make sure that nothing suspicious *did* happen?"

"We will talk later," Adam said, his eyes scanning the room. "Not about this . . . but you know . . . about your Nancy Drew tendencies."

"There are no Nancy Drew tendencies," I said. "I really am genuinely curious if it was an accident or not. It just occurred to me that my brain is now wired to automatically think something suspicious is always going on. So, I was inquiring to give myself some peace of mind."

"I can't take your statement," he said, instead of responding to my explanation. "So, it'll have to be Higgins. He'll be over in a minute."

I huffed. "Fine."

"Lana?"

"Yeah?"

"Is your hair going to stay like that?" He jerked his chin upward and smirked.

I narrowed my eyes at him. I knew that for my sake he was trying to make light of an uncomfortable and heavy situation, but I wasn't much in the mood. "You're lucky you're on duty." I folded my arms and turned my back to him.

I heard him chuckle softly before walking away.

CHAPTER
6

Once I was finished giving my statement to Adam's partner, Detective Matthew Higgins, I was permitted to leave. I hadn't really known what to say, and there wasn't much for me to contribute.

I reviewed my arrival at the salon, seeing June, then Millie showing up, and of course, the fallout that then occurred with them screaming at each other. Though it was just my own speculation, I did tell Detective Higgins that June seemed to be hyper aware of Millie's presence and the expression on her face had been of a sinister nature. His pen paused when I said that, and I imagined he was wondering if he should write that down verbatim or not.

When he asked if anything had seemed out of place, my mind went blank. Had it? Aside from the two women practically ready to jump down each other's throats, it did seem like just another day at the salon. I concluded things had seemed normal and told him as much.

His final question involved what exactly I remembered about the time immediately before and after the power went out. I remembered hearing a splash, which I realized now was the nail lamp hitting the water. A scream, no doubt Mildred Mao's. And then I heard a huge popping noise, now understanding that must have been some type of electrical short, and immediately the power blinked and fizzled off. I remembered hearing something slam . . . maybe a door, but I couldn't be sure about that because once the lights went out, I was completely discombobulated.

Detective Higgins asked me to spell "discombobulated" for him, and then questioned the existence of the word before officially thanking me and sending me on my way.

I decided to stop at the noodle house and talk to my sister since I was almost positive that Kimmy had gotten her all riled up with half stories and wild theories. And depending on my mood after that, I might stop to pick up a doughnut or seven from Shanghai Donuts because, let's face it, after an ordeal like the one I'd just been through, who didn't need a little comfort sugar?

The lunch rush was about an hour away and the restaurant was empty except for Vanessa Wen, who was sitting at the podium, reading a book, and blowing bubbles with her gum.

"I see you're feeling better after your stomach flu."

She slapped the book shut when she saw me. "Hiya Lana . . ." She drifted off as she scrutinized my hair. "What's going on—"

I held up a hand. "Don't even ask. Jasmine couldn't finish, the end."

She gave me a salute. "Right. Sorry about your luck."

Though Vanessa's casual dismissal and lack of curiosity about the salon situation wasn't what I had expected, I decided to be grateful that I didn't have to explain anything to her. My attention was caught instead by her book. It was rare to see her with one. "You're reading *1984*?" I couldn't keep the shock out of my voice.

"Yeah, my friend Simone was talking about Big Brother, and I was like, who the heck is Big Brother?" She smacked herself on the forehead. "Like, how would I know that, you know? So, she told me to read this book and everything would make sense and stuff."

"I see." I replied. "Well, don't let me interrupt your reading."

Her eyes widened. "Really? You're letting me fluff off at work?"

"Reading is good for you, so I approve of you spending your slow time on this. But"—I held up my index finger—"make sure that the dining area is clean at all times, and do not ignore any of the customers. Got it?"

She gave me another salute. "Thanks, boss."

"Is Anna May in the back?" I asked.

"Yeah, she's cooking until Lou gets here."

Without saying anything else, I headed to the back of the restaurant and through the swinging doors into the kitchen where I found my sister wrapping spring rolls.

She lifted her head as the doors open. "Lana, thank god, what the heck happened? I tried to text you . . . have you checked your phone? Kimmy came running in here rambling about a crime scene at the salon and said you were trapped inside."

"No, I haven't checked my phone yet; I left the salon and came straight here."

She wiped her hands on her apron and came around the counter to talk with me. "So? You still haven't answered my first question. There are all kinds of stories circulating around the plaza, but no one knows what actually went on in there. I've heard there was a robbery, that someone had a heart attack, then a seizure, and then some weirdo said that someone was poisoned with hair bleach."

I shook my head. "None of that is true. This place is going to turn into a circus. A heart attack or a seizure wouldn't even make sense for a crime scene. I swear, what is wrong with everyone?"

My sister stared at me impatiently. "Well . . . what really happened then?"

"Mildred Mao was electrocuted while she was having a foot bath."

Anna May gasped. "Are you kidding me? That almost sounds like one of those *Final Destination* scenarios."

Surprised at my sister's choice of pop-culture reference, I blanked for a second. "There isn't much to go on so far. The police took our statements and let us go after we finished. They mentioned getting in contact if there were any more questions once everything was reviewed. And that, as they say, is that."

"Thank god you're all right. I was worried you were hurt somehow."

Again, I was surprised by my sister's response. There weren't many occasions when Anna May and I expressed genuine concern for each other. Usually our feelings toward the other were something along the lines of annoyance or frustration. I didn't want to admit it, but she was making me feel a little sappy. "No, I'm completely fine. Except my hair . . ."

"Well, be thankful that's all you have to worry about." She pivoted and moved back to her work area, grabbing another spring roll paper. "Mom doesn't know anything yet, but I'm sure she's going to call you later. I figured she doesn't need to know anything right now. That should buy you some time."

Now I was genuinely shocked. "Who are you and what have you done with my sister?" I asked playfully.

"Oh, stop it. I can't be nice to my little sister?"

"No," I said. Her pleasant behavior was weirding me out, especially considering the last time we talked, she was lecturing me on my lifestyle choices. "You're supposed to scold me and tell me that I bring this negativity into my own life, and that if I hadn't been going to dye my hair some weirdo shade, this would have never happened."

"Honestly, Lana, you're being kind of dramatic this morning. As if I even talk like that."

All I could do was stare at her in amazement. "Okay . . . well, I just wanted to check in with you before going home. I'm going to hibernate with this hair until tomorrow."

"Yeah, don't show up to dim sum like that, you'll never hear the end of it from Mom." Anna May chuckled.

"No kidding." I sighed. "Anyway, I'm going to stop at Shanghai Donuts and grab a few munchies before going home. I'll see you tomorrow."

"Watch your sugar intake, little sister. You've been eating there a lot lately. If they had one of those loyalty cards, you'd have gotten a ton of free doughnuts by now. And all those calories are going to go straight to your mid-section."

"There's the sister that I know and love," I said.

"Good to know you weren't possessed by the nice-sister fairy."

Her eyes darted up from the spring roll she was finishing. "Get out of here before you wear this spring roll home on your head."

On my way out of the plaza, I picked up a half dozen doughnuts from Mama Wu. Her name was Ruth, but no one called her by her first name outside of the older generation. It was a relief to see her. She didn't go in much for the whole gossip bit, so I didn't have to worry about anything I did or didn't say to her. Another small blessing was that I hadn't run into any of the Mahjong Matrons before leaving.

That's when it dawned on me that Pearl and Opal had been at the salon during the incident. Yet I didn't remember seeing them after the fact, and I wondered how they had handled everything. I was sure that they would spread the news quickly to the two who were missing. I also found that to be a little odd in itself, since you rarely, if ever, saw the four widows without one another.

Fifteen minutes later, I was situated in my favorite parking spot at home, and I had six doughnuts that I wasn't entirely sure I was going to share with Megan. I planned on brewing a pot of coffee and sitting in front of the TV indulging in a good Netflix binge. I had a lineup of shows that I wanted to watch, and it had been too long since I'd had a day to just lounge around the apartment without feeling a sense of guilt attached to it.

When I walked in the door, Megan was at the

kitchen table with her laptop, drinking a cup of coffee. Kikko had been dozing on the couch, and my opening the door had woken her up. She lazily glanced around the room, looking a little disoriented from her nap.

Megan's eyes fell immediately to the doughnut box in my hand. "What happened?" she asked.

"Why do you assume something happened?"

"Because by the size of the box, I can tell you have a half-dozen doughnuts in there and the look in your eye tells me you plan to eat all six by yourself."

"Oh, did you want one?"

She pursed her lips. "Again, I ask . . . what happened?"

My shoulders sank and I trudged to the table, setting the box down opposite her laptop. "Do you remember Mildred Mao? The lady I told you about who always sues everyone?"

"Yeah, isn't she the one who got into the car accident with June Yi yesterday?"

"She's the one."

"What about her?"

"Well, she was electrocuted at the hair salon today."

Megan gasped. "Oh my god, that's terrible!" She closed her laptop and gave me her undivided attention.

I sank into the chair across from her. "I can't even tell you how unnerving the whole thing was. We were all just sitting there, pop music playing in the background, women gossiping, and then boom, the lights went out."

"Wow, so the power went out from the electrocution or what?"

"Yeah. That's the thought anyway. Jasmine went to check the breaker box and when she got the lights to

come back on, one of the salon workers found Millie dead in her chair."

Megan covered her mouth, her eyes wide with horror. "I can't even imagine."

"Trust me, you don't want to."

"Are you okay?" she asked. "I can understand the doughnuts now."

"Aside from being a little shaken up by things, I'm okay. Adam was called in to the crime scene, so he's back on another case. He barely got a break."

"Did he say anything to you?"

I tilted my head at her in a gesture of impatience. "It's not like I didn't try to get something out of him, but you know he didn't."

"Right, well, you never know . . ."

I rose from my chair and headed toward the coffee maker. There was still a half pot left. Grabbing a mug from the cabinet, I poured myself a cup. "Jasmine gave everyone their visit for free today," I said, trying to lighten the subject. "She's going to come by and finish dyeing the bleached parts. Everything happened right in the middle of her putting the color in my hair."

"Ah, that explains it," Megan said, pointing at the side of my head that wasn't dyed. "I wasn't going to bring it up, considering what happened. I thought maybe the dye didn't take or something."

"Hopefully she can get over here first thing in the morning before I go to dim sum with my family. If I show up like this, my mother will talk about it for the entire duration of the meal."

"Your mom would have a field day with this, that's for sure. Maybe you should cancel this week."

"Are you kidding? If I cancel, she'd lose her mind.

I better be sick to cancel. And then she would show up here to assess just how sick I am."

"True." She nodded. "So, getting back to this whole Millie Mao thing. What's the game plan?"

"Game plan?" I asked. I finished putting the cream and sugar in my coffee, grabbed two napkins, and sat back down at the table, passing the extra napkin to Megan. I decided I would share my doughnuts with her after all. "What do you mean 'game plan'?"

"Well, like, are you going to put together a list of people who were in the salon?"

I sighed. "Funny, you should say that. June was at the salon this morning. And she and Millie got into an argument right in front of everyone."

Megan eyes widened. "They did, did they? This is the fastest case we've ever solved."

"Calm down, detective." I opened the pastry box's lid and plucked out a Boston cream doughnut. This helped Kikko gather her senses. She flopped off the couch and came scuttling over to sit at my feet, hoping for a crumb to fall her way. "Oh, I see how you are," I said to my dog.

Megan grabbed a glazed doughnut and leaned back in her chair. "What do you mean, 'calm down'? This is what we do."

"Not this time," I said before taking a giant bite out of my chocolate-covered pastry. "First of all, we don't know for sure that it was even murder. And second of all, this is Millie Mao and June Yi we're talking about. I do not want to get mixed up in anything that involves either one of them. Any way you look at it, it's a disaster waiting to happen."

"Yeah, but—"

"No 'buts' Megan." I said as firmly as possible. "Even if we find out that it's murder, I want to stay out of it. This time, *for sure*, we are one hundred percent, absolutely not getting involved."

CHAPTER
7

After Megan left for her shift at the Zodiac, I decided to spend my alone time finally diving into my book. Since I was house bound anyway, it seemed like the best possible option, and my Netflix marathon could wait until later that night. Kikko and I spent most of the afternoon and early evening on the couch surrounded by blankets with the air-conditioning blasting.

Around seven o'clock, Adam came over. In one hand he was holding a pizza box, and in the other, a brown paper bag that was suspiciously shaped like a bottle of alcohol.

"Bad day?" I asked as I opened the door.

He kissed me on the cheek then stepped into the apartment. Kikko was immediately at his feet, straining her neck to smell the delicious scents of pepperoni and cheese. "To say the least," he replied. He ambled into the kitchen, setting down the pizza box and the paper bag. "Just when I thought I was going to get a break from work."

I followed him into the kitchen. "But it wasn't

murder, right? It was just an accident, wasn't it?" My voice sounded desperate and hopeful. And I hated it.

He looked over his shoulder at me, his hand on the paper bag. "No, it definitely wasn't an accident. For the sake of us both, I was hoping it was, but I'm sorry to tell you that's not the case."

The very statement gave me an immediate stomachache.

"The crime scene unit acted out a few scenarios of someone potentially tripping over the cord of that nail lamp," he began to explain. "None of them managed to get the nail lamp to fall in the nail tub. Then they tried a few other scenarios with someone bumping into the table, or even knocking it over with their hands. Nothing came up right. The trajectory was all wrong. And I shouldn't even be telling you this, but I'm tired and don't want to argue. The only workable scenario they came up with is that someone flung the nail lamp off the table so it would fall in the water, and in turn the power went out, which was either intentional to help them get away or a lucky accident they used to their benefit."

"Yeah, but maybe it was a fluke?" I crossed my fingers behind my back. "A freak accident that can't be replicated."

"And why doesn't Jasmine have any cameras in that place?" he asked. He opened the paper bag and pulled out a bottle of Jack Daniels.

I shrugged. "No clue. I guess she's not very worried about anything happening there. It's not from a lack of money, I can tell you that. She definitely has the means to pay for a security system—the place is always packed with women, and her services aren't exactly cheap."

He grumbled to himself and opened the bottle, then dug around in my cabinet for a highball glass. "Well, it would be nice if these people had more cameras. It would make my life a lot easier. With the way things are nowadays, everyone should have at least one camera in their business. I hope she plans to get one after this nonsense."

"You know, I thought of something after I left earlier today. Did you or Higgins interview the Mahjong Matrons at the salon?"

He set the bottle down and turned to face me. "You mean those snoopy ladies who are always at the noodle shop?"

"Yeah, Pearl and Opal were both getting their hair done while I was there this morning."

His brow furrowed. "No, they weren't questioned. They weren't on our list of witnesses and I don't remember seeing them."

"That's so weird, I saw them there. Not even ten minutes before it all happened."

He turned back around and poured a decent amount of whiskey into his glass. "They probably left right before the incident and you just didn't realize it." He assessed my hair again but didn't say anything.

I shoved him to the side with my hip and reached into the cabinet for some plates. "If you're going to drink like that, you better eat this pizza ASAP." I handed him a plate before opening the box and grabbing two slices for myself.

Once we had some food and our drinks, we migrated to the couch where Kikko did laps around the coffee table in excitement. I know she was craving a piece of pepperoni.

He bit into his first slice and pointed at the TV.

"Let's just veg out on some random shows and forget about today. I really don't want to think about it anymore."

I turned the TV on and opened Netflix. My mind was beginning to do that thing it does when something doesn't sit right with me. When situations like this would arise, I began to have montages of events that seemed significant to me. Like the fact that June Yi was present when this whole thing happened and sitting not even five feet away from Millie.

Then again, it was almost too obvious. If June were to do something scandalous, why would she do it in front of so many women, especially at Asia Village, and especially the day after an accident with the recently deceased? Which made me wonder then, was this a great opportunity for someone *else* to exact revenge on Millie? Did someone know that both women would be at the salon at the same time that morning?

Of course, then, there always is the idea of hiding in plain sight. It would be so ludicrous of a thing to happen that it could actually happen, but who would be willing to take that chance? Was June that bold?

"Hey, Earth to Lana . . ." Adam nudged my knee with his leg. "Are you in there?"

"Huh?"

"You're doing that thing where you bite your lip and stare into outer space . . . which usually means trouble."

"No, just random thoughts," I said, shifting my eyes away from his interrogating glance.

"Uh-huh." He patted my leg. "Try not to think about it. Let's find something to watch."

"Okay," I said with a sigh. Now that I knew this was a murder investigation, I didn't know if I could

just let it go. But I had to and really should. Not just for my own sanity, but for Adam's.

"Oh, and babe . . . ?"

"Yeah?"

"Don't pick a murder mystery."

I woke up the next morning a little earlier than usual for a Sunday. I was really anxious to have my hair finished prior to meeting my family for dim sum. I didn't know when Jasmine would be getting here, but she knew my family's tradition for Sundays, and had assured me she could be here with plenty of time to complete my dye job. It worried me a little that I hadn't heard from her yet, but I was trying not to overthink it.

I walked Kikko and made coffee, then put on my makeup and a temporary shirt for the dyeing process. I picked out what I would wear to dim sum, and by the time I finished, there was still no word from Jasmine.

I decided it was time to give her a call. While I waited impatiently for her to pick up her cell phone, I assessed myself in the bathroom mirror. My hair didn't look too bad unfinished, did it?

The harsh yellow strips peeked through the dark strands of my hair, and I concluded that I looked like a blonde-highlight job gone terribly wrong. Worse that it was only on one side of my head, so it wasn't even a consistently bad dye job. I sighed as her voice mail picked up, then left her a message, trying not to sound impatient or frantic. I knew that she'd been through a shock, and my anxiousness wasn't going to help matters. Plus, in the grand scheme of what was happening, how important was my hair crisis?

I poured myself another cup of coffee. Adam was

still sleeping, and so was Megan. For now, it was just me and Kikko pacing the living room together. Finally, my phone rang, and I nearly jumped at the sound.

"Hi, Jasmine," I said, trying to sound both cheerful and calm. "I hope I didn't call too early."

"Not at all," Jasmine muffled into the phone. "I barely slept last night."

"I'm sorry to hear that," I replied. "I wish I could say something that would help."

"It's okay, I'll be fine," she said, not at all sounding like she meant it. "I don't think I can make it in time though. I forgot to text you last night and tell you that I need to meet with one of the detectives this morning to discuss . . . some of the particulars of you know what."

"But I thought they went over all of that with you already?"

"Apparently there's more they want to go over with me." She sighed. "Is it okay if I come by later this afternoon? The salon is closed because they're waiting on some results back from the crime lab. They're not sure if I can open again right away. So, I'm completely free once I'm done at the police station."

"Sure, no problem," I said through gritted teeth. Smiles could be heard over the phone, so I hoped she couldn't tell that mine was fake.

"Thanks, Lana. I really appreciate your patience." She said goodbye and hung up.

I called my sister right away and told her that I was thinking about cancelling.

"Are you crazy?" my sister responded. "You know Mom is going to call you and give you the third degree. Just wear a hat or something."

"You even said yourself yesterday that I shouldn't

show up to dim sum like this. And you know Mom isn't going to let me get away with wearing a hat at the table. It's rude."

"Well, yeah, you definitely *shouldn't* show up to dim sum with that hair." Anna May groaned. "But you know the rules, Lana—no cancelling unless you're violently ill or out of town. You're just going to have to suck it up. The end." And with that, my sister hung up on me.

I returned her groan even though she couldn't hear me. Sometimes it was hard for me to believe that these types of scenarios still went on in adulthood. How old would I be before these family obligations didn't feel so . . . well, obligatory?

Worse things have happened, I told myself and sulked into my room.

Adam stirred from the bed as I walked in, and he turned to face me. "Morning dollface. Is Jasmine on her way?"

"No." I sat down at my vanity and assessed my hair again. "She has to go to the station and talk to Higgins, so she can't come until later."

"So, you're going to cancel dim sum with your family then?"

I whipped around on my stool. "Are you crazy? I can't cancel dim sum; my mother will have my head on a platter."

"That serious, huh?" he chuckled.

"You've met her. You tell me."

"Fair." He swung his legs over the edge of the bed and rubbed the sleep from his eyes. "Well, I guess I'll get out of your hair then. No pun intended . . ."

"Oh no," I said, turning back around to face the mirror. "You're coming with me today." If he thought

for one minute that I was gonna go this alone, he had another thing coming.

My parents are kind of on the old-fashioned side. Mostly my mom. I always made wisecracks about how things went down in the "old country"—that country being Taiwan—and all of my friends thought that I was kidding. But, in truth, I was always only half joking. There were many things a proper young lady shouldn't do, and dyeing their hair weird colors and thus creating unnecessary attention was one of them. Oddly enough, my grandmother—who came from an even more traditional time—was okay with my hair and loved that I was constantly changing the color.

We arrived at Li Wah's on the East Side of Cleveland at eleven o'clock on the dot. I tried my best to cover up the peekaboo highlights that weren't completed, but the yellow strands kept poking out and my hair looked like an experiment gone terribly wrong.

Adam grabbed my hand and gave me a reassuring squeeze as we entered the restaurant. I expected everyone to be staring at me, but no one seemed to notice, and I was thankful that people were preoccupied with their dim sum selections.

The hostess smiled at me, her eyes momentarily traveling to the left side of my head, and then pointed toward the back of the restaurant where my family was already seated. Everyone here knew us because we'd been coming every Sunday since both Anna May and I had moved out on our own.

For the first time ever, my mother wasn't facing the door, and I realized that's why she hadn't been scream-

ing my name across the restaurant like she normally did.

"Hi, everyone," I said, as we shimmied around the table to the open seats between my sister and my dad.

I took the seat next to my sister, and Adam pulled out the chair next to my dad. The two men exchanged a brisk handshake as Adam sat down.

My mom, Mrs. Betty Lee, assessed me, and her mouth dropped open. "Ai-yoooo. . . . Lana . . ." She pulled on her own shoulder-length black hair. "What happened to you? Did you have an accident at the beauty shop? Your hair looks so bad today."

If there was any one thing you should know about my mother, it was that she didn't mince words to spare feelings. Not even on your worst day.

I glanced at my sister. By the expression on her face, I could tell she hadn't told my mom that I'd been at the salon when Millie Mao had been electrocuted.

My grandmother, who was sitting next to my mom, tugged on her arm for my mother to translate.

With a sigh, I went through the play-by-play of how my hair appointment was unexpectedly interrupted.

My mother gasped and quickly relayed the story to my grandmother in Hokkien—the Taiwanese dialect my family spoke—and then my grandmother gasped as well.

A-ma had only been in the country for a few months, and since she knew practically no English, my mother was often her translator. She was a petite woman, not even reaching five feet in height, and I had my doubts that she weighed more than a hundred pounds soaking wet. Her predominantly gray hair was always pulled back in a tight, classic bun at the nape of

her neck. Though her hair was long, she never wore it down. And the most notable feature she possessed was her smile, because her two front teeth were solid silver.

My dad was the first one to actually produce a sentence. "Good grief, Goober, are you okay?"

Adam chuckled at my dad's pet name for me and I pinched his leg under the table.

"Yeah, I'm fine. I was on the opposite side of the salon when it happened," I explained.

My dad, William Lee, the tallest of our little clan, towered over us four ladies by almost a foot. He was the solo white guy in our immediate family photos, and people were often surprised to find out he was my father. Even though my sister and I were both only half Asian, it seemed as if that part of our gene pool had taken over our features more and more as we aged.

"Why must you do your hair like this?" my mother asked. "You are such a beautiful girl, and you always do these funny things."

By "always do," she meant the rebellious phases I had gone through in my teenage years.

"It's going to be fine, Mom." I reassured her. "Jasmine is coming over after I leave here to finish up my hair."

"Yah, but it is gray. Why would you do this? One day you will be gray anyway. Look at A-ma."

Even though my grandmother had no idea what we were talking about, she smiled at me anyway, and her two silver front teeth sparkled. When she'd first come to the United States, I thought it was going to be a temporary visit, but now it appeared she planned to make it permanent. My mother was in the process of helping her learn English, and she was going to begin the process of getting her a Green Card.

If you asked me, I didn't really think that my

mother was the appropriate party to be teaching my grandmother English—her own speech was still quite broken after all her years here. But she was currently the person with the most availability. Between me now running the restaurant, my sister doing her whole becoming-a-lawyer thing, and my dad still being active in the real estate world, my mom was the only one who could dedicate the time. From what my sister had told me, our dad was helping when he could, and that made me feel a little better.

"If you did not go there to dye your hair, this would not have happened," my mother lectured.

"I still get my hair *cut* there," I reminded her.

Thankfully the food cart came by and I signaled down the server before my mother could lecture me any more about my hair.

My mother was usually the one to select the food, so I let her do the honors. She knew all of our favorites, and the only time she really let someone else pick anything was if there was a guest present.

Quickly she rattled off all the items we wanted off their dim sum menu: noodle rolls filled with shrimp, pork dumplings, sticky rice in lotus leaves, turnip cakes, fried tofu, chicken feet (yuck!), and BBQ spareribs specially for Adam.

My mouth watered as I followed the plate with the noodle rolls on them. They were one of my favorite dim sum items. I was so focused on them I almost didn't notice that my mother forgot to order some spring rolls. Almost.

"Excuse me," I said, waving my hand at the server. "Spring rolls too, please."

He nodded and told me he'd be right back with a fresh serving.

I assumed once we got situated and filled our plates with food that my mother would continue her unsolicited advice about my hair and then trickle into other areas of my life, but it didn't happen because my sister made an announcement that took everyone's attention off of me.

"So . . ." my sister said, wiggling her butt in her chair. She straightened her back and tapped the chopsticks she held on the edge of her plate. "I have something rather exciting to tell everyone."

"Is it about your internship?" my dad asked.

"It is. Well, sort of." She smiled wide, showing all of her teeth. "As you know, I only have about a week left there."

"So, you're going to be coming back to help out more at the restaurant then?" I asked. I had been working so many extra hours at the noodle shop and I was getting a bit on the burnt-out side.

My sister huffed. "Yes, but this isn't about that," she said.

"All right, well out with it," I replied, waving my chopsticks at her to continue.

She gave me an evil side-eye and then turned her attention back to the table as a whole. "Well, Henry and I . . . that's the law firm partner I've been telling you guys about . . . he and I have been seeing each other."

My dad tilted his head at my sister. "By seeing each other you mean . . . romantically?"

My sister blushed. "Yes."

My mother's eyes lit up like a Christmas tree. "You are going out with a lawyer?"

"Yes, Mother . . . but—"

My mother clasped her hands together. "Oh, this is good news. I can't wait to tell everyone."

"Mom, you can't," my sister said a little too harshly. When she realized her tone, she tucked her chin in. "It's a secret."

I scrunched up my face. "Why is it a secret?"

"Well, you know, work romances and everything. I'm an intern, after all."

"So, Mommy cannot tell anyone?" My mother immediately deflated at the realization that this oh-so-amazing news would not be shared with her closest friends, who I'm sure she suspected would all be envious of her wonderfully successful daughter.

I slid a glance at Adam, but he seemed more preoccupied with his spareribs than with what my sister was saying.

"But," I interjected, "you'll be done working there next week, so why would it have to be a secret after that?"

Anna May's eyes shifted down to her plate. "Henry said we'll discuss the particulars later. It could affect me getting a job there later on down the line if we're romantically involved."

I studied my sister's face and felt my spider sense tingling. She was lying about something. "Don't you want that job?"

"There are other firms," she mumbled.

"Interesting," I replied, digging back into my shrimp roll.

"Why do you have to make it sound like a conspiracy? I just wanted to share it with my family, okay? I'm excited. It's been a long time since I've gotten involved with anyone, and it actually seems really promising."

Anna May said, her voice turning into a subtle growl. "Is that so horrible?"

I held up my hands in surrender. "No, nothing wrong with it at all. Sorry you took it that way. Geez."

That's what I said out loud, but truth be told, that is not what I was thinking. My sister was definitely hiding something, and I had a feeling it wasn't just a workplace romance.

CHAPTER
8

That afternoon when I got back to my apartment, I had a little time to waste before Jasmine came over to finish my hair. She texted me while I was driving home and said she'd be over within the hour, once she grabbed some needed supplies from the store. I decided to do a search on this Henry Andrews character my sister was dating while I waited. Most of what I found were stories related to court cases. I did find a few photos of him, and I had to say he was an extremely attractive man with sandy blond hair and light green eyes. He had a crooked smile that produced large dimples in his cheeks, which I could see being very endearing to my sister. I found a Facebook profile, but it was set to private, so there was no fun to be had there.

Nothing of interest popped out at me, but I was still bothered by the expression I'd seen on my sister's face. Between her refusal to make eye contact with me and the fact that I knew her well enough told me that she was leaving out part of the story.

There aren't a lot of reasons to hide a relationship,

but I could think of a few and I didn't like the idea of any of them. Knowing my sister and her high standards, I really hoped she wasn't getting mixed up in something that she shouldn't be a part of.

For the time being, I'd have to let it drop. There were more pressing matters at hand besides what my sister was up to with her new, secret beau. I had plenty of time to worry about it later.

Since I was already trying to dig up dirt, I searched the Millie Mao case to see what information had made it to the media. Even though I wanted nothing to do with it, I was still curious about the details.

The article I found was basic and didn't offer much. It stated the tragedy, then mentioned there were some inconsistencies that needed to be investigated. The source promised to report more as the story developed.

The hour was up before I knew it, and when there was a knock at the door, I assumed it to be Jasmine. Kikko rushed to investigate the noise, snorting and yipping along the way. She pushed her nose to the crack of the door and gave a good sniff.

I shooed her out of the way and took a quick peek out of the peephole just to be sure that it was in fact my hair stylist. Once I confirmed it was her, I unlocked the door.

The usual pep that Jasmine greeted me with was absent. Instead, she gave me a weak smile and shuffled into my apartment with a somber "Hi, Lana."

She carried an oversized, hot pink tote bag that had the salon's logo on the side.

I shut the door behind her and smiled. "How'd it go at the station?" I kept my voice light and airy, as if I were asking about dining at a new restaurant.

"Fine, I suppose." She shrugged the tote bag off her

shoulder and set it down on the kitchen table with her purse.

Kikko had followed our new guest to the table and sniffed at her feet.

Jasmine glanced down at Kikko but didn't make an attempt to lean down and pet her.

"Well . . ." I moved past her into the kitchen and pointed to the coffee maker. "Want some coffee or anything?"

"Just some water would be nice." She slumped into the chair adjacent to her bag. "What if I told you I think I saw something odd that day?"

I had my back to her at the time, prepping a cup of coffee for myself. But I set down the mug and turned to face her, leaning against the kitchen counter. "Like what kind of odd?"

She sucked in a breath. "Like June Yi lingering near the bathroom right before everything happened."

This conversation might need something stronger than coffee, I thought. "When you say, 'right before,' how literal are you being?"

She ran a hand through her loosely curled, brown-tinted hair. "Within a minute of the lights going out. That's all I can remember. I was mixing some dye near the back of the salon and I noticed her standing near the bathroom as if she was waiting for something. At first, I thought she was waiting for someone to come out of the bathroom, but then I realized that the door was open, and the light was off . . . so . . ."

I took a deep breath through my nose and let it out slowly. Then I focused back on my coffee. Normally this was the time that I would sit and ask myself whether or not the person in question was capable of doing the horrible deed they were being accused of.

And more often than not, I felt torn about that possibility or at least had some sense that it was a ludicrous idea.

But this time . . . well, let's just say I could envision June being that evil. And that thought didn't sit right with me.

"Lana, say something," Jasmine begged. "Anything. Tell me I'm nuts and no one we know is that sinister."

I filled my coffee cup before answering her, giving myself some time to think through what I wanted to say. Truth was, we did know people that sinister. And maybe her mind was blocking those memories from her, but the past wasn't something I could easily forget. "I'm not sure what to tell you, but I will say not to let your thoughts run away from you. Everything happened so fast and you may be remembering it wrong." I finished preparing my coffee with cream and sugar, grabbed a bottled water out of the fridge, and joined her at the table. She took the bottle from my hand with a nod of thanks, and untwisted the cap.

Kikko had retired to the couch, most likely bored because there wasn't any food present. "You did your part, Jasmine. Now let the police do theirs."

She cocked her head and pursed her lips. "Really? Lana Lee is saying this to me?"

I smirked. "What am I supposed to say?"

"For one thing, I totally don't believe your true feelings are to not let my thoughts run away from me. Also . . . it's June. Come on."

I understood where Jasmine was coming from. She was one of the few people that usually knew I was snooping around in one thing or another well before anyone else did. Partial blame for that could go to the Mahjong Matrons, who were at the salon regularly and filling the stylists and Yuna with gossip whenever they

could. The salon was, for the most part, their home base for the rumor mill. Of course, most of it was speculation on the Matrons' part. With that being said, their speculation was usually correct.

"As far as June is concerned," I started, "we do know she's a miserable woman and it's plausible she could snap one day, but you have to remember we are talking about murder. That's pretty extreme and we can't just assume something that horrible, even if it is June, without any facts to back it up."

"What if I told you that Millie threatened to sue June for so much money that it would jeopardize their bakery?"

Now *that* caught my attention. "What do you mean? Where on earth did you hear that from?"

"The Matrons, of course," Jasmine replied.

"But aren't we talking about a minor fender bender here?" I asked, completely confused. "I know she mentioned something about June paying for her medical bills too, but how could any of that total up to harming the bakery?"

"Supposedly she was planning to sue her for emotional distress, defamation of character, *and* her physical injuries. Apparently, this rivalry has been going on for a long time, and Millie claimed she had a long list of items to accuse June of."

I shook my head. "I still don't get it."

"I didn't at first either," Jasmine admitted. "From what I heard, Millie said that June has been out to get her and trying to hurt her any way she could for months on end. She thinks that June hit her car on purpose and that her verbal abuse was finally turning physical."

"Can you really do that? Isn't that technically considered speculation?" I leaned back in my chair. This

whole thing seemed flimsy to me, and I couldn't figure out what to make of it.

"Well, according to Millie she could and was planning on it."

"It had to be an empty threat," I said. "Would June really fall for something like this?"

"I have no idea. But it got me thinking, what if all of this is Millie's own fault?"

"How so?"

"What if she made it so June would hit her on purpose, and she'd have something physical to go on? And she underestimated June's temper and this . . . outcome."

"Do you know how much Millie threatened to sue her for?"

"A half a million dollars."

"What? That's absurd!" I practically screamed the words, and Kikko jumped off the couch and scurried away in the direction of my bedroom.

"The Matrons told me that a recent mahjong tournament was involved. A big one. Like championship big."

"How come I haven't heard anything about this?" I asked. "I feel like this would have floated all over Asia Village by now."

"Maybe it just never made it to you," Jasmine said. "It definitely was mentioned in the salon. Millie was furious. June said that Millie was stacking the tiles to her benefit and it disqualified her from the contest right before she won two hundred fifty thousand dollars."

"Whoa, that's a lot of money. I had no idea you could win that much at tournaments."

"Same here. Since then I've found out you could win up to a million dollars if you're able to make it all the way to the final four."

"Okay, so that's a quarter of a million. But I don't see where the rest of that comes from . . ."

"Apparently the rest is a combination of whatever she had planned for the lawsuit. This was the only info I heard after the accident. If there was more discussed, I didn't hear of it. You know how busy I get at the salon. I move in and out of conversations so quickly." Jasmine let out another sigh. "Come on, let's get started on your hair. I'm sure you have things to do."

"Not really," I admitted, feeling the disappointment of cancelled plans with Adam rising to the surface.

We made our way into my tiny bathroom and covered the floor with old newspaper. While she prepped the dye, I changed into a ratty old T-shirt and sweatpants.

"You know what I don't understand," I said as I walked back into the bathroom.

"No, what?"

"If all this is true and none of it is embellished, then why would June risk doing something like this in such a public place?"

Jasmine put down the toilet lid and patted the top, gesturing for me to sit down. "I don't know, I kind of wondered that myself. The only thing I know for sure is that June definitely had a motive. And if she really was harassing Millie for months on end, it's very possible this threat of a lawsuit is just the thing that sent her to the breaking point."

CHAPTER
9

To my dismay, the metallic gray in my hair didn't give me the excitement or pleasure I thought it would. Jasmine had been real pleased with it once she was finished, but I found it to be a little drab and lackluster. Only I couldn't figure out why, considering it looked just like I thought it would according to the picture I'd selected.

As I got ready for work on Monday morning, I assessed myself further in my vanity mirror as I applied smoky gray and black eye shadow. I thought it might make my hair appear more vibrant, but the effect was not as I hoped.

I couldn't understand why this was bothering me so much, but I decided it must be so I wouldn't think about more pressing topics, like the situation with Millie Mao, or the sidewalk sale meeting I was going to have with Ian later that morning.

The drive into work was pleasant, and traffic was light. I loved morning drives in the summer. There were no school buses or bustling parents rushing to get

their kids to school on time. I dreaded the fall season and all the chaos it would bring to my morning commute.

When I pulled into my parking spot, I saw June and Shirley Yi getting out of Shirley's car. I guessed that June's car must be in the shop. The twins seemed to be arguing about something, and June flailed her arms emphatically while they walked toward the entrance. I stayed in my car a few extra minutes so I wouldn't run into them and be subjected to some kind of weird interaction.

Once the coast was clear, I hustled into the restaurant, finding my way through the darkened room to the back near the kitchen where a row of light switches brought the dining room to life. There was something serene about being in an otherwise busy establishment before anyone else. Almost as if you had a freedom with the surrounding space that no one else was privy to. When I was a little girl, I would zip around the tables in zigzag patterns until my mother scolded me for running indoors. Her cautionary advice was always that I would crack my head open on the side of a table or chair at any given moment.

Through the kitchen and into the back room—a sort of employee hangout complete with an old ratty couch greater in years than myself, an outdated television set, and a small dinette table with two chairs—you could find my office. Or to be more accurate, a broom closet. Yes, it really was that tiny. But it had served my mother through three decades of running this restaurant, and now the torch had been passed on to me.

Somehow, we still managed to fit a medium-sized desk, two wobbly guest chairs, and three filing cabinets in the cramped space. When you moved around

the desk, you had to shimmy sideways—but it's not like I spent my time pacing in here. Usually to Peter's dismay, I did all my best pacing in the kitchen.

While I waited for Peter to arrive, I went through some of the paperwork that had been left for me over the weekend. Anna May had made some notes about ingredients we were running out of, and the fact that more pairs of chopsticks were missing. This had been an ongoing problem, and I had no idea if people were sticking them in their purses and pockets or what.

When I was finished, I went out to the dining room and straightened up until I heard Peter knocking at the door. He waved through the glass when I turned my head and signaled to him that I was on my way.

"You gotta help me, man," Peter said, rushing into the restaurant. "I don't know what to do."

"Okay . . ." I sized him up, noting his agitated state, which was very unlike him. There wasn't much that ruffled his proverbial feathers. "What's up?"

"Kimmy wants us to move in together." He whispered it as if Kimmy could hear us talking from two stores over.

"Really?" I followed behind him as he made his way to the kitchen. "But you guys haven't been dating all that long. It seems a little rushed, if you ask me."

"That's what *I* said," he replied, looking at me over his shoulder. "And she almost ripped my head off for saying it."

"How did all of this come up? Did she just bring it up out of the blue or were you guys talking about relationship stuff?"

We were now in the kitchen where he began every morning with first putting on his apron. He then switched out his ratty Alkaline Trio hat embroidered

with the band's logo—a heart with a skull in the middle—for a plain, black baseball cap he kept here and wore instead of a chef's hat.

"I told her some stuff," he said, his eyes focused on the grill. "And then bam, she was like, dude, we should live together, and then I was like, dude, whoa."

"Told her what stuff?" I asked.

"You know . . . stuff."

I folded my arms. "No, I really don't. . . . What stuff?"

He turned away, hiding his face from my scrutiny. "Like love stuff."

I started to giggle involuntarily. It was so cute to see Peter being emotional.

He whipped around to glare at me. "See? That's why I didn't want to say . . . you're gettin' all weird about it."

I covered my mouth. "No, I'm not. It's just cute is all."

"Don't call me cute . . . that's even weirder than you giggling like a schoolgirl."

"Okay, okay. Sorry. I promise that I won't giggle like a schoolgirl or call you cute anymore."

"What am I gonna do, Lana?" He huffed and started to turn on the appliances. "I'm not ready for that and she's taking it personally. But it's just . . . I don't know . . . it doesn't have anything to do with her. I like having my own space and the idea of living with someone is going to take a little bit of time for me to get used to. That's why I don't have a roommate. I don't know how you do it."

"Did you explain that to her?" I asked.

"Yeah, but she doesn't believe me. She said that I

must not actually love her if I don't want to wake up with her every morning."

"Hmmm. . . . Well, I can try talking to her for you if you'd like . . . but she's going to have to bring it up. Otherwise, she'll know you talked to me about it and that will really set her off."

"Good point."

"Try not to worry about it for now," I said. "Maybe she's upset about something else and it came out in the wrong situation. Right now, we have to get ready for the Mahjong Matrons." I glanced at the clock. "They'll be here before we know it."

At nine a.m. sharp, the Mahjong Matrons arrived. You could set your watches to their punctuality. But to my utter surprise, only Wendy and Helen walked in.

I greeted them with a pleasant smile, but also with curiosity. "Where are Pearl and Opal?" I turned my attention to the entrance, where I thought they might have fallen behind.

Wendy and Helen exchanged a glance.

Helen replied, "They're not feeling well today." She left it at that, and they continued on to their usual table without further explanation. Outside of her love for gossip, Helen was an otherwise no-nonsense sort of woman. She was loud and assertive and often acted as the mother hen of the group, doting on the others and making sure they were taken care of.

I followed behind them, unsure of what to do. This was completely unprecedented. Since I had started working at the restaurant, all four women had always come in and ordered the same thing every day without

fail. Now with only two of them here, I didn't know the proper protocol.

The four of them were like a well-oiled machine. Each one contributing something slightly different to the mix and complementing the others with their various attributes. Not seeing them together as the typical foursome we all knew and loved made me wonder if the two by themselves almost felt as if they were missing a limb.

They must have sensed my confusion because Wendy, the most sensible and patient of the four, looked up at me and said, "We will still be ordering the same thing, Lana. And we will also take some wonton soup to go for Pearl and Opal when we leave."

I nodded and zipped back to the kitchen without saying anything. The situation had me at a loss for words. When I was sure the swinging doors were closed, I hissed at Peter. "Hey . . . guess what?"

"The Matrons are here . . . yeah, yeah, I know."

"No . . . well, yeah they are. But Pearl and Opal are missing."

Peter dropped his spatula. "Really?"

"Yes, really." I tiptoed around the counter, unsure of why I felt like I had to sneak around. "Helen said they aren't feeling well."

"Wow, this is one for the books," he said with a chuckle. "So, what do they want to eat then?"

"Same thing, and then add a container of wonton soup for two to the order. They're going to take it to go."

Peter picked up the spatula and threw it into the sink. "Do you think it's sad we're completely shocked by this?"

"Not really," I replied. "I've never seen it happen."

"The planets must be out of alignment, or some-

thing like that." He chuckled to himself and opened the fridge, pulling out the ingredients for their usual breakfast of rice porridge, pickled cucumbers, century eggs, and Chinese omelets with chives.

As I prepared tea for Helen and Wendy, I pondered if the other two women were sad to miss their daily outing to Asia Village. Although, surely the two present Matrons would keep them fully updated on anything that went on in their absence. And that would include what I found when I returned out to the dining area. June's sister, Shirley, was standing in the lobby area near the hostess station. Another unprecedented event, as neither of the Yi sisters ever came into the noodle shop. Maybe Peter was right and there was a planetary shift that was causing everything to go bonkers.

I signaled to her to give me a minute while I dropped off the tea with Helen and Wendy. The women thanked me with a gleam in their eye that told me they were fully aware that Shirley was on the premises. I'm sure both of them had their ears tuned into our conversation.

Shirley was a little on the plain side. Really, both of the Yi sisters were. Shirley wore next to no makeup, often appearing pale and tired. Her salt-and-pepper hair was usually pinned up with plain barrettes, and the neutral-colored outfits she chose always hung loosely on her small frame.

I greeted her with my customer-service smile. "Hello, Ms. Yi. How can I help you today?"

"Miss Lee," she returned, bowing her head ever so slightly. Her hands were folded in front of her and she rubbed one thumb with the other. "I was wondering if I may speak with you in private."

The warning bells in my head went off. I could only

imagine what she'd want to talk to me about. There weren't a lot of reasons for us to communicate with one another. I kept my fingers crossed that it had something to do with the upcoming sidewalk sale. Glancing over my shoulder at the Matrons, I said, "I'm the only one here right now and I can't leave the dining room unattended for too long. Maybe you could come back later? Nancy will be here soon, and I could meet with you then."

"Very well," she replied, sounding a little impatient. "I will come back around ten thirty or so."

Once Shirley left the restaurant, Helen waved me over. "Lana, what did Shirley want from you?"

"She didn't say," I told her. "She wanted to talk to me in private, but I can't really do that right now."

The two women nodded at each other and I wondered at their unspoken understanding.

Wendy rested a hand on the table and gazed at me with genuine concern in her eyes. "Lana, whatever that woman has to say, please be careful. The Yi sisters are not to be trusted."

CHAPTER
10

Something about Wendy's warning left me a bit unsettled. In a way, I wanted to ask more questions, but at the same time I didn't. Instead of stressing myself out about something that hadn't happened yet, I told myself I could always have the Matrons elaborate at a later time. It wasn't like I didn't know where to find them.

They left with their carry-out soup for Pearl and Opal, and I had to admit I was little stunned that they didn't try to linger and wait around for Shirley to return.

The time passed uneventfully until Nancy arrived. It was comforting to see her warm smile and delicate features as she entered the restaurant. Aside from being Peter's mother, Nancy Huang was one of my mother's best friends, and an honorary auntie of mine and Anna May's. I've known her all my life as a gentle spirit who continuously encouraged and supported me as I grew into adulthood.

Not many in my mother's generation were big huggers, as their societal background in Taiwan leaned

more on the formal side when greeting family or friends. But Nancy was a hugger and she always made it a point to hug me upon arrival.

"Lana, how are you?" she said, giving me a delicate squeeze. "Your mother told me that you were at the beauty shop getting your hair done when Mildred Mao was . . ." She released me from the hug, held me at arm's length, and studied my eyes. "You are okay, yes?"

I nodded and gave her what I considered to be a convincing smile. "Yes, I'm okay. I appreciate you asking."

Her smile widened. "And your hair looks so beautiful. Does your mother like it?"

"I think you know the answer to that."

She laughed. "Yes, I do."

The restaurant was empty and would mostly likely stay that way until lunchtime. Nancy assessed the dining area. "I see it is slow. Is there anything that needs to be done? You still have to meet with Ian this morning?"

I nodded. "Hopefully it won't take too long. We're going to meet at Shanghai Donuts for a little bit. Everything is good here, but we could use some more wrapped silverware."

"I will do this for us," she said. "Now you go and talk with Ian. I will stop to say hi to Peter before I start. See you when you get back."

She disappeared into the kitchen, and I made my way out of the restaurant and headed over to Shanghai Donuts, where I found Ian waiting for me at one of the bistro tables near the picture window.

I acknowledged him before stepping up to the counter. Ruth Wu was standing behind the cash reg-

ister ready to greet me with a pleasant smile. She was one of those cozy women everyone considered to be their mother. Her rosy cheeks and kind demeanor had instantly won me over, and I often found my day incomplete if I didn't stop by and at least say hi. Of course, I always ended up with doughnuts to go, and on the rare occasion that I didn't buy anything, she always sent me away with a few glazed doughnut holes.

"Good morning, Mama Wu," I said cheerfully. "How are you today?"

"I am doing well, Lana." There was concern in her eyes as she regarded me. "How are *you* doing?"

"Oh, I'm fine," I reassured her.

At this point, I felt like a broken record. I had spent so much time convincing everyone that I was okay, I was beginning to wonder if I actually was.

"Please remember to take care of yourself. You are always working."

"I promise I will. I even spent the rest of Saturday lying on the couch and just relaxing with a good book."

She nodded with approval. "What would you like today? The usual?"

I turned my head slightly in Ian's direction. "Yes, but make it a large coffee. I have a feeling I'm going to need it."

We shared a giggle before she went to prepare my order.

When I had my Boston cream, a few doughnut holes, and my coffee, I made my way over to the table where Ian was waiting and sat across from him. He was dressed in a light gray suit and pastel pink shirt, which I felt a lot of men couldn't pull off. But with his skin tone, it worked. "Okay, I'm here. What's up?"

He eyed my plate. All he'd ordered was a cup of green tea. "I don't know how you eat all of that on a regular basis and keep your figure so . . . thin." His gaze traveled up to meet my eyes before he quickly looked away.

I shrugged. "Anna May assures me that my day is coming." I puffed out my cheeks and rolled my eyes.

Ian pursed his lips. "Well, your sister is a tad on the rigid side, isn't she?"

It could have been my pending unplanned meeting with Shirley Yi, but I was not in the mood for small talk. "Ian, out with it. What are we doing here? I've heard some rumors I'd rather not be true." I bit into my Boston cream and savored the sweet custard that oozed from the center of the doughnut. I could eat these every day and never tire of them.

He wrapped his hands around the mug in front of him. "I had a feeling it would get back to you that I wanted *you* to be in charge of the sidewalk sale."

"So, it is true then?" I asked with a full mouth.

"Of course. Who else could I possibly entrust with something this important?"

"How about yourself?"

"I have some other things that need to be attended to and I can't give this the attention that it deserves." He drummed his fingers on the side of the mug, his eyes focused on something out in the plaza. "Besides, you're really good at coordinating things like this."

I groaned. See what happens when you're good at things? People expect you to do stuff.

Ian cleared his throat and took a sip of his tea. "Donna has me working on a few different projects and I have my hands full. I know that I can count on you to see this sidewalk sale goes off without a hitch."

I wanted to protest and tell him that my hands were equally full. But if Donna had him running her errands or doing whatever it was that she made him do, I knew he was going to be in chaos mode, and truth be told, I didn't feel like dealing with the attitude that would come along with it. He would be barking orders up and down the plaza ruining everybody's day until the sidewalk sale was over. "What do I have to do?" I asked with clear reluctance in my voice.

"I took the liberty of making you a list of things that need to be done. Everything is on here." He pulled a folded-up piece of paper out of his inside jacket pocket and slid it across the table.

"Oh goody," I said with fake enthusiasm. I unfolded the paper and skimmed over the list of items that were now my problem. "I don't understand why we had to meet for coffee just to go over this. You could have easily given me this list on Friday when we spoke."

A sly smile spread over his lips. "I prefer to do business the old-fashioned way. You know, take the time to sit together face-to-face and have a conversation like civilized human beings. I wasn't going to spring this whole thing on you while we walked to the parking lot."

I raised an eyebrow at him, unconvinced. "Uh-huh."

He held up a hand. "Lana, please, I've accepted the fact that you've chosen Detective Trudeau, and at this stage, my feelings for you are strictly professional."

His eye twitched when he said "Detective Trudeau," but I decided not to point that out. "Okay, well, I should be getting back to work then."

"Just one more thing before you leave. . . . I wanted to discuss the situation that happened with Mildred Mao and June Yi the other day."

"What's there to discuss?" I asked, popping the last of the doughnut holes into my mouth.

"Exactly," he replied. "I don't want to make a spectacle of this whole situation, so it's best if it isn't discussed at all, is that clear? We've had enough issues around here as it is."

I leaned back in my chair. "Excuse me? Me? Tell the Mahjong Matrons. . . . They're the ones who would make a spectacle out of the whole thing. You can't actually think that I could control the rumor mill around here, do you?"

"Lana, you are a prominent figure in this plaza. And everyone knows that you were at the salon that day—"

"Yeah, and who you do think spread *that* around?" I asked, my cheeks getting warm.

"I understand that, but don't encourage any talk about it is all I'm saying. You don't want to give them more ammunition to keep the gossip flowing."

I rose from my seat and grabbed my coffee. "Ian, I don't make it a point to stick my nose in other people's business. Especially anything that has to do with either of the Yi sisters."

His mouth dropped. "Shall we talk about your track record?"

"You're not innocent in that, you know. There's been plenty of times you've asked me to look into things to help speed the process along, so don't act like I'm a willing participate in all of these shenanigans."

He stood and began following me out of the shop. "Just promise me that you'll stay out of it this time. I think it would be the best course of action."

I waved goodbye to Mama Wu before leaving. "Yeah, yeah, you can believe I don't want any part of this."

And that statement would have probably been more convincing had Shirley Yi not been waiting for me right outside the doughnut shop.

"Shirley!" Ian greeted her with a little too much oomph to be convincing.

She scrunched her eyebrows at me, and all I could offer in return was a shrug.

"Hello, Ian," she replied, sounding unsure.

"What can we help you with?" he asked.

"I have a meeting with Lana," she replied plainly.

His eyes slid in my direction. "Ah, well then, I won't keep you two ladies from your meeting." He turned to face me. "I will speak with you later."

I huffed. "Fine."

Shirley shook her head as we watched him walk away. "He is a very strange man. Handsome, but strange."

"You're tellin' me," I said with a snort. "Um, I mean the strange part . . ." It took me a moment to realize that I had an unnatural comfort level at that particular moment, and it caught me off guard. If any conversation took place between the Yi sisters and me, it was always formal and proper—and filled with a rigid undertone.

"Are you available to chat now, Miss Lee?"

"Yes, let's talk in my office," I said, returning to the formal ground I was used to.

She followed me into the restaurant, and we passed Nancy on the way toward the back. Nancy didn't say anything, but her eyes shifted between Shirley and me several times. Peter gave me a similar glance as we passed through the kitchen.

When we were in the privacy of my office, and

Shirley was seated in one of the visitor chairs, she said, "You have a very clean kitchen. I am impressed." She folded her hands neatly in her lap.

"Thank you," I said with a sense of pride. "Would you like anything to drink?"

She held up a hand. "That won't be necessary."

I sat down across from her in my chair and folded my hands in front of me on the desk. "What can I help you with, Ms. Yi?"

"I know that you are aware of the situation with my sister, and I have come to ask for your help."

"Excuse me?" I leaned forward.

"I know of your tampering with other situations that have happened around here, and I would like you to do something similar for my June."

"I don't know that I would call it tampering," I replied, forcing a chuckle. "More like assisting."

Ignoring my correction, she continued, "She is being very stubborn, and I do not know how to help her. I fear she will cause more trouble for herself, and this will lead to trouble for both of us."

"I'm not sure this is the best idea," I said. "I feel that I should at least be up front with you since you've come to me with this . . . dilemma. But I know that your sister doesn't like me very much, and quite honestly, I didn't think you liked me much either. So, I'm completely surprised by all of this."

Originally when she'd asked to speak with me, I assumed it was to tell me something similar to what Ian had said—for me to keep my mouth shut. I hadn't expected her to ask me for help. When we were done with our meeting, I would have to check and see if hell had indeed frozen over.

"Please, Miss Lee, I don't know who else to ask for

help. June does not have to know that I've come to you. I can pay you if you wish."

I held up my hands and waved them emphatically. "Oh no, I wouldn't take your money. I'm not a private investigator or anything. I'm just a restaurant manager."

Her chin dropped and she stared at her hands, rubbing the top of one with her thumb. "If you could consider helping me with this, I would very much appreciate it. The detectives have already started asking questions and are looking into the claims that Mildred made against June. Mildred's brother is now coming forward and telling the police that he feels June is guilty, and the stories do not sound good."

I took a deep breath. "I hate to ask this, but do you think that June is guilty?"

Her eyes slowly met mine, and there was a sadness in them that hurt my heart. "The stories do not sound good," she repeated.

I rubbed the side of my neck and stared at the calendar on my desk. I didn't know what to say. This definitely wasn't something that I would willingly sign up for on my own. I didn't even like June Yi. And, not to mention I'd promised myself that I'd sit this one out. "Can you give me a day to think about it?" I wouldn't have even gone that far, but the expression on her face was just too much for me to handle.

She nodded, a sliver of hope crossing her features. "Yes, that is acceptable. I will speak with you again tomorrow."

We both stood from our chairs, and I followed her out through the restaurant. She thanked me before she left, and I stood at the hostess booth watching her cross the footbridge back to Yi's Tea & Bakery where

her sister June was waiting for her and had no idea of what was going on.

Nancy joined me at the hostess station and put a gentle hand on my shoulder. "It is most unusual for a Yi sister to step into the noodle house. What did Shirley want from you?"

I let out a dramatic exhale. "You wouldn't believe me if I told you."

CHAPTER
11

Shirley's request had weighed on me for the remainder of the day. I couldn't decide what the right thing was to do, but I had a feeling sticking my nose in any Yi family business was not the answer. Did I think June was guilty, and was that why I didn't want to meddle? Or was it something more along the lines of pettiness and I simply didn't like her. After all, she had never been nice to my family. And now I was supposed to help her?

The mature voice in my head tried to give me a lecture on putting aside my personal feelings, but the bratty side was much more vocal. I thought about when my family and Peter had been under the microscope during Mr. Feng's murder investigation—both Shirley and June had snubbed us, assuming right away that we'd been guilty. I think if June Yi could have arrested Peter herself, she would have. *And* probably slept just fine that night.

Megan was still home when I arrived, and I was thankful for her presence. If there was anyone who

could help me with this moral dilemma, it was my best friend.

After I'd given her the lowdown, she took a few minutes to mull the situation over. "First of all, I can't believe we are still contemplating this to begin with. It should be a no brainer. We're wasting precious time."

"But it is a 'brainer'—for several reasons."

"Well, Lana, there's only one reason you should be considering right now. And that is, do you want to stoop down to their level?"

"No, but . . ." I started to come up with a sound explanation for why I shouldn't interfere with the police investigation, but I couldn't seem to find one.

"If we had never gotten into this sort of thing to begin with, I'd tell you to absolutely stay out of it," Megan said matter-of-factly. "But we have, and we know how to get things done. So, dismissing things this time doesn't seem very fair. And why do I always have to be the one to convince you of these things?"

"Because when things go sideways, I can blame you for getting me into this mess," I joked.

Megan threw Kikko's duck at me, hitting me on the shoulder. "You're not funny, Lana Lee."

I picked up the duck and threw it back at her. "I think I'm quite humorous."

"Uh-huh." She rose from the couch and made her way to the kitchen table to grab her purse. "Listen, you know deep down that you have to help June, whether or not you like it . . . or her, for that matter."

"Ugh, I hate when you're right." I groaned and flopped over sideways, planting my face in the couch cushion.

"Start digging," she said, turning the door handle. "I won't be home until three a.m., so we'll talk more

tomorrow." With a final wave, she shut the door behind her.

Kikko joined me on the couch and nudged my hand with her nose. I scratched behind her ears and smiled at her smooshy face. "Did you hear that, Kikko? We have some detective work to do."

For purposes such as these, I keep a handy-dandy notebook tucked underneath my mattress like teenagers often do with their diaries. I kept it hidden because if anybody ever found my notes, they were liable to think I was a crazy person. Sometimes, when I read through it, I started to wonder about that myself.

With little to go on, I jotted down a few brief thoughts I had on the pending situation with June Yi and her relationship—that I was aware of—with the recently deceased Mildred Mao. I made a note about Millie's brother and his involvement in placing blame squarely on June. I also included the little bits of info I'd gotten from Jasmine. However, I couldn't even manage to fill up half a page, and after pacing around my room for a while, I decided to call it quits.

My true work would begin after having another conversation with Shirley. If there was anybody who could tell me the nitty-gritty about June, it would be her twin sister.

I was anxious to get my day started that Tuesday morning, and I mumbled to myself about potential scenarios while I put on my makeup, or as I liked to call it, my war paint. My biggest hiccup with what I knew so far was that June was seen by Jasmine meandering around the ladies' restroom right around the time the power

went out. If she had been the one to knock the nail lamp into the footbath, how would she have successfully made her way back to her seat without stumbling on something along the way?

I wanted to consider that this whole thing was just a nasty accident and the person who tripped over the nail-lamp cord didn't want to come clean. But I couldn't ignore the fact that Adam said the crime-scene techs couldn't replicate the scenario as an accident. Someone would have had to physically lift the nail lamp off the nearby table and drop it into the footbath.

The only people that I could think of off the top of my head who would be able to pull something like that off in the darkened salon *and* find their way around without tripping on something would be someone who worked there. An employee would know the place like the back of her hand. I could certainly maneuver the noodle shop blindfolded.

I didn't want to think that though. I liked everyone at the salon and had known them all for quite a while. It was hard to even think about any of them actually carrying out this plan.

Then I realized that wasn't entirely true. There was one person at the salon that I didn't know anything about. And that was this Samantha person who I had never seen until the day of Millie's murder. I contemplated the chances that this new person at the plaza could be the guilty culprit. Who was she and what motives could she have?

My drive to the Asian shopping plaza was equally fraught with haphazard thoughts on what could have possibly happened that day. When I pulled into my parking spot, I realized that I had worked myself into a frenzy. I didn't know what my main problem was,

but this particular ordeal was aggravating me a little too easily.

Asia Village was fairly quiet as I entered. Most of the shop owners had yet to arrive, and I let the calming energy of my surroundings remove some of the chaos I was feeling from my overactive imagination.

I stopped in front of Asian Accents and studied the inside of the salon through its wall of windows, hoping to decipher how much light someone would have to see from the back of the salon. The answer to that was "almost none." The front of the salon was sectioned off from the rest with a floor-to-ceiling shelving unit filled with styling products and shampoos. A sliver of light would make it to the back, but it wasn't enough to afford anybody a great view of things. Especially if it was an overcast day and limited sunlight came through the plaza's skylights.

I remembered the day being pretty sunny, but I also remembered feeling like someone had thrown a pillowcase over my head as the lights went out.

With a sigh, I made my way down the cobblestone that covers the plaza's floor and followed it to Ho-Lee Noodle House. I unlocked the doors and let myself in. From the inside of the darkened restaurant, I scrutinized Yi's Tea and Bakery, wondering how I would get in contact with Shirley without interference from June. Even though it was Shirley's idea to leave June out of it, I agreed with that decision wholeheartedly and preferred that she didn't know something was up.

I didn't have to wait long to find an answer to my question, however. Shirley must have seen me come in, and a minute later I saw her slip out of the bakery and shuffle over the footbridge.

As she approached the door, I opened it enough for

her to sneak in. She took hold of the door, shut it, and peeked out the window back at the bakery. "Oh good, I don't think June noticed where I was going."

"What did you tell her?" I asked.

Satisfied with her escape, she turned around to face me. "I told her that I forgot something in the car. So, I only have a few minutes. What have you decided? Will you help me?"

We stood in the darkened dining area and I felt like an actress in a noir movie. "I'll help you," I replied plainly.

Shirley clasped her hands together and held them close to her heart. "Thank you, Miss Lee. I truly appreciate this kind act."

"Well, even though we haven't always gotten along, I still want to help if your sister is being wrongly accused. I know how that feels." I gave her a pointed look, but I didn't know if it would be lost on her in the dark.

She tucked in her chin, breaking eye contact. "Yes, I can understand your feelings." Looking back up at me, her expression sincere, she said, "Your kindness will not be forgotten, Miss Lee."

"Please, call me Lana," I said in return. If we were going to work together, there was no need to be so formal.

She gave me a delicate smile that barely moved the corners of her mouth.

"I will need your help to get started though. I don't know much about your sister or her life."

"What do you need to know?"

"For starters, who do you think did this?" I asked.

She crossed her arms and took a moment to think. "I'm not sure."

"Who hates your sister?"

She appeared taken aback by this question. "Why would you ask something like that?"

"Well, it's very possible that someone was trying to frame your sister. Considering what happened the day before, and then both of them being at the salon, it's an angle I should check out."

"Yes, but how would they know that both June and Millie would be at the beauty parlor that day at the same time?"

"It could have been a coincidence and the person took the opportunity while they had it. It might have been a heat-of-the-moment situation."

"But you just said 'considering what happened the day before.' That would make me think this was planned out more carefully."

I wanted to groan. A big, loud groan of frustration. Instead, I took a moment to count to five. "Right now, I have no ideas on what actually happened, but it would help to know if anyone hates your sister, just in case this was some kind of setup."

She turned her head away from me. "This is a waste of time."

"Not if it's going to help June," I reminded her. I feared she didn't want to give me a list of people who disliked June because the list would be severely long.

"Whoever did this was out to get Millie, and they did. That is what you need to focus on. My sister does not have anything to do with this."

I didn't want to argue with her anymore, so I decided to go along with this for the time being. I could always ask the Mahjong Matrons for info about June later. They had to know something I could use. "Okay, well do you know who hated Millie then?"

Her eyes slid in my direction, but she still kept her face turned away. "Everyone."

Change that previous groan into the need to scream. I counted to five again. "'Everyone' is too general. Is there anybody in particular that sticks out?"

She took a moment before answering. "You might want to ask your precious Mahjong Matrons about that."

"The Matrons?" I asked, slightly jarred by this response. "What is that supposed to mean?"

"Didn't you hear about the mahjong tournament?" she spat. "It's been the talk of the plaza for weeks."

"I heard a little bit about it, yes."

"Well, they are the ones who told on Millie for cheating. Not June. Everyone thinks it was June because she could not keep her mouth shut after it happened. June told everyone that she was glad that Millie got caught, so people assumed that it was her who went to the referees, but it was not."

"How do you know that it was the Matrons and not June who first told them?"

"June told me."

"June told you?"

Shirley's arms fell to her sides and she turned now to glare at me with an icy stare so intense it rivaled any expression my mother had ever given me in my twenty-eight years. "Yes, she told me, and I believe her. My sister would not lie to me. This I know to be true."

There was a knock on the windowpane of the restaurant door, and both of us jumped at the sound.

It was Peter. I huffed, clutching at my chest. I could feel my heart racing as I unlocked the door to let him in.

"Good morning, Peter," I said, attempting to act as

though Shirley Yi and me talking in the dark was totally normal.

"Uh . . . good morning?" He glanced between the two of us. "Hello, Ms. Yi."

She tipped her head slightly. "Peter."

Peter's eyes met mine, and I had a feeling we'd be having an equally frustrating conversation once Shirley left.

Shirley broke the silence. "I must be going, Miss Lee. I will speak with you again soon." Before opening the door, she skimmed the plaza, and finding it satisfactory, she slipped out and scurried toward the main entrance, no doubt to keep up appearances with her sister should she happen to notice what direction she was returning from.

I locked the door once again and sighed heavily. Peter was standing behind me and I could feel his eyes boring into the back of my head.

"Lana . . . what the heck are you up to now?"

CHAPTER

12

"I don't believe you," Peter replied. "I know you better than you think, and I don't buy it for a minute. And don't think I forgot about the fact that she stopped by and you talked with her yesterday too. Something is up, and I have a few guesses what it might be."

We were now standing in the kitchen and he had his back to me as he started prepping the appliances for open. I'd just got done telling him that Shirley and I had been talking about sidewalk sale related topics. Nothing suspicious going on at all.

"I'm offended," I returned, trying to act the part.

He turned around, his eyes giving away the growing impatience I'm sure he was feeling. "Yeah right, man. Just tell me."

Telling him the truth wasn't going to benefit me in this situation but trying to keep up this lie would belittle our friendship. "All right, fine. She feels that June is being falsely accused and asked me if I would help her figure out who killed Millie Mao."

He turned back around without saying anything.

"Peter, don't be mad at me. I didn't want to get involved this time. You know they're the furthest from my favorite people on the planet. If she hadn't asked me to do them a favor, I wouldn't have even considered it."

"So, what if she asked you? You don't owe them anything. They sure didn't help *us* out when *I* was being interrogated."

I took a step forward, my voice turning into a pleading whine. "I know. But can you try and understand? If I refused her based on the fact that I don't like them, then I'm just as bad as they are."

"Do whatever you want," he mumbled. "But don't expect me to help with anything that involves the two of them. If you ask me, June Yi is probably the guilty party. That woman is a miserable witch."

I wasn't going to bring up the fact that Peter had never really helped me with any type of investigating. At this point, who needed to split hairs? "I agree, it's possible considering the type of person she is. . . . But something doesn't sit right with me about it. Would June really do something this bold so close to their accident? I mean, she had to know that people would look at her as the guilty party."

"It could happen though. What evidence do the police have? Nothing, that's what. You're still trying to see the good in people, and that's why you don't want to believe it happened the way it did. That ship has long since sailed for me." He pulled an assortment of metal containers out of the refrigerator below the counter that sat next to the grill. "Especially when it comes to people like June Yi."

"Can you at least try and see what I'm saying

though? For one minute, put your personal feelings aside. Don't you think it's kind of obvious?"

"Maybe that's the point. It's so outrageous that it's true."

I had considered the same thing myself, and even though I had, I didn't want to admit it to Peter. "Well, either way, I told Shirley that I'd help, and I plan to at least try."

"You're a better person than I am," Peter said. "And no, I can't put my feelings aside. They thought I killed my own father. Me, Lana. Me."

I checked the time on the clock that hung by the double doors. It was just about time to open the restaurant, and the Matrons would be here any minute. I definitely needed to get some information out of them today.

Even with Peter being none too happy with me, I knew that I'd have to let it go for the time being. He'd either get over it or he wouldn't. My hope was that he would eventually come around to at least accepting the fact that I couldn't sit idly by even if that's what I wanted to do. It just wasn't right.

I slipped back out into the dining area and flipped on the lights, giving the room a quick once-over as I headed up front to unlock the doors.

Within minutes of opening the door, Helen and Wendy walked in. Pearl and Opal were missing yet again.

I greeted the two ladies with my customary smile and followed them to their usual table. "How are Pearl and Opal feeling?" I asked.

Helen, situated in her seat, looked up at me with a sad expression. "They are both still very ill. We will

be taking them soup again today. Hopefully they will feel better soon."

"I'll put in your order," I said and headed back into the kitchen.

Peter gave me a nod of approval; we didn't need to even discuss the Matrons' regular order at this point. "We'll need more soup to go."

His hands stopped moving over the grill where he'd begun to work on the Matrons' onion-and-chive omelet. "Pearl and Opal are not here again?"

"Do you think it's odd?" I began preparing a tea-kettle for the two women.

"A little," he replied, continuing with the omelet. "I've never known them to ever be sick or miss a day at Asia Village."

"Shirley said something weird to me this morning," I began.

Peter held up his metal spatula like a stop sign. "No way, man. I don't want to know anything about it. I just said to you not even a half hour ago that I want no part in this."

I sighed. "Fine."

He returned my sigh with a groan. "Ugh. . . . What? What did Shirley say that was so weird?"

"She said that I should talk to the Mahjong Matrons about Millie Mao . . . that they were the ones who told on her for cheating in the mahjong tournament, not June."

"Yeah, but so what? If they did, they had every right."

"True . . . but . . ."

"But what?"

"But then why is it a secret? And why do people think that June was the one to do it?"

He shrugged. "Who cares? It probably doesn't mean

anything, and Shirley is just trying to throw you off track. Maybe it was even June's idea to have Shirley come ask you for help."

"I don't know. Maybe." I finished prepping the tea and headed back out into the dining area. I had the people I needed to ask right in front of me. No sense in waiting.

I smiled at the two Matrons once again and set their tea on the table. Helen picked up the kettle and poured out two cups.

"Would you ladies mind if I asked you a question?"

"Not at all," Helen replied. "You know you can always ask us anything, Lana."

"I heard something that surprised me and just wondered if it's true."

Wendy blew lightly on her tea, then turned her attention to me. "What is it, Lana?"

I gripped the edges of my tray. "Is it true that you guys were the ones to report Millie Mao cheating during the mahjong contest?"

The two women looked at each other, their eyes widened, and then both of them set down their teacups. Helen was the one to respond first. "Where did you hear this?"

In the time since I've begun questioning people, I've learned that whenever a person answers your question with another question, especially in this context, there is usually truth to what is being asked. "Someone mentioned it to me in passing," I replied nonchalantly. It didn't seem like the best idea to out Shirley this early in the conversation.

"I see," Helen glanced down at her teacup. "Well . . ."

"If you did, there's nothing wrong with that," I added. "I was just wondering, because everyone is under the

impression that June was responsible for that, including Millie, and I thought that was kind of weird. I don't know what the big deal would be, especially if she was actually cheating."

Wendy inhaled deeply. "To be honest with you, Lana, a group of players noticed that she was cheating. It was not one person or another, but several of us were asked."

"If that's the case, then why is June being singled out? Who was the one to make the original claim?" I had directed my question to Wendy, so I was looking right at her waiting for some kind of tell. But out of the corner of my eye, I swore that I saw Helen make some type of facial gesture at Wendy to keep quiet.

"I believe this is her own doing," Wendy answered.

Helen interjected. "Yes, she has done this to herself. She was very vocal about her dislike for Millie and spread through the plaza that Millie was a cheater."

Their collective answer bothered me because I didn't feel my question had been truly answered. Were they in fact saying that June was the one who started it all or merely taking credit?

The bell sounded in the kitchen, signaling that their order was ready. I excused myself and headed back into the kitchen to fill my tray up with their food. When I returned to the dining room, I noticed the two women seemed to be having an argument of some type and harsh whispers were being exchanged in Mandarin.

I'm not sure why they stopped their back-and-forth when they noticed me coming—it wasn't like I could understand what they were saying. Their abrupt silence only led me to further believe that they were feeling paranoid about whatever they were saying.

"Is everything okay?" I asked as I began setting down their various plates of food.

Wendy's smile was a little overcompensating. "Yes, my dear, everything is wonderful as always. We were just curious as to why you were asking these questions about June and the mahjong competition."

After I set down the final plate, I took a few steps back from the table so I could observe both of their facial expressions. If one signaled the other or even kicked the other under the table, I'd be able to see it. "I guess I was just curious since June seems to be taking all the heat for what happened, and it's being used against her in this murder investigation."

The two women regarded each other, but both of their faces held no telltale signs.

"And as much as I'm not a fan of June, it doesn't seem right to me that she would get blamed for something she didn't do. I mean, Millie was planning on suing her over this."

Helen seemed to bristle from this statement but said nothing about it. She grabbed the soup ladle from the giant pot of rice porridge and scooped a few servings into her bowl.

Wendy reached for her chopsticks and stared blankly at the food in front of her as if she couldn't make heads or tails of the plate's contents. "I can understand this frustration, Lana. However, any trouble that June has gotten herself into is her own trouble, and you should not worry yourself with these matters."

"This is true, but—"

Before I could explain anything further, Helen interrupted. "Would you please make sure that Peter has our soup to-go order ready as soon as possible? We

are in a hurry this morning and need to be on our way shortly."

"Of course," I said with a polite nod. It was clear that I was being dismissed. So much for being able to ask anything.

As I walked to the kitchen, I felt more discouraged and scattered with every step. I tried to cheer myself up by remembering that old and rather strange saying about there being more than one way to skin a cat.

When Nancy arrived for her shift, I ducked into my office so I could think without being interrupted. The disappointment of failed questioning with the Matrons really bugged me. They were supposed to be the eyes and ears around this place, and they had managed to offer nothing of use. I wondered about that and about the little breadcrumbs that led in their general direction.

Were Pearl and Opal really even sick? I was starting to have my doubts at this point and entertained the notion that maybe I should verify their supposed illness myself. I could use my concern with their absence at the plaza, bringing some food delivery as my cover to see them.

This thought also brought me to the conclusion that I needed an insider to the tournament who wasn't the Matrons. I'd have to find out from someone else who might have been present and cross my fingers that they would be a little more forthcoming with me.

I definitely needed to talk with Millie's brother at

some point—maybe he could help point me in the right direction. Although from the way Shirley told it, he was gunning for June as the guilty party too. Would he be honest with me or did he have blinders on when it came to seeking out the truth?

It would probably also be beneficial to talk with the person that Millie got into a car accident with prior to the incident with June. Jasmine had mentioned there'd been a lawsuit involved in that situation too.

The first thing I really needed to do was talk with Jasmine and ask her for a client list from that morning's appointments. I decided since business was slow, I could run over to the salon real quick without anybody wondering what I was up to. And by "anybody," I meant Peter.

I hurried through the kitchen before he could stop me for conversation and explained to Nancy on my way out of the restaurant that I would be right back. For all they knew, I was heading out to grab some doughnuts from next door.

The salon was dimmed and only half the lights were on toward the back. I tried the door, but it was locked. I could see Jasmine moving around near the employee door, and I knocked hard enough on the glass to get her attention.

She jumped, dropping the broom. When she realized it was me, she held a hand to her chest and took a deep breath before coming to the front door to greet me.

"You scared me half to death, Lana," Jasmine said, ushering me in.

"Sorry, I wasn't sure if you'd notice me standing out here."

She locked the door behind me and headed back to

where she'd been before I interrupted her. "Probably not. I've just been thinking about what to do about this whole thing."

Following behind her, my attention shifted to our surroundings, and a mini montage of the last time I'd been here played through my mind. I tried to shake it away because the most prominent of memories from that day were of Millie Mao and her slack jaw. I shook my head, trying to physically discard the memory. "What to do about what thing?"

She picked up the broom and gripped the handle with both hands as if this would keep her together. "The police just released the salon back to me late last night. They said they've gotten everything they can from the crime scene. And now I'm here and I want to tear the entire inside of this salon apart and start from scratch. But I feel almost as if that's a little suspicious."

"Why would it be suspicious?"

"Because what if people think I'm trying to cover something up by changing everything around?" She began to sweep at nothing. From what I could see, the floor did not appear dirty. "But at the same time, who wants to come here now? Are they going to sit in the same spot that Mildred Mao was killed in and have a footbath?"

"I see your point," I said, my gaze traveling to where the foot spa chair in question used to be. "Did you order a replacement chair then?"

"Yes, but do I want it *there*? Should I move everything around so it all looks different and no one who was here that day can relive the awfulness that took place? Me, included."

"Well, it's something to consider." I didn't know

if she wanted me to affirm that it wasn't suspicious. I could see both sides of the argument, so I decided just to leave that portion of her worries unanswered. "If it makes you feel better, people went back to the Bamboo Lounge after what happened there." A handful of months ago, the owner of the Bamboo Lounge, Penny Cho, was worried about the sustainability of her business after a well-known food critic was murdered in her party room. It had taken a little while, but eventually things went back to normal.

"I guess," she said, releasing an exaggerated sigh. "Anyway, what brings you by? I'm sure it wasn't to listen to me ramble on about nonsense."

I laughed. "Well, I'm here for you if you need a good ramble. But I actually came by to help you."

She tilted her head. "How's that?"

Okay, so I wasn't being completely honest. Usually in these situations I had ulterior motives. I wasn't here to help *her* specifically, but if I could figure out what really happened, it would benefit all invested parties. There was nothing like a stray killer on the loose to really muck things up for everyone. After all, what if this person planned to continue coming to the salon? I'm sure that idea would spread in the minds of the other salon patrons in no time.

I opened by explaining as much, and then went into how I could maybe find the guilty party through the appointment list from that morning. I, of course, made it seem as if it was solely for her advantage and had absolutely nothing to do with June or Shirley Yi.

She finally stopped sweeping. "Do you think that would really help?"

"I do," I replied, feeling confident that I was telling the truth in that instance. I really did think it would

help. Whether it actually did or not was another story entirely.

"Okay, I can print out the info for you, but don't tell anyone that I gave it to you, or I could get into a lot of trouble."

"No problem, if I end up talking to anyone on the list, I'll just say that I saw them with my own two eyes that morning."

She gestured for me to follow her into the back room where she showed me to her office. The computer on her desk was already on and it only took her a few seconds to print out the schedule from that morning.

When she handed it to me, I skimmed over the information quickly, noting Pearl and Opal's scheduled times. "The Mahjong Matrons were here that morning. Did you by any chance notice what happened with them?"

"What do you mean?" she asked.

"They left pretty quickly, didn't they?" I tried to ask without accusation in my voice, but it didn't come out quite as purehearted as I'd hoped.

Jasmine searched my face for some type of explanation. I'm sure that she was wondering how I could insinuate such a terrible thing. Who didn't love the Matrons? But her answer surprised me. "Yuna did tell me later that she saw Pearl leave alone, she said she was sick or something, and would be back to pay at a later time. I don't know when Opal left. And I wasn't that concerned about it because I know for a fact that they'd never stiff me."

"Interesting," I said as I folded up the list and stuffed it in my back pocket. "Neither Pearl nor Opal were on the list of people interviewed by Adam or his partner . . . so . . ."

Jasmine's eyes widened. "Wait a minute. You don't think either one of them would be involved, do you?"

Really, I didn't. But something felt odd about their timing, and I hoped that it was only coincidence. "Let's just keep this whole thing between us until we know more," I said. "I would hate for anyone to be falsely accused and then more problems get started because of it."

"Believe me, Lana, when I say that my lips are sealed about *everything* that happened that day."

As I left the salon, I couldn't help but feel her ending statement had a double meaning that I didn't fully understand.

CHAPTER
14

I returned to the restaurant and was relieved to find that neither Peter nor Nancy questioned my whereabouts. It was nearing lunchtime, so Nancy and I straightened up the dining area in preparation for customers, but both of us kind of knew there wouldn't be many because it was such a beautiful day out.

With a little time to waste, I reviewed the list that Ian had given me for the end-of-summer sidewalk sale. It was pretty straightforward, and the bigger-ticket items all involved advertising. He wanted flyers made and ads placed in local newspapers and magazines. I jotted down a few notes on where to fit that into my schedule and threw down a suggestion for the plaza to start a Facebook page. I almost didn't write it down because I knew that somehow, yours truly would have to be in charge of that too.

While I was finalizing my scribbles in the margins, my mother walked in. She seemed perplexed and I wondered if she'd had a bad afternoon at the casino.

"Hi, Mom." I folded up the paper and stuck it back

under the hostess counter with my purse. "Come by for some lunch?"

"No." She scrunched her nose and scanned the restaurant, shaking her head in disapproval.

"What's wrong? And where's A-ma?" It was rare to see my mother without my grandmother in tow.

She turned her attention back to me. "A-ma is visiting with Mr. Zhang at his store."

Mr. Zhang, an extremely kind and wise man, was the owner of Wild Sage herbal shop, and he had become smitten with my grandmother. From what I understood, they spent a lot of time talking about the old days . . . although, I couldn't tell you if his old days were the same as my grandmother's old days because no one knew exactly how old he was.

"Okay, so what's wrong?" I asked again. "You don't look happy."

"Me and A-ma went to have lunch on the East Side. We went to the House of Shen." She paused and waited for my reaction.

My mouth dropped. The Shen family were our rivals, and it was a long-standing rivalry at that. Even before I was born, my mother's distaste for the Shen family had been solidly in place. I couldn't imagine what would make her go there. So I asked, even though I wasn't sure I wanted to know the answer.

She pursed her lips. "A-ma said she would like to try their food. I told her that they are not nice people, but she said the restaurant looks very nice and she would like to see. So, we go."

She paused again.

"Mom . . . come on . . . what happened?"

"It is beautiful inside. They have new everything."

Her attention drifted back to our restaurant, the look of disdain never faltering.

The inside of the noodle house had always been red and black with accents of gold. And though we had made minor updates over the years, it hadn't changed all that much.

"I wouldn't let it bother you, Mom. People love our food and that's what matters. Our business is doing really well—you see the books, you know."

"Yes, but it could be better. We could have more business," my mom replied. "I would like you to fix this."

"Huh?"

"You have good style," my mother said, much to my astonishment. "I would like you to fix Ho-Lee Noodle House to make it look more new."

Before I could protest, Nancy came up front to say hello to my mother. The two women began ranting to each other in Hokkien, and I caught a little of what they were saying. My mother was basically repeating what she'd just told me about the House of Shen. Without acknowledging me any further, they walked away and disappeared into the kitchen, leaving me somewhat stupefied.

Great, more stuff for me to do. I almost swore out loud, but thankfully caught my tongue right as a customer walked in.

Toward the end of my shift, the idea of checking in on the sick Matrons became more appealing. I decided to give Megan a call and see if she'd be interested in tagging along. She happily agreed but said that she had

only a small window to work with because she was heading in for a shift soon.

She met me in the plaza's parking lot, where I stood waiting with my carry-out bag of egg drop soup, white rice, and moo shu chicken. I'd gotten Pearl and Opal's address from Mama Wu at Shanghai Donuts who was impressed by my generous act of delivering them food while they were ill. I felt a slight pang of guilt lying to her about the real reason behind my supposed kindness, but deep down I knew it was for a good cause.

"So, what are we going to do once we get there?" Megan asked as I sped down Center Ridge. Opal and Pearl lived just down the street from the plaza in a condo development off the main road.

"I was thinking I'd go to the door, and maybe you can see what's going on through the window. If it looks like a sick-people environment."

"A sick-people environment?" Megan asked.

"Yeah, you know, like tissues everywhere, maybe they're camped out in the living room. That sort of thing."

"Uh-huh."

"What? It's a good idea."

"What if they invite you in?"

"They won't," I replied. "Especially if they're supposedly sick."

A few minutes later, we pulled up in front of the condo. There wasn't really a driveway for me to park in, so I drove a little ways past it and found a row of five parking spots that thankfully had a slip open for me.

"Maybe I'll just wait in the car," Megan suggested, craning to look out the window toward the condo. "What if someone sees me snooping in their window?"

"There's a giant bush in the front, you can hide behind that."

Megan groaned. "The things I do for you, I swear. You owe me big-time."

"Yeah, yeah. Let's go."

We got out of the car, and while I headed for the walkway, Megan walked around the front lawn and disappeared on the other side of the bush.

I took a deep breath, clutching my bag of takeout, and rang the doorbell. It seemed like several minutes had passed before anyone answered the door, but in fact, it had only been a matter of seconds.

It was Opal who opened the door. She appeared to look perfectly healthy, maybe a little pale, but she also had no makeup on, and I wasn't used to seeing her like that. Obviously puzzled to see me there, and though being a familiar face, she only opened the door enough to poke her head out. "Lana, what are you doing here?" Her eyes traveled down to the bag in my arms.

"Hi, Opal," I said, putting on a cheery smile. "Helen and Wendy told me that you and Pearl were sick, so I thought I'd bring you a care package." I held up the bag. "Some soup and moo shu chicken with white rice. I thought it would be good comfort food."

"Oh well, thank you, Lana," she said, opening the door just a sliver more to extend a hand. She took the bag from me and then returned the door to the small opening it provided before. "You truly did not have to go to any trouble for us. We have plenty of food here, but I appreciate your kindness."

"It's no problem. How's Pearl?" I tried to peek over her head into the house, but it was no use. There was a step up into the condo, so she already had a height advantage over me.

"She is doing much better, thank you. I suspect we will be returning to the plaza soon."

I heard a thunk and a rustle near the front bush. Opal paused and seemed to be focusing her attention on where the noise was coming from.

To distract her, I started to ramble. "It's just been so odd without the two of you coming in for breakfast. Me and Peter hardly knew what to do with ourselves." I threw in a forced laugh, and it sounded terribly fake.

But it worked. Opal turned her attention back to me. "Yes, I imagine so."

We stood there awkwardly, and I was unsure of what I could say to keep the conversation going. I had already asked how they were doing and offered the bag of food. As I'd suspected, there was no offer to ask me inside.

"Lana, I'm sorry to send you away, but it is not a good time right now . . . with us being sick. Please forgive me, and I will tell Pearl you said hi."

"Oh sure, no problem. You guys take care of yourselves." I continued to smile as she shut the door.

I let out a deep sigh, my shoulders sagging with the air I released. Hopefully Megan had seen something in there that was proof of their illness, because it didn't look like Opal was all that sick to me.

I walked back to the car as if I'd come alone and waited patiently for Megan to return.

When she opened the door, I started the engine and wasted no time pulling out of the parking spot. "Well?" I said.

"Nothing. I didn't see one tissue box, one blanket . . . nothing."

"Did you see Pearl in there?" I asked, turning out onto the main road.

"Nope, no sign of Pearl either. Maybe she was hiding in her bedroom."

"Maybe," I said, my thoughts moving a mile a minute. I felt unsatisfied with our experimental adventure. But there was one thing that could get written in my notebook: *It was doubtful that Opal and Pearl were sick.*

I dropped Megan back off at Asia Village where she'd left her car, said goodbye, and headed toward home, feeling more agitated than I'd felt in a while. Everything was starting to come crashing down on me. There was too much on my plate and not enough time to handle it all. How was I supposed to update the restaurant, head the sidewalk sale, *and* figure out what really happened to Millie Mao? Oh, and I couldn't forget Peter's request to find time to talk with Kimmy about their relationship woes.

When I got home, I walked Kikko and tried to clear my head. One thing at a time, Lana. Maybe I could stall on the restaurant updates. It's not like I needed to do this right now. And what exactly was it that she even wanted me to do? Were we talking about a complete makeover? Or did she just want some updated decorations to spruce the place up?

I hopped on Pinterest when I was finished walking Kikko and searched "Asian décor ideas." I felt frivolous. I needed to figure out murdery stuff instead. The Mao case was more pressing of an issue, and redecorating of the restaurant could wait.

Switching gears, I pulled the list from Jasmine out of my purse and reviewed the names of the salon clients once again. I had completely forgotten about it,

but Evelyn Chang was among those present that morning. Our interaction had been so brief, it had slipped my mind. She was someone that I knew would talk to me, and that brought me a sense of joy. Evelyn being a good friend of Donna Feng's, I knew I had an in. Donna would surely assist me with getting a meeting with the rich housewife. On top of that, I'd been to Evelyn's house once before, so she was already familiar with who I was. It was perfect.

Breaking out my notebook, I updated the info that I had and listed my true starting point with Evelyn. Everything prior to this moment felt like a false beginning. I had been getting nowhere fast, but this little glimmer of hope would be enough to carry me into the next day.

CHAPTER
15

When I woke up Wednesday morning, the first thing I did was call Donna to see if she could get me an appointment to talk with Evelyn. She, of course, had questions of her own, because if anyone knew about my digging and snooping around, it was Donna. I'd helped her a couple of times in the past on some personal matters involving the law, so we didn't have many secrets from each other at this point.

After I explained the situation, she said, "Of course, dear. I'll see if she can meet with you as soon as possible."

"I really do appreciate it," I replied. "I am getting nowhere fast with this whole thing."

"Well, honestly, if you ask me, Lana, I would say June is most likely the guilty party."

"You think so? Everyone that I talk to keeps saying that."

"Absolutely. June is a wretched woman, and always has been. I wouldn't doubt her completely losing control of her senses. She's like one of those women you

see in documentary films about people who finally snap because their dry cleaning came back wrong and that was the last straw."

"Why is she such a nightmare anyway?" I asked. I really didn't know anything about the Yi sisters when you came down to it.

"From what I understand, she was held back in life because of her sister, Shirley. And I say 'held back' as sarcastically as possible."

"Held back?"

"Yes, I guess June wanted to be an actress of some type, but she felt obligated to take care of Shirley, who used to be extremely sick all of the time. Not sure about the details of her illnesses, but the last thing June wanted to do was stay in Cleveland or work in a bakery, I can tell you that much. Their parents died while they were still very young, and it changed June's life. I can see that straining a person, but I'd like to think if it happened to me, I'd handle it much better."

"So, in simple terms, she's bitter and takes it out on everyone else?"

"Precisely, my darling. I've seen people bitter about much less. But the road not taken will plague the best of us."

We hung up after she promised again that she would contact Evelyn right away. I thanked her for her help and left for work after scribbling on a Post-it to let Megan know I'd stop by the bar later that night for a visit. We needed to discuss the particulars about the pending case, and her work schedule was getting in our way.

The workday was humdrum and the time passed slowly. When Nancy arrived for her shift, I decided to swing over to China, Cinema and Song to finally

pay Kimmy a visit. I needed to tackle something on this to-do list successfully, and maybe talking with Kimmy would get the ball rolling.

I entered the Asian entertainment store and was welcomed by Teresa Teng playing over the speaker system. I was a little surprised by the choice, considering the Taiwanese singer was often more popular with the older crowd, and on top of it, Kimmy definitely enjoyed listening to more upbeat music.

Either Kimmy's mother was working that day, or Kimmy was really depressed. But it was in fact my friend I found behind the sales counter.

Kimmy Tran and I have been friends since we were little kids, what with our family's businesses only one storefront away from the other. We'd spent a lot of time playing Barbies and running around the plaza in haphazard circles to our parents' dismay. As we'd gotten older, we didn't really fit together anymore, but despite the fact we were night and day, she was a lifer in the friendship department.

Kimmy glanced up from the magazine she was flipping through as I approached the counter. "Lee, what brings you by?" Her voice was deflated, and the typical sass she carried with her was non-existent. I could also tell by the fact that she barely wore any makeup and that her normally shiny black hair looked dull and was tied in a sloppy ponytail as if she'd just crawled out of bed.

"Just wanted to stop by and say hi. You okay?" I asked.

"What's there to be okay about?" She closed the magazine, slumped on the stool that was behind her, and folded her arms across her chest. "Don't say anything because I know you two are best buds, but you're

the only person I know around here that doesn't spread gossip faster than the *National Enquirer*."

I did my best to pretend I was totally clueless, but I knew what was coming.

She puffed out her already chubby cheeks and then let out an exaggerated huff. "I think I'm going to end things with Peter."

Okay, apparently, I actually *was* clueless, so it wasn't hard to look shocked. I hadn't realized their disagreement had become this serious. "Why? What happened?"

She told me the story of her asking Peter to move in together and him saying he wasn't ready. I was relieved that there were no variations in the stories they told. "He's just such a jerk, Lana. I mean, then don't tell me you're so in love with me and blah-blah-blah."

I wanted to tell her that I could understand why she was upset, but at this early stage in their relationship, I kind of felt like she was overreacting. Me telling her that, however, would get us nowhere. "Maybe it's just too soon to be thinking about moving in together. I wouldn't break up with him over it. . . . You guys need more time to develop and evolve."

"Lana, I'm not getting any younger, and I want kids . . . and I want to be in a relationship where things are going somewhere. Not this stagnant . . . crap." Her cheeks were starting to turn red with agitation. "We're almost thirty. Don't you want that stuff with Detective Hottie Pants?"

I groaned. Megan was to blame for Adam's nickname, and though I'd tried hard to discourage people from calling him that, it hadn't happened so far. "Actually, I'm okay with the rate things are going. I don't want to rush into anything, you know? Kids aren't

something that I think or worry about, so I can't say that I relate with you on that aspect. Regardless though, it's not like your biological clock is on its last leg. There's still plenty of time for all that."

"Thirty, Lana, we're two years away from thirty."

"Look at Anna May," I said. "She's thirty-one and she's not married."

"That's your example?" Kimmy asked. "Your sister . . . don't even get me started on your sister. She could use a few how-tos on how to loosen up. And maybe spend a little time in the dating department. Maybe that's what she needs—"

I dramatically put my hands over my ears. "La la la, I don't want to talk about Anna May in that way. Ever." I also didn't want to tell Kimmy about my sister's new relationship. I also technically couldn't say anything since it was supposed to be some kind of secret.

Kimmy smirked. "Fair. Anyways, yeah, I don't know now, Lana. Peter is a great guy, but what is really happening here? He's afraid of commitment . . . that's all I can see."

"I wouldn't say that. I think you should give it more time. Really. I mean, you haven't even been together for six months yet."

She scowled and leaned forward on her stool. "Are you taking his side right now?"

"No . . ." I knew I had to choose my words carefully. Kimmy was somewhat of a ticking time bomb when she became defensive. "I just think you need to give things time to develop and see where it goes . . . naturally. Twenty-eight isn't that old. It's nothing, really. A drop in the bucket."

"Says you," she scoffed. "Whatever. I don't want

to talk about it anymore." She stood up and threw her hands in the air. "Let's talk about something else. Tell me what's going on with the whole Millie Mao thing. That'll keep me preoccupied for at least twenty minutes."

"Why do you assume I know anything about the Millie Mao thing?"

"Because you're you," she said plainly. "Now out with it."

I sighed. I didn't want to tell her anything, but I didn't want to leave on this awkward disagreement about Peter either. "There's not a lot to tell really. Shirley did ask me to help out though . . . she claims that June is innocent. So far I've gotten nowhere with it."

"That rotten woman probably did do it," Kimmy said, lifting her chin. "I wouldn't put it past her at all. She'd kill us all if she had the chance."

"There has to be something redeeming about her." For the record, I sounded completely unconvincing.

"Doubt it . . ." Kimmy trailed off, and her line of sight ran along the far wall near the movie racks.

That's when I knew that my friend was holding out. "What aren't you telling me?"

"I did see something strange . . . but I don't know if it's related to what happened or not."

I gawked at her. "Well, duh, tell me."

She squirmed on her stool. "I saw Opal pacing near the main entrance doors, it seemed like she was waiting for someone—"

"Did you see who?"

Kimmy clucked her tongue. "Yeah, if you would let me finish my damn sentence."

I held up my hands in defense. "Okay, sorry. Continue."

"Anyways, she was pacing, and she kept checking around the corner at the salon. I don't know what her problem was, but she seemed kind of nervous. Then I saw Pearl pull up and she ran out of the plaza. A few minutes later, the cops came walking in."

I felt a pit forming in my stomach. After seeing Opal at her house the previous day and being less than convinced that either she or Pearl was sick, it was hard not to think that what Kimmy was telling me confirmed my suspicions. But it was just a coincidence, right? Yes, it had to be. I was still unwilling to believe any of the Mahjong Matrons would be capable of doing something like that and that the rest of them would cover it up. They were all just the sweetest old ladies. "Did she look sick to you?"

"Sick?"

"Yeah, you know . . . like maybe she had the stomach flu or something."

"It's hard to say . . . she did seem kind of pale. But the only thing I couldn't figure out is why didn't she just go to the car with her sister to begin with?"

When I got back to the restaurant, I found myself wishing that I was someone else, because this case wasn't something I wanted to be a part of anymore. I didn't want to believe that any foul play involved the Matrons, especially Opal. She was the most soft spoken of the bunch, and the gentlest. The whole thing had to be a misunderstanding. For my own sanity's sake.

I was in my office going through sales slips when I received a text from Donna telling me that I could meet with Evelyn at four o'clock that afternoon. It was an hour before my shift ended, but I was sure that

Nancy wouldn't mind me taking off a little early, considering how slow it'd been the entire day.

A little bit of relief washed over me as I thanked Donna once again for her help. There was potential in talking with Evelyn, and I was hoping she would give me something that could take that small part of my brain away from the thought that one of my favorite customers was possibly a murderer.

CHAPTER
16

I pulled up to Evelyn Chang's expansive home in Rocky River with five minutes to spare. She lived in what I could only refer to as a mansion. I didn't actually know the qualifications for a house to be a legit mansion, but if the house had wings, I'd say that counted.

The first time I'd ever visited the Chang residence was to speak to the maid in order to find out some much-needed information about a case I was working on at the time. I wouldn't have thought that close to a month later, I'd be back to ask more questions, and this time to speak with the lady of the home.

I rang the musical doorbell and waited for the housekeeper, Susan, to answer the door. So, it threw me off guard when Evelyn was the one to greet me.

"Hello, Lana." She gave me a dazzling smile and stepped to the side. Her hair and makeup were exceptionally well done considering she was just lounging around the house. Dressed casually in a fuchsia floral knit tank top and khaki capris complete with diamond

studded flip-flops she appeared to be the epitome of a relaxed housewife enjoying a gorgeous summer day. "Please come in. Susan took the kids shopping for an upcoming camping trip so we could have some privacy. From what I understand, the conversation that needs to be had is quite on the serious side."

I walked in with the same amazement I had the very first time. "It is. Thank you for meeting with me, Ms. Chang, I really do appreciate your time."

"Don't mention it," she replied, signaling me to follow her. "You know I just adore Donna and I'll do anything to help a friend of hers."

She led me to her private library, and my mouth nearly dropped to the floor when I saw her collection of books. The shelves lined an entire wall and were floor to ceiling. They were jam-packed with both Chinese and American novels. I think I gasped out loud because she chuckled and said, "I'm somewhat of a collector. Do you like to read?"

I nodded in return. "Do I ever."

"What do you like most of all?" she asked, moving to a group of leather chairs in the center of the room. There was tea service for two set on the round mahogany coffee table that sat between the chairs.

"Mysteries are my favorite, but I'll read anything," I told her.

"I'm a romance woman myself." She sat gingerly on the edge of her chair and poured tea into two cups. "I'm sorry, I assumed you'd want tea. Would you prefer a soda or water instead?"

"No, tea is fine, thank you." I took the seat across from her.

"Now, what can I help you with?" she asked once we were both settled with our tea. "Donna didn't go

into any particulars; she said you'd go over everything once you arrived."

"Well, besides being serious, the topic is also kind of delicate, so if you don't mind keeping it between the two of us, I'd really appreciate that too."

"I completely understand, Lana. And, I am absolutely a believer in discretion."

I took a deep breath. I didn't level with many people about this sort of thing, so I was a tad on the nervous side. My hands were sweaty, and it wasn't from the teacup. "I'm looking into what happened with Mildred Mao," I began. "And then I remembered that you and I ran into each other at the salon that day. So, I was wondering if you might have seen or known anything that didn't get passed along to the cops?"

Evelyn set her teacup down on the coffee table and shifted uncomfortably in her seat. She put her hands between the seat cushion and her thighs. "I had a feeling it might be something of this nature. Donna mentioned to me that you were helping her from the very beginning with her own situation. Which I truly commend you for, by the way. It's quite a task to take on. And you don't have to worry, I won't tell anybody about that either."

"Thank you. I figure the fewer people know, the better."

"But I have to ask. Don't you find this sort of thing rather dangerous? Or worry that you'll bark up the wrong tree? I don't think I need to remind you that things did get a little complicated with Donna . . . dreadful, really."

"It can be somewhat risky at times, but there's something in me that can't seem to let these situations slide."

She nodded and the expression on her face told me that she respected my answer. "I didn't see much, to be honest with you. I was on the other side of the partition, but I did see June get up right before the lights went out, so I know she was in the vicinity. And I did tell the police about it in case it was relevant."

"I see." I took a moment to think about that. It matched up with what Jasmine had said as well. "Do you think that June would be capable of doing something like this?"

Her eyes moved side to side like a pendulum as she contemplated my question. After what seemed like an eternity, she finally answered. "Yes, I would have to say so, unfortunately. I do feel bad for that poor woman—you can tell that she absolutely detests everything in sight. But alas, we make our own misery, don't we?"

"Donna mentioned something about her feeling obligated to take care of Shirley."

Ms. Chang picked up her teacup and took a delicate sip. "Yes, she's always been very protective of her sister. That's the only thing that shocks me about this whole thing."

"What do you mean?" I asked.

"If she is guilty of this, well then who would take care of her sister while she's whisked away to prison? Perhaps she didn't think of that in the heat of the moment, but if she did harm Millie Mao, it was a bad judgment call on her part. They have no other family."

"I see." If Anna May and I had only each other, would we be less willing to take risks in fear of leaving the other? I would assume so. "Okay, so let's pretend that it wasn't June, just for a minute. Who in the salon do you think would be capable of murder?"

"With Mildred Mao's reputation?" A nervous laugh escaped from Ms. Chang. "My dear, she has made quite a few people feel murderous, I can tell you that. Especially within the mahjong community."

My stomach sank. I didn't like where this was going. "Yes, but anyone specific that might have been there that day?"

"Actually yes, two people to be exact."

My stomach was flip-flopping all over the place now. I didn't want to hear what she said next.

"Well, first there's Opal . . . and then there's Lynn Ming to consider," Ms. Chang replied.

I cringed at the mention of Opal's name, but the second name caught me off guard. "What happened with them?"

"Well, the Mahjong Matrons and Millie have a checkered past. Millie always wanted to be part of their group, but they never allowed her to play with them. They said she was a dishonest player. And apparently, they were right. Opal seemed to be the most adamant about leaving her out of their group, however."

"Opal?" I was shocked by this and tried to imagine the quiet and good-natured woman that I knew acting out in anything that resembled an adamant manner.

"Evidently she had very strong feelings about it. She promised to keep Millie out of their group at any cost."

"And what about this Lynn Ming woman? What happened there?"

"Millie and Lynn play in the same mahjong group, so you'd assume they were friendly with one another. But from what I've heard, Lynn has never cared for Millie and they would get into all kind of arguments.

Lynn tried at one time to have Millie kicked out of their group, The Tile Tigresses . . . not sure if you're familiar with them?"

"Really, kicked out?" I'd heard of the Tile Tigresses before in passing. They were at the top of the leader board in the Cleveland area and competed with the Matrons on a regular basis. I would say, though, that the Matrons beat them eight of the last ten times.

"Yes, Millie was always threatening to sue people on opposing teams for one thing or another. I'll tell you, I've never met someone who was so accident-prone. Someone was always hitting her car, or spilling hot liquids on her, and one time she even claimed another player tripped her with their cane while she was walking by a mahjong table. She broke a leg that time and was out of commission for quite a while."

"Interesting."

"You don't know the half of it. I've heard so many absurd stories about the woman, you'd think it was a comedy show instead of real life."

"Do you happen to know who her last car accident was with before June Yi?"

Evelyn froze. "Her last car accident? What would that have to do with anything?"

I shrugged. "It's possible that they may have been looking for revenge after a lost lawsuit. . . . I'm assuming they lost since Millie was caught bragging about it. Or they could know of something that may be useful."

"I see. Unfortunately, I'm afraid I don't know the name or the circumstances behind that situation."

"It was worth a shot. No one seems to know any details about it. How about family? Do you happen to know her brother?"

She winced. "Jeffrey Mao? Talking to him might

not be a good idea. He's not exactly in the best mental frame of mind right now. Her brother has always been a little on the illogical side, much like her. And considering what just happened with Millie, I can only imagine that his behavior is worse than normal."

"Still, I'd like to talk to him if I can. He could help give some insight into potential rivalries that none of us are aware existed."

"I wish I could help you, but I don't know much about the man. He spends a lot of time at the community center on the East Side over on Rockwell Avenue. And I'm afraid that's all I know about him. I still don't advise speaking with him though. I think it would end up making more trouble than it's worth."

I couldn't think of anything else to ask, so I committed the information she'd given to memory while we finished our tea. It wasn't as much as I'd hoped to learn, but it was better than what I came with, which was a big fat nothing.

When it was time to say goodbye, she walked me to the door.

"You've definitely been very helpful," I said. "I think I have everything I need for right now. Thank you again for taking the time to meet with me today."

"I'm glad I could provide you with something useful. Like I said, anything to help a friend of Donna's. And please, take my warning about Jeffrey seriously. We wouldn't want to agitate the situation further."

"I'll keep it in mind. But just one more thing before I go," I said as I passed through the threshold and stepped out into the muggy August evening. "How did you know all this about the mahjong players and Lynn Ming?"

"Well, Lynn is Jasmine's grandmother, of course."

CHAPTER
17

I sat in the car staring out my windshield for a good
five minutes while I processed what Ms. Chang had
just told me. Lynn Ming was Jasmine's grandmother.
Duh. It didn't even occur to me when she said the name
because the surname Ming was so common. Also, I'd
never met Jasmine's grandmother or known that she
was a mahjong player for a local team.

It started to eat at me that Jasmine hadn't mentioned
the fact that her grandmother was at the salon that day,
or that she had close associations with the woman
who was murdered in her very own salon. I began to
think about the things she'd said to me in regard to not
wanting to remember that day and that keeping things
between her and I would not be a problem.

She didn't seem too reluctant about giving me information, but then again, she was hiding a very suspicious aspect of the whole thing. Why wouldn't she
mention her grandmother was there? Or even introduce us? Jasmine and I had been friends for a long
time, and it would be a natural thing to do.

Even still, the last person I wanted to think would be guilty of some ill doing was a grandmother. And my stylist's grandmother no less.

I put the car in gear and maneuvered my way out of the driveway, heading for the Zodiac. I needed to consult with Megan before my head exploded.

When I arrived at the bar, I hadn't expected to find Adam there. He was seated on his usual stool, his eyes glued to the flat-screen TV overhead. It was tuned to a news station and a sophisticated-looking anchorwoman in a blush pink suit talking on mute while a news banner scrolled across the bottom of the screen.

I despised watching the news these days. There was always some awful to-do that dominated the airwaves all day. Months ago, I decided to shield myself from the bombardment of daily disastrous happenings of the world. Didn't anyone have anything positive to say anymore? Besides, I didn't need the extra stress. I had plenty of my own coming right from Asia Village.

Hopping up onto the stool next to Adam, I planted an over-exaggerated kiss on his cheek before planting my butt on the seat. And though I thought he'd jump in surprise, he barely flinched. Instead, he turned his head slowly to face me with that dreamy smile he often dazzled me with. "Hey there, dollface."

"No one's gettin' the jump on you," I said with a smirk.

"I should hope not. That's kind of the point. Also, I saw you comin' before you even opened the door." He put an arm around the back of my chair. "I've been expecting you. It's a little late for you to be getting out of work, isn't it?"

"Expecting me? How'd you know I was coming?"

He shrugged. His attention turned back to the TV. "Megan told me. I only stopped in for a quick beer, but I figured I'd stick around and wait for you."

"I stopped at Ms. Chang's house for a little bit after work," I admitted. On instinct, I was going to come up with a story of some kind about how I had to run to Target for feminine items, because let's face it, that would be the end of *that* conversation. But we were doing this new thing where we were up front with each other about everything . . . even the uncomfortable things that I was normally used to hiding from him. Like sticking my nose where it didn't belong.

"Oh?" His eyes slid in my direction. His curiosity was piqued.

"Yeah," I replied, leaning my body over the bar. "Where's Megan? I could use a drink."

"She went in the back room right before you came in."

I drummed my fingers on the counter.

"Well . . ." he said, squeezing my shoulder. "Tell me what happened."

"It was no big deal; I just went to Ms. Chang's to see if she knew anything about what happened to Millie Mao."

"I thought we agreed that you wouldn't meddle with cases when I was the lead detective? These graying temples are escalating fast."

"I happen to like it. It's very becoming on you," I teased. "And I said I'd *think* about it. I never actually agreed to it."

He groaned. "So . . . what did you find out then?"

"That Millie's brother is just as crazy as she was, and Jasmine's grandmother was at the salon that morning."

"I thought there might be a relation there, but I didn't want to assume."

"Have you talked to her brother, Jeffrey, yet?" I asked. I was guessing that he had, and if he had, he wasn't necessarily going to tell me about it, but I had to try. Adam wasn't in the habit of talking to me about any of his cases.

"I did. Interesting man," he responded. "A little on the tightly wound side though."

"Did he say anything that might insinuate that June isn't guilty?"

"*Isn't* guilty?" Adam scrubbed his chin with the back of his hand. "You know I can't talk about this with you," he said. "Why do you insist on making things complicated?"

"Because what else would I do with my spare time?"

He leaned his head back and stared at the ceiling. "I think you should give this up. And I'm not saying that because of the whole danger aspect with you snooping around. I'm saying it because it's a waste of your time and I'm sure you could occupy yourself in other ways. Didn't you mention something about wanting to learn the piano? That would keep you busy."

"Maybe I will. But that's not really the point, is it? Why do you say that I'm wasting my time? What do you know that you're not telling me?"

"I don't want to get ahead of myself here, but most likely this June Yi woman did it. I don't know how we're going to prove it, but let's just say she's being a little too vocal about how happy she is now that Mildred Mao is dead. She definitely had a solid motive. But we're lacking the proper evidence to go forward. No one saw anything of use, there are no usable fingerprints,

and Jasmine's decision to not install a camera is really workin' my last nerve."

His response left me with a variety of emotions. The first one being pure amazement. He was *actually* sharing snippets of information with me. Like I said, he'd never done that when he was working on a case, especially when the case involved people that I knew directly. The second was relief because he didn't mention Opal being guilty of anything. Although, why would he? She wasn't even there when he arrived on the scene. And though Kimmy had seen her pacing outside of the salon right before everything happened, and I thought I knew what I knew, well, it wasn't much to go on. So even though I shouldn't take it into consideration, I was still going to put his lack of interest in her in the plus column for the time being. But the third, well, the third emotion was sheer and utter surprise. Was he of all people so quick to eliminate other prospects just because it *seemed* like June was the most likely party? It was not like him at all.

I started to say as much, but he stopped me by holding up a hand. "There's no current reason for us to look elsewhere. Nothing strange has come up and we can't just go chasing down leads without some type of reason."

Did I put Jasmine's grandmother on the spot right now? Could I do that to her? To Jasmine? My conscience told me no. Sure, Lynn Ming didn't like Millie, but was there a strong enough hatred there for her to act on it? Did I have any plausible evidence whatsoever? No, all I had was some gossip from a member of the Asian community. Whether it was factual was yet to be seen. I would have to do what I always did, which

was to check it out for myself before stepping on any toes. If anything came of it, I could tell Adam then.

Megan came out of the back room with a large tray of food in colorful baskets. I watched as she sauntered over to one of the bar top tables and placed food in front of the four patrons who were occupying it. She smiled before leaving—she looked to be asking them if they needed anything else—and then returned to the bar, ditching her tray as she came toward where we were sitting.

"Well, hey there, bestie," she said in a chipper tone. "It's about time you showed up. Detective Hottie Pants was getting more anxious with every minute."

Adam blushed.

"Stop calling him that. I won't be able to get his head through the door on the way out."

Megan laughed. "So, how'd it go . . . at work?"

"It's okay, I told him where I really was."

Megan sighed relief. "Alright, give me the details then. What do we know?"

I gave her a summarized version of my visit with Ms. Chang but skimmed over the part where Lynn Ming and Millie were constantly at each other's throats.

She embellished a low whistle. "Either grandma was very naughty that day or you're gonna have to look into a new stylist."

"Megan!"

"What? I'm just being honest. It's weird that Jasmine didn't even bring up that her grandmother was there that day."

Adam looked between the two of us. "Wait a minute here. You guys think that sweet little old lady did this?"

It concerned me a little that Megan agreed with me about Jasmine's grandmother without me even saying anything about it. Megan and I usually saved the more detailed conversations for when it was just the two of us. And I didn't want to draw unnecessary attention to Lynn Ming at this stage if I didn't have to. "No, I didn't say that. I don't even know what she looks like and I'm sure it's not important anyway," I said, attempting to appear dismissive.

He snorted. "Trust me, she didn't do this."

"Fine," Megan replied indignantly. "Then my money's on Jasmine. I knew she was too perfect with her flawless makeup and to-die-for curls. It's just not natural."

I rolled my eyes. "She's a stylist—of course she looks like that."

Megan blew a raspberry. "Whatever. I'll get you a drink. . . . Be right back."

Adam turned to me, his index finger tracing a circle on my shoulder. "Babe, for real. You're wasting your time with this whole thing. Just let me handle it. Higgins and I will come up with a way to get this straightened out, and June will be in orange before the first snowfall."

"I think you're underestimating one tiny fact."

"Oh yeah, and what's that?"

"That I'm always right about these things."

CHAPTER
18

Adam and I said our goodbyes in the parking lot of the Zodiac. He needed to get a good night's sleep because he had a long day ahead of him, and I wanted to tinker in my notebook and figure out my best course of action.

After I got home and handled Kikko's tinkle needs, we hunkered down on the couch with a bag of chips and my trusty notebook. I didn't like any of my options, and I knew that the next thing I would need to do is talk with Jasmine about her grandmother being at the salon. Then, I would need to track down Millie's brother, Jeffrey, and see why he was so hell-bent on blaming June Yi for what happened to his sister. I felt like there had to be more than I was seeing.

A bout of fitful sleep followed. I woke up several times, feeling continuously uneasy about the upcoming conversations I would need to have. I dreaded my next encounter with Shirley where I would have to admit that I didn't have a ton of useful information to help her sister in the long run. Everything was speculation. Then again, wasn't it always?

Around four a.m., I finally found myself on a positivity kick and willed myself to believe that I was going to find the answer, solve the murder, have a successful sidewalk sale, and update the restaurant's interior to my mother's exact liking.

My alarm clock went off too soon, and I trudged out of bed, shuffling my way to the coffee maker. The sun was streaming through the blinds and I dug my sunglasses out of my purse before taking Kikko on her morning tinkle adventure. The air was humid and thick, and I knew it was going to be another sticky day.

The Village was quiet when I arrived, and upon entering the enclosed plaza, I noticed the lights were off in the salon. I didn't see Jasmine moving around anywhere inside, so I'd have to find time throughout the day to stop and see her. I'd been hoping to see her before the day got started so I could get it out of the way.

Across the pond, I saw the Yi sisters darting around their bakery and wondered if Shirley would stop by again for another secret morning meeting. I really hoped not.

While I waited for Peter to arrive, I began to design the flyer for the sidewalk sale, purposely trying to keep my mind busy with something different. As I listed the names of the businesses that would be participating, I paused halfway through and focused back in on Asian Accents, which was at the top. What would happen if Jasmine or her grandmother were guilty? Would the salon close? If Jasmine was some type of accomplice, *then* what would happen?

I didn't want any of those scenarios to be true. And I also didn't want it to be Opal either. So that left June at the top of my list. Part of me felt guilty for wanting it to be her in the end.

It was getting close to Peter's arrival time, so I abandoned my flyer creation and headed to the dining room to straighten up and wait for him.

"What did you do, Lana?" Peter said when I opened the door for hm.

"Huh? What do you mean? I didn't do anything." I shut the door as he stormed in the restaurant clearly flustered.

"Kimmy said she's not sure about me anymore. When I asked you for help, I wanted to *stay* in the relationship, not get out of it."

"Don't blame this on me," I said, becoming a little agitated. "*She* was the one who came up with that all on her own. I tried to tell her she was overreacting and needed to slow down."

He sighed. "Man, I'm sorry. I'm just so stressed out by this whole thing. All we did last night was talk about our feelings." His chin dropped and he sulked to the kitchen. "I feel like I'm on some kind of probationary period or something."

I followed behind him, trying to be optimistic. "Maybe this is just a phase. She seems really focused on the future and setting the foundation for a family."

"Dude, I know." He pushed the swinging door to the kitchen wide open, and it hit the counter behind it. "Like, I don't even want to think of that stuff right now. I can barely take care of myself, you know?"

"This could be pressure coming from her parents. Has that come up at all?"

"Your guess is as good as mine. She hasn't said anything about her parents. Man, they better not have said something about grandkids or whatever. My mom is always going on about how she wants a grandson. Double ugh." He threw his apron on, and switched ball

caps. "I thought we were havin' fun and seeing where things would take us. I thought maybe I'd give her a key to my place or something like that."

"Why don't you suggest that then?" I said. "Maybe it'll be enough to satisfy her for the time being. It shows commitment and trust."

"I don't know, I'm almost afraid to bring it up after the way she acted the other night . . . and last night."

"I think you should do it anyway, and be cute about it. You know, put it in a little box and give it to her as a present. Tell her it's the key to new possibilities."

He started to nod in agreement as the suggestion became more attractive. "You know, that idea isn't half bad. Maybe I'll give it a shot. It's like, kinda romantic and stuff."

"Good, now I better get out there and open the door. The Matrons will be here soon and I'm anxious to see if Opal and Pearl are with them today."

"Why is that buggin' you so much anyway?" he asked, turning on the cooking equipment.

"The last time I saw Opal and Pearl in the plaza it was at the salon." I said it slowly to see if he would jump to any conclusions. When he didn't respond, I continued. "Which was the morning of Millie's murder."

Still nothing.

I went on. "And both sisters seemed to disappear pretty quickly right before everything went down."

He still stared.

I huffed. "And neither one of them has shown up at Asia Village since that day, claiming to be sick." I didn't include the fact that I had stopped at their house to drop off food or that Opal didn't seem all that sick when she answered the door. Peter had already left

that day, and Lou had been the one to make their take-out order for me.

Finally, his eyes widened, and then he burst out into laughter. "Hold on, are you telling me that you think one of those sweet old grandmas killed Millie? You're pullin' my leg."

"It's a possibility," I whispered, now feeling unsure of myself. It did seem ludicrous when he said it out loud.

"There's no way, man. No way at all." He shook his head. "You really are way off this time, Lana. If one of them is the killer, then I'm Bruce Lee's long-lost son."

After Peter had a good laugh at my expense, I headed out to the dining area and did my final check of all the tables and chairs before opening the doors for the day. Per usual, the Matrons walked in at their regular time, and I was happy to see that all four ladies were in attendance.

I greeted the two previously absent sisters with a bit too much zeal, and I crossed my fingers that it didn't come off as fake or suspicious because I felt like both might be a possibility.

As I dropped off their tea, I couldn't help but stare at Opal. Despite Peter's previous bout of laughter, I couldn't shake the feeling I had and began to wonder again if I'd pegged her all wrong. They do always say it's the quiet ones, and Opal fit that profile to a tee.

She seemed to notice me staring at her and cocked her head upward. "Is everything all right, Lana? You appear to have seen a ghost." Her voice was undemanding as ever, barely above a whisper, and had there been other patrons present, I wouldn't have heard her speak.

"Oh yes, everything is fine," I said, trying to appear reassuring. "I was just about to ask how the two of you are doing and if you and Pearl enjoyed the food that I dropped off."

Helen and Wendy were clearly caught off guard by my mention of dropping food off with the sisters. Which meant, neither one of them had bothered to bring it up. Was I now reading too much into everything? Or did it mean something that they'd kept silent about my visit.

Pearl answered for the both of them. "We are doing much better, thank you. And we appreciate you stopping by with food for us. It was very unexpected and very nice of you. We must have caught the stomach flu that has been going around the Village. It seems as though everyone we know is getting it."

Helen, who was pouring the tea, added, "We felt incomplete without the two of you. Things weren't quite the same."

Wendy nodded in agreement. "It is good to have both of you back."

I smiled again before walking away to give them time to talk with one another while I thought about what to do next. I pretended to wipe off some menus at the hostess station until Peter rang the bell, signaling that their food was ready.

When I was back at their table, I decided to try for some seemingly innocent conversation. "So," I said, as I set down a plate of pickled cucumbers. "You two really left just in the nick of time on Saturday. You would have gotten stuck at the salon for hours."

The group of women all froze and exchanged glances, but no one said anything.

I decided to keep going. "I was stuck there for

about four hours . . . didn't leave there until after one o'clock."

"Lana," Helen said. "Our food is getting cold . . ."

I glanced down at my half-filled food tray. I had stopped putting their dishes on the table.

"Right, sorry," I said, shaking my head. I reached for the bowl of century eggs. "But you ladies were probably long gone before there was anything to be seen, huh?"

"We were," Pearl replied stiffly. "Opal started to feel ill shortly after we saw you and I went to get the car right after."

Opal nodded but didn't add anything to Pearl's explanation.

"It's too bad about what happened really," I went on. "The police don't have enough evidence to charge anyone. And wouldn't it be a shame if Millie's murder went unsolved?" I waited patiently for their reactions. My main focus was primarily on Opal. "The murderer could be roaming the plaza as we speak."

"Lana, it would appear that we're out of tea," Helen announced. "Would you mind refilling the pot for us? We all seem to be very thirsty this morning."

I wanted to scream, but instead, I nodded with the grace of a true hostess and took their empty tea pot. "I'll be right back."

Hurriedly I prepped a new teakettle for the four women. Peter ignored me as he bobbed his head along to the heavy metal music playing on his kitchen radio. The Matrons were without a doubt hiding something. I had never seen them this unwilling to talk about something so gossip-like the entire time I'd known them.

I returned to their table yet again, my cheeks beginning to hurt from all the fake smiling I was doing and

placed the fresh teapot on their table. "Here you are, ladies." Normally, I would have told them to let me know if they needed anything further and left them to their breakfast. Instead I stood there, waiting for someone to say something. Anything.

"Lana," Opal said with a gentle smile. She rested her chopsticks on the edge of her plate, folding her hands neatly on the table. "I can see that this situation with Millie Mao is upsetting you, but I would like to assure you that everything will be okay. You do not have to worry about this."

The other ladies nodded in unison.

Helen reached for the fresh pot of tea, her hand rattling as her fingers closed around the handle, betraying her otherwise calm demeanor. "Yes, soon enough the police will find the evidence they need to arrest June Yi."

CHAPTER
19

I couldn't tell if what Helen said about the police finding the evidence they needed against June sounded almost like a promise or more like a concern. But my imagination often ran away with me and I didn't know at this point if I was hearing what I wanted to hear. Not that I *wanted* to hear that, but the idea was definitely at the forefront of my mind. It was totally possible she was simply stating an obvious conclusion with no meaning behind it at all.

In some ways I wished that I could talk to Opal alone—without her being able to hide away in her house—to see if she would unintentionally give away any clues.

After Helen's declaration, I excused myself and let the ladies enjoy the rest of their breakfast. I didn't want to be so annoying that they would be discouraged to come back, making my snooping even more difficult than it already was. If Opal was, in fact, guilty and I pushed too hard, they may decide to start having breakfast elsewhere.

Once they'd left, a few other customers came in for some steamed pork buns and dumplings. Business was light and time passed at a casual pace. Once Nancy arrived, I slipped into my office to prepare a produce order and finalize the flyer I had started earlier that morning.

When the lunch rush was over, I decided to head over to Asian Accents to see if Jasmine was available.

The salon seemed to be back to normal and was bustling with customers. Yuna was manning the receptionist desk and swayed her body to the rhythm of the music as she wrote something down in what I gathered to be the appointment book.

She was never without her oversized earrings, and I noted that today's pair were bright yellow suns with kawaii-style smiley faces on them. Her yellow tank top matched their color perfectly. Her unicorn-streaked hair was pinned up in two buns on top of her head, and delicate wisps of hair and thick bangs framed her face.

"Oh, hi Lana," she said, looking up from the counter. "I didn't see you in the appointment book today. Did you need a trim?"

"No, I'm not here to have my hair done, I actually came by to see Jasmine. Is she around?" I craned my neck to glimpse behind the wall of shampoos and conditioners that the reception area stood in front of. "I was hoping to talk to her about the sidewalk sale."

"Oh! Right. The sidewalk sale. We have a ton of summer-themed polish we're going to put on sale. Gotta make room for those cozy fall vibes, am I right?" She beamed with excitement. "There's a new shipment that just came in and I can't tell you how in love I am with this new burgundy color that we're going to carry. Women are going to go crazy for it!"

I mustered a half smile. Here I was faced with yet

another person who seemed to be so thrilled for fall to begin, and all I saw was a precursor to winter, snow, and icy roads.

"She should be right out. She had to take a call from a client in her office. You're welcome to hang out with me up here while you wait."

While I'd been peeking around the product wall, I happened to notice Samantha, the new girl who'd been taking care of Millie. I had yet to talk to her, and now was just as good a time as any. "I'm actually gonna go introduce myself to the new girl, if that's okay with you."

"Sure thing! She's a peach. You're really going to like her."

I would be the judge of that, I thought. I said good-bye to Yuna and headed over to the nail station where Samantha was touching up her own manicure. Her fiery red hair was impressive, and a small part of me wished I could pull off a full head of daring hair color the way she did. But then I did a mental calculation of the upkeep and concluded I was better off with my peekaboo highlights.

"Hello there," I said, pulling pleasant vibes all the way from my diaphragm. "You're Samantha, right?"

The young woman lifted her head to acknowledge me. She was attractive in her own right, but her features were a bit too sharp for my liking. Both her chin and nose came to points, her cheeks were sunken in and accented with a heavy hand of bronzer along the bone. The sour expression on her face told me she wasn't entirely entertained by my presence. "Yup, that's me. Are you here for a nail appointment?" She assessed my outfit—a black A-line skirt paired with a shimmery capped-sleeved blouse and wedged black sandals—and I picked up on her sense of disapproval.

I almost gasped at the thought of her greeting a customer this way. But I held it in and continued with my fake smile. "No, actually I just wanted to introduce myself. I'm Lana . . . I'm a client of Jasmine's and I manage the noodle restaurant here." I pointed behind me in its general direction. "Ho-Lee Noodle House."

"Oh," she replied, appearing uninterested. Her attention turned back down to the nail she was working on. "It's nice to meet you."

"Likewise," I said, forcing the word to come out as sincere as possible. "How do you like working at the salon so far? You started about a little over a week ago, right?"

"Yup. It's been a trip so far," she said, chuckling to herself. "These women are a bunch of gossipers. I've never seen anything like it before."

"Where are you from?"

"Pittsburgh. I went to college there, but I'm originally from Akron."

"Oh . . . what made you move to the Cleveland area instead of going back to Akron?"

She stopped for a minute, inspected her nail, and then looked up at me. I was fully prepared for her to ask me why I was being so nosy, but instead she said, "Family."

She said it so bluntly, I didn't think I was going to get much else out of her, so I felt I should just get to the point.

"That must have been something else to deal with, someone being electrocuted your first weeks on the job. Crazy, right?" Inner groan. I sounded so unconvincing, even to myself. I might as well have said, So how 'bout them Indians? Which is another thing you'd never hear me bringing up casually—Cleveland sports.

Her overly plucked eyebrows rose and then crunched together. "Yeah . . . crazy."

I rocked back and forth on my heels. This was so awkward; I envisioned an Acme-style black hole appearing beneath my feet and swallowing me up, just like in the old Looney Tunes cartoons. Wishful thinking.

We stared at each other for a minute before her attention turned back to her manicure. While I tried to come up with something clever to say, the door to the backroom opened and Jasmine stepped out. I sighed a breath of relief.

"Lana!" Jasmine seemed to be back to her old cheerful self and greeted me with a hug. "Have you been waiting for me long? I wish someone had told me you were here. I was just talking with my grandmother."

My pulse started to quicken. "It's okay, I don't mind waiting."

She released me from our embrace and held out a hand in Samantha's direction. "You met Sam, I take it? The newest member of our team."

Immediately Sam's head popped up and the disapproval that had been on her face was replaced with a bubbliness I hadn't thought she'd be capable of. "We did. Lana was nice enough to come introduce herself to me. I can't tell you how great it's been with everyone being so nice since I've started working here. You were right about the family-like environment. I am loving it more and more every day."

If I'd been sitting down, I would have fallen out of my chair at that exact moment. Who the heck was this girl? Instead of putting my foot in my mouth, I smiled and nodded as if I was in total agreement.

"Lana," Jasmine said, giving my arm a gentle squeeze. "What can I help you with? Need a trim? Your bangs are looking a little long, but you told me you like them that way. I could cut more?"

"No, I came to talk to you about the sidewalk sale, if you have a free minute."

"Oh right. I almost forgot about it with everything else going on. Well, let's go into my office and we'll talk about the particulars in there."

I said goodbye to Samantha, who grinned up at me. I began to feel a little self-conscious, so I turned around and followed Jasmine through the back door. But I couldn't help myself and as the door began to close behind us, I took a quick look back at Samantha.

Yep, she was still staring at me.

"So, the sidewalk sale is three days long, right?" Jasmine asked when we were back in her office.

I wasn't really paying attention to what she was saying, I was still thinking about the way that Samantha had been eyeballing me. And what was with her cheerful act? Was she putting on airs for the boss?

"Lana?" Jasmine asked, leaning forward in her seat.

She was sitting behind her desk, and I was on the opposite side staring at her closed door as if I were waiting for it to start talking. Her office was much like mine in that it was small. But it was very put together—unlike mine—with a spotless white lacquer desk, pink and gray décor, and if my olfactory senses were correct, she had some type of diffuser or incense releasing a calming scent of jasmine. Go figure.

"I'm sorry," I said, bringing my attention back to the topic at hand. "Yes, it'll be three days long. I'm

putting a little blurb next to the name of each business on what they'll be featuring at their table. Yuna mentioned that you were going to be displaying a lot of summer-themed nail color."

"Oh yeah, nail polish galore, and on top of that, a bunch of hair treatments, some facial mud masks . . . and what are you really here for?"

"Huh?" I felt my cheeks warm. "What do you mean?"

"You could have easily texted me about this," she pointed out. "But you chose to come by and talk with me in person . . . so, spill it, sister."

I should have known that Jasmine would see right through me. It wasn't like she didn't know me well enough to know when I wasn't being up front.

I had spent a lot of the day beating around the bush, so straightforward seemed to be the direction I needed to take. "Why didn't you tell me that your grandmother was at the salon that day?"

She looked taken aback by my question and I had a feeling that was because it came out in an accusatory tone. "I didn't know that I needed to . . ."

Okay, maybe not that straightforward. "I think that came out wrong. I didn't mean it like *that*."

"Then how did you mean it?" she asked. A trace of anger was slipping into her voice.

"I guess I thought you'd mention it. You know my family," I said, hoping to recover from my poorly worded question. Maybe I wasn't the best at being up front when it came to these particular types of scenarios.

"Your family works here," was her reply. "I see them all the time so it's natural that I would know them. My grandmother seldom comes here, and when she does it's usually on Saturday mornings to get her hair done.

You're not always here on Saturdays, so there are few chances for you to have a run-in with each other."

"True. I'm a little surprised is all. I would have loved to meet her."

"Like I said, she comes in most regularly on Saturdays. If it's such a big deal to you, I'll make it a point to introduce the two of you next time she's here."

I couldn't help but note her hostility, and it made me wonder—if there was nothing to be guilty of, then why was she taking this tone with me? As delicately as I could, I asked, "Are you aware that your grandmother and Millie play on the same mahjong team?"

Not a muscle moved on her face as she spoke. "Yes, the Tile Tigresses. They've known each other for years. I don't see what that has to do with anything."

"Nothing, I suppose. I didn't realize they knew each other is all."

"Apparently there is a lot you're not aware of that you seem to think involves you."

"Jasmine—"

"Look, Lana, let me save you some trouble here," she began. She tucked her hair behind her ears. "Yes, my grandmother Lynn and Millie know each other and don't have the best history with each other. But that's no reason for anyone to assume she did anything wrong that day."

"Why would you automatically assume that's where I was going with this?" I was only mildly offended that she would jump to that conclusion because that was, in fact, why I was there.

"Because I know you, Lana. And since I already know that you're looking into things, I can safely say I know where your mind is at. The only thing that shocks me is that you didn't realize my grandmother

was here sooner. After all, I did give you the list of appointments that day."

"Well, Ming is such a common name. I didn't think much of it at the time."

She ignored my comment and continued. "Regardless, my grandmother is not guilty of anything and I didn't tell you she was here because I knew this is exactly what you were going to do. I'm not going to sit and speculate with you on how my grandmother might have done something wrong because I know in my gut that she didn't do anything." Jasmine broke eye contact as she said this last bit, and I wondered if she truly meant it.

"Do you honestly think I want to even entertain the idea?" I asked, starting to truly feel offended. "It's not like I want to accuse your grandmother of anything. But I can't have a blind eye either just because we're friends. That wouldn't exactly be me playing fair now, would it?"

"Fine, then don't have a blind eye. . . . I don't care what you do. But the extent of me helping you is over."

I didn't know what to say, so I stood from my seat, my eyes traveling down to my feet in shame. "I'm sorry that I offended you. That was never my intention in all of this."

"You don't have to apologize," she said without sounding the least bit convincing. "You're a good friend and have been a faithful client . . . but maybe right now until this is sorted, I should just consider you a client."

I couldn't really say that I was completely shocked by her behavior. I was kinda sorta suggesting that her grandmother might have some involvement in something nefarious. Who would take that accusation lightly?

I know that if anyone even looked sideways at my grandmother for a split second, I might be motivated to pop them one right in the kisser.

"I shouldn't have come by," I said, feeling a mountain of guilt weighing down on my shoulders. I headed for the door, wanting to be anywhere but in this room that suddenly felt suffocating.

As I twisted the knob to open the door, she stood up. "Lana, I know you mean well, and you just want to figure out what happened. But I have to say . . . you're way off on this and maybe you should stay out of it this time. You've got a lot of pressure on you right now and I don't know that you're thinking clearly at this point."

I gave her a solemn nod and headed to the front of the salon, refusing to make eye contact with Samantha as I passed by her. I'd had my fill of interactions for the day. But, before I could make it all the way out of the salon, Yuna stopped me.

"Did you get to meet Samantha?" she asked.

"I did." I paused for a moment and considered if I should take a chance with Yuna. She was always friendly, so what were the chances of her scolding me too? "Hey, so, how do you like working with her so far?"

"Ohmigod, she's totally awesome. She has so many interesting stories about living in Pittsburgh. She's a really fun person to talk with."

"That's great," I said. "She seems to fit in well here."

"She really does." Yuna smiled. "I'm so glad it's working out for her, too. It's gotta be lonely to move to a city and have absolutely no family or friends near you."

CHAPTER
20

So, Samantha had lied to me about her family situation. Gee, that wasn't suspicious at all. I'd half-heartedly dismissed the thought of her involvement early on in my investigation because a new employee at the salon who started working there shortly before one of their patrons ends up murdered seemed all too ridiculous. And on top of that, it just so happened to be one of her clients? Come on. But maybe I had been too quick to disregard the possibility.

Samantha was turning into someone that I definitely needed to investigate further. I should have asked Yuna what her full name was before I left the salon. But if I went back right now, it might raise suspicions. Especially if Jasmine had wandered up front after I left, or Samantha happened to be nearby. I could try searching her through the salon's Facebook page. Perhaps they'd done an introductory post when she first started working there to welcome her to the community.

The restaurant was very much the same as how I'd left it. Uneventful. A table of four businessmen

lounged near the back appearing thoroughly entertained with themselves.

Nancy was at the hostess station relaxing on the stool and watching the activity out in the plaza, which was really nothing extraordinary.

"There you are," she said as I approached the counter. "I was wondering when you'd be back. Helen is here to speak with you. She is waiting at the Matrons' usual booth."

I directed my attention to that part of the restaurant and sure enough, there was Helen all by her lonesome. "Huh, what is she doing here?"

"I'm not sure. She asked to speak with you, and I told her you would be right back. She did not say anything more."

I shrugged. "I'll go and see what she wants. Let me know if you need anything."

"No rush, business has been slow since you left."

I headed over to greet Helen and found her staring at the table as though she might burst into tears at any moment. When she realized it was me walking up to her, she closed her eyes and inhaled deeply. "Oh good, Lana, you are here."

"Yeah, I'm sorry to keep you waiting. I had to step out for a minute and handle some business."

"I really need to talk to you." She extended her hand, grasping for the tea pot, but it shook uncontrollably as she tried to wrap her fingers around the handle. It reminded me of how she'd been jittery earlier as well.

"Here, let me," I said to the elderly woman. I reached for the teapot and filled her half-empty cup. "What has gotten you so upset?"

She glanced up at me and then back down at the cup. "It is about Opal and Pearl. I'm afraid. I need your

help and I do not want the other Matrons to know that I'm here."

I felt queasy. I flipped over the unused teacup and poured some for myself. I took a sip and let the warm liquid travel down my throat, hoping that it would calm my nerves. "I'll help any way I can," I said with genuine concern.

Her eyes began to tear, and I wished that I had a tissue to offer her. "I suspect that Opal and Pearl have some type of involvement in what took place at Asian Accents last Saturday. I do not wish to think such ill things of my closest friends, but there is too much that I question about what happened that morning."

I was worried about this exact scenario. The scenario where I couldn't ignore the truth behind my seemingly ridiculous notion. Here I'd been this whole time still holding onto hope that there was no way either sister could have anything to do with Millie's death, but now here was one of their own saying that it might be possible.

I also knew the emotions that Helen was currently feeling, as I had been put in this exact position myself when Peter had been under the microscope regarding his father's death. It was a horrible way to feel and I wouldn't wish it on my own worst enemy. Yes, that's right, I wouldn't even wish this feeling on Jackie Shen.

"Can you tell me what makes you feel this way?" I asked as gently as possible. "Did something happen?"

"I do not believe that either lady was sick." Helen confided. "Wendy and I went to their house each day to bring them soup, and both of them seemed to be fine. They were also in quite a rush to have us leave. We haven't ever hidden anything from each other, but this time I fear that they are guilty of lying."

It matched my experience of visiting Opal and Pearl, which wasn't making me feel any better. "I see. So, they didn't say anything unusual that would give you that impression?" I was keeping my fingers crossed for something other than them not appearing sick. It was possible to have the stomach flu and not look ill on the outside.

"No, nothing was said. But we all know each other well enough to know when the other isn't being honest, and this is one of those times. I can feel it in my bones, Lana. Something isn't right about this."

I took a moment to consider that. "What can you tell me about the situation that happened with Millie Mao and the accusation of her cheating during the mahjong competition?" I figured since Helen was now approaching me for help in sorting this whole thing out, she would be more forthcoming than she was the last time I tried to get information.

"Opal was the first one to see it," Helen said. "She said she noticed Millie shuffling the tiles in an odd manner, almost as if she were isolating a specific grouping of them. Then she swore she saw her drop a tile or two into her lap."

"Did anybody else see this happening?"

"A few other people assumed she was cheating because she won so many times in a row, but no one saw what Opal saw. At least not to my knowledge."

"So how did June become involved then?"

"A group of players suggested to the referees that Millie was cheating. June was one of them and was more persistent than anyone else in getting the point across. Millie was under close watch at that point. And then two matches later, the referees said there

vas proof she was stacking the wall in her favor and told her to leave the playing room immediately. She was disqualified from going further into the tournament."

"So really, the only thing June did was speak up?" I asked. At least that was the way it was sounding to me so far.

"This is only one small thing between the two women. June and Millie have always been enemies. This has a lot to do with Millie's brother, Jeffrey."

"Millie's brother? How so?" I asked.

"A long time ago, June liked Jeffrey and wanted to marry him. They were very close friends, and after a while they began to spend time with each other . . . romantically. Which was to be kept very much a secret because women did not do such things openly back then like they do now."

"Wait, what?" I had a hard time imagining this. June liked someone? Romantically?

"Yes, she liked Jeffrey very much, and it would seem he felt the same way about her. But Millie did not want her brother's attention to go to someone else, so she begged him not to continue seeing her. Millie was the only one who knew the true nature of their relationship at the time."

I sat back in the booth, and sighed. Today was certainly turning into quite the day. "Okay, so that would lead me back to June having a motive. It starts there with Millie disapproving of their relationship—she interferes, and June knows it. Then a rivalry begins, it gets heated, and now here we are." I spread my arms out with a flourish.

"This is quite possible," Helen said. "If I am lucky,

then June is guilty of the murder. I know that it is horrible of me to say such a thing, but I hope you can understand why I would feel this way."

"I do actually," I told her. "You don't want it to be your friend. Who wouldn't understand that? But, then why are you so concerned if you know this about June? Wouldn't knowing this ease your mind?"

She took a sip of her tea before speaking. "Because this story becomes more complicated. You see, Pearl and Millie used to be friends a long time ago. But many bad things began to happen, and the friendship disappeared quickly."

I massaged the back of my neck. "Wait . . . Pearl and Millie were *actually* friends at one time?"

"Yes, at that time, we were all friends. However, Opal did not like Millie. Opal has always had this way about her where she can sense things from somebody just by watching them, and she did not trust this woman from the beginning. But Pearl befriended her anyways, thinking that her sister was simply jealous of her new friendship.

"We would often play mahjong together, but Millie was still an outsider to our group. The four of us have always promised each other that we would be in agreement when it was time to add another member."

I nodded as I followed along. "And since Opal didn't like her, I'm guessing that's why it didn't happen?"

"You are correct. Opal would not stand for it. Wendy and I were indifferent. At first, Millie seemed to be okay. But then, she began to become more and more angered by this. She even tried to cause arguments between Opal and Pearl, but their sisterhood is too strong for anything like that to happen. Still, she

tried to get in our good graces, and she knew that we liked to share gossip with each other."

"Let me guess," I said. "She told you about June's relationship with her brother?"

Helen nodded. "You are correct again, Lana. She told all of June's secrets, things that a woman should never betray another woman with. It was very dishonorable."

"But you didn't tell the whole plaza, right?" I gaped. Even though I knew the Matrons never intended to hurt anyone's feelings, it seemed almost cruel to expose June's private relationship.

Helen shook her head. "No, this we did not tell, Lana. We would never do such a thing to June. But she believes that we did, and so many enemies were created from this one lie. When Pearl made it clear that Millie would never be a part of our group, Millie told everyone about June's relationship with Jeffrey and said that we were the ones who told everybody. June, of course, believed this and has never spoken to any of us since. Many times we have tried to tell her that it wasn't us, but she refuses to believe it.

"June was so ashamed, she said she would never trust anybody at Asia Village again." Helen leaned back against the booth, staring out the window into the plaza. "After that, Opal became furious that Millie would blame us in such a way, and she promised that karma would find Millie and punish her for her wrongdoing."

Now things were starting to come together. "So, this isn't just about the tournament and cheating. This is personal."

"Yes, I fear this to be true, Lana."

"And you think that Opal decided to hand out karma herself after all these years?"

"Opal is a kind woman, and I have never known her to be a violent person in any way. But she does believe in honor and I worry Millie cheating at the tournament was more than Opal could handle."

CHAPTER
21

I left work and went home that evening not wanting to know any of the things I knew. This whole ordeal seemed more challenging than I was able to handle. The sensation of feeling lost was overpowering and my brain scrambled to find logical answers to the information I had learned throughout the day.

Megan was presumably at work, so once Kikko was walked and taken care of, I sat down at the kitchen table with my laptop and did a search on Asian Accent's Facebook page. I wanted to entertain an idea that wasn't my stylist's sweet old grandmother or one of my regular customers. And I still felt borderline about June because she seemed to be the all-too-obvious choice, and though anything was possible, I was hoping she wasn't quite that stupid.

I scrolled down the page searching for fire-engine red hair and sure enough, I found a "Welcome to the Team!" post giving a short bio on our woman of the hour, Samantha Hui. It mentioned that she'd moved from Pittsburgh to Cleveland and had gone to school

for business before finding her passion in cosmetology. She was twenty-six years old and hoped to one day have her own salon.

From there I did a Google search of her name and age to see what I could find. Which was a big nothing. I did find her name attached to the University of Pittsburgh, confirming that at least that part of her story was true, but that was about it. I also checked her name on the county's website, just to make sure that she didn't have a record. Zero finds. And I even did a search for her time in Pittsburgh, but found nothing.

Thirty minutes later, I was still staring at my computer screen, zoning out and wondering about what to do next when Megan walked in the door.

"What are you doing here?" I asked, surprised to see my roommate home at a reasonable hour.

"We were slow, so I decided to take off. They seemed to have everything under control." She was carrying a takeout bag, and as she neared the kitchen, I could smell the tangy aromas of BBQ. "I assume all you ate were noodles today, so I brought you something different to munch on." She plopped the bag on the table.

"Yes, thank you," I said, reaching for the bag and sticking my nose in the opening. "Ooh, there are potato wedges too."

"Carbs are wonderful, aren't they?"

She grabbed two plates from the cupboard, napkins, and two cans of Coke. "How's the case coming along?"

I took the plate she offered. "Not great, everything feels so helter-skelter and I don't know what to do at this point. I just keep walking around all day asking

myself who could have done this. The more I think about it, the more turned around I get."

"What do you suppose is different this time?" she asked, sitting across from me.

Kikko, smelling the food, was now on high alert and danced at my feet. I tore off a small piece of potato wedge, and she lunged upward on her hind legs to nab her fried treat.

"I'm not sure, I guess it's that I'm being pulled in too many different directions. I'm supposed to handle the sidewalk sale, update the restaurant, *and* figure out who the killer is." I sighed as I bit into the remainder of the potato wedge. "And don't forget—also *run* said restaurant. Oh, *and* somehow help Peter and Kimmy reconcile their differences."

"Huh?"

"Ugh, forget it. Kimmy is being ridiculous. That's all you really need to know."

She laughed. "Why am I not surprised? It's Kimmy. And, your mom really picked a horrible time to spring this on you."

"Well, it's not like she knows that I'm trying to solve a murder. I can't exactly tell her that either."

"This is true." Megan bit into a chicken wing. "Okay, run everything by me. Tell me what you got."

As patiently as possible, I went over all the details I had thus far. I told her about what I'd learned from Helen, my interaction with Jasmine, and my brief meet and greet with Samantha. When I was done, we sat in silence, enjoying our chicken wings.

Megan unfolded a wet nap she'd dug from the bottom of our takeout bag. "I still think it's June, and the situations with these other people are just coincidences. June has the most to gain from Millie's death."

"I suppose. I still want to talk with Millie's brother and try to track down the person she got into a car accident with. Maybe that person wanted revenge."

"Could be. But then that means that person would have to have been at the salon that same day and time."

"I know . . . and maybe they were."

"Don't you think Millie would have made a scene about it though?" Megan asked.

"Not if she didn't see them before they saw her."

"True enough."

The takeout containers were now empty and so were our plates. Megan got up and cleared the table while I stared at my laptop some more.

Megan sighed as she watched me zone out in front of the screen. "Why don't you let me take over the Internet search duties? You know I always have better luck with the technology portions anyway. Watching you is almost painful."

"Sure," I agreed. "Be my guest. My eyes are starting to blur anyway."

"We'll figure this out, Lana. Don't worry. You may not like the outcome, but we'll figure it out."

The next morning as I readied myself for work, I considered what I might say to Jeffrey Mao when I approached him. I knew that he frequented a community center on the East Side near Rockwell Avenue—the location of Cleveland's original Chinatown—where a lot of people went to have tea and play mahjong together. I'd learned this little tidbit from Evelyn Chang during our previous conversation. And though she'd warned me to stay away from him, I had to at least try to find out something of use from him.

When the Mahjong Matrons arrived at Ho-Lee Noodle House for their daily breakfast, I had a hard time looking any of them in the eye. I didn't know what to think about Pearl and Opal, and I felt like if I shared too much eye contact with Helen, the others would know something was up. I busied myself with mundane tasks around the restaurant while they ate. I must have put up a good performance because none of them asked me if anything was wrong or why I was being quieter than usual.

Ten minutes after they left, Ian came storming through the door. As he approached the counter, he adjusted a silver cufflink, and straightened his suit jacket. "Good morning, Lana. I came to check on your progress with the sidewalk sale promotions. How is that going?"

I winced. "Ugh, I'm sorry, I completely forgot to have the flyers printed. But they're ready to go. I'll stop and have them made today."

His brows furrowed. "Lana, I'm surprised at you. I assumed you would have this well under way by now. This isn't like you at all."

I sucked in my lips and held my tongue. I wanted to tell him that maybe he should do it himself and leave me alone. But I knew it wouldn't get me anywhere, and I didn't have the mental capacity to start an argument with him. So, I just said, "I've had a lot going on, but I'll take care of it."

"Fine, I'll check in with you tomorrow," he warned.

I nodded. "See you then."

Only after he'd gone did I realize I had my "in" with Jeffrey Mao.

* * *

I didn't know why I hadn't thought of it sooner, since I'd used this tactic before. Pretending like you needed to be somewhere because you were dropping something off was always a good way to get your foot in the door.

With Nancy manning the dining room, I'd taken off for lunch under the guise of handling the sidewalk sale for Ian. Technically, I wasn't lying. Now, I stood in line at OfficeMax and waited while their copy machine created five hundred of the flyers that I'd designed. The flyer included a professional photo of Asia Village's exterior and listed all of the businesses that were participating in the sale. I also added the fact that we had a karaoke lounge in case anyone felt like singing their lungs out after splurging on sale items. Ho-Lee Noodle House would also be participating with half-off appetizers and lunch specials.

Once I had my stack of flyers, I headed for Rockwell Avenue, practicing my "casual" face. My biggest giveaways were always the facial expressions I made and could never seem to keep under control. I was getting better at it, but if I didn't prepare myself, who knew what I'd divulge with my telltale eyes.

I found some off-street parking, put money in the meter, and tried to walk where there was some shade. In a few short hours, the entire street would be barricaded, and tents, tables, and lighting equipment would cover the road and sidewalk for the weekly night market event.

The community center was toward the middle of the row of Asian businesses that lined the street. It sat next to Emperor's Palace, one of my favorite restaurants, and I thought about stopping in for some dim sum.

Focus, Lana. Flyers now. Dumplings later.

Cleveland Asian Community Center was a decent-sized establishment, plain in design. On the right side of the main room was a low-sitting bar made of Formica, and vinyl stools with metal posts for legs that were drilled into the floor. It was reminiscent of an old coffee shop, and I wondered if perhaps at one time it had been.

The linoleum floors were scuffed, but otherwise clean, and the air was scented with sandalwood incense that burned at a small Buddhist shrine in the back.

Inexpensive card tables were scattered around the open space to the left of the room, creating a somewhat jumbled environment. The area was filled with people playing mahjong, cards, or checkers or lounging with the familiar faces of friends.

There was a welcoming vibe in the air, and I felt comforted by the fact I didn't feel like a complete outsider. I had my stack of flyers in my arms, and I took them to the counter and sat down on one of the empty stools next to a petite elderly woman with short gray hair who was drinking a can of Apple Sidra through a bendy straw.

"That's my favorite pop," I said to her with a smile.

She grinned in return. "It is always nice on a hot day."

A middle-aged woman with stringy hair in a floral blouse sauntered over to our end of the counter. "Can I help you with anything?"

"Yes," I said, straightening in my seat, appearing to look official. "I was wondering if I could have a can of that Apple Sidra, and if I might leave some of these flyers here." I held them up with some bravado. I'm

from Asia Village and we're having a sidewalk sale at the end of the month."

The elderly lady next to me gasped with excitement. "Oh, I love sales! Can I have one of those?"

"Sure." I handed her one of the flyers. "I run Ho-Lee Noodle House, and if you stop by, you get half off all appetizers and lunch specials."

The woman behind the counter nodded in approval. "We have a table near the back where you can put them." She walked away to get my apple soda.

"I haven't been to the West Side in ages," the woman next to me remarked. "I don't go as many places as I used to."

This was common among Clevelanders. We had our sides of town, our preferences, and there was much pride in the areas we resided in. And though we were all about fifteen to twenty minutes away from each other, we acted as if it meant traveling to the ends of the earth.

"Well, if you stop by, I'll throw in some free dumplings for you," I said.

She gave me a toothy grin. "I think I'll have to take you up on that."

The woman with the stringy hair returned with my can of Apple Sidra and passed it along with a wrapped straw. "That'll be two dollars."

When she was gone, I turned back to the elderly lady. "I was wondering if you might help me find someone. They're a friend of a friend and I wanted to say hi since I'm on this side of town."

"Who are you looking for? I can try to help."

"His name is Jeffrey Mao; do you know him?"

Her eyes widened a little bit. "Jeffrey?" She lifted a

hand to her ear and made circles with her index finger. "He's a little on the cuckoo side."

With a nervous laugh, I said, "I've heard that."

"Especially since his sister was murdered. Didn't that happen at your plaza?"

I blushed. "I'm sad to say it did."

"Well, he is ready to sue the salon. He has been talking about it all week. Every day he comes in and talks about it. I guess he and Mildred use the same lawyer. Right now he is trying to go after some woman named June Yi, and then after that he will go after the salon . . . or try anyway. I'm sick of hearing about it."

"I can imagine. It's kind of a depressing subject too."

"Who do you know that is friends with him? Especially on that side of town."

Uh-oh. I hadn't thought that through. Who would be friends with him who went to Asia Village? Not many people were a fan of his because his sister was such a troublemaker. "Ummm . . . I don't know if you would know her. Evelyn Chang."

"Oh, Evelyn." the woman smiled and nodded. "Yes, I know Evelyn. She comes here all the time. Matter of fact, I just saw her yesterday."

My heart skipped a beat. I hadn't seen that coming. "Really?" I wanted to say more, but I couldn't muster any other words.

"Yes. That's odd that she asked you to say hi for her . . . she spent all her time with him yesterday when she came by."

CHAPTER 22

After my elderly informant pointed him out, I thanked her and rushed out of the community center to call Donna. The woman probably wondered what the heck I was doing, but I didn't have time to worry about her opinion of me. I had to find out if Donna knew that Evelyn was good friends with Jeffrey Mao.

I found a tree that looked as though it'd just been planted, it wasn't very big, but provided enough shade to keep me out of the scorching sun. I entered Donna's name into the search bar on my phone and pressed CALL when her information came up.

She picked up on the second ring and after she said "Hello," I blurted out a string of words that I hoped made sense.

It took Donna a moment to respond. "Well, yes of course, they're friends, but I wouldn't say they're overly chatty. Are you sure this old woman said that Evelyn is there on a regular basis? I can't even imagine what she would be doing at a community center of all

places. She is quite refined . . . a country club would be more up her alley."

I shook my head as if she could see me. "No, the woman said that Evelyn is there all the time, and that she has been there a lot this past week. She's been spending all her time talking to Jeffrey Mao."

"My word," Donna replied. "I don't even know what to say, Lana. You don't suppose she is involved with this somehow, do you? A woman of Evelyn's status . . ."

"Anything is possible. But what would her motive be?"

"I don't know, dear. As far as I know she shouldn't have one. Like I said, she is quite refined, and being mixed up in something like this isn't part of her personality."

"Do you happen to know who Millie got into an accident with before the whole thing happened with June?"

"Not a clue. But I can try and find out for you. I do have a few sources I could try."

"Thank you. Call me as soon as possible if you find out anything useful."

"I will, but . . ."

"But what?" I was facing the community center and as Donna started to go on, I noticed that the man my new friend had described as Jeffrey Mao was leaving the establishment and heading down the street. "Donna, I've got to go. Jeffrey's on the move."

"Okay dear. Well, call me back and let me know what happens."

I hung up without saying goodbye and jogged across the street, keeping an eye out for traffic. I stayed a few hundred feet away from Jeffrey as he ambled casually

down the sidewalk. To my utter dismay, he turned into the entrance for the House of Shen.

I stopped dead in my tracks and thought about whether it was worth it to agitate myself by going inside. There was little to no chance that my arch-nemesis, Jackie Shen, wouldn't be there. She worked about as much as I did.

After much back-and-forth, I decided to take one for the team. I didn't want to waste time coming back here the next day to follow around Jeffrey Mao for the perfect opportunity to talk with him. As it was, I still didn't know what I was going to say.

I mentally pulled myself together, ran a hand through my hair to smooth it out, straightened my shoulders, and strolled into the House of Shen like this was the best day of my life.

I will give the House of Shen credit for their excellent ambiance. Their restaurant was styled with an air of 1920s Shanghai accented with modernized adjustments. The lattice woodwork was well placed and used to separate different sections of the restaurant. The same design was also used on each dining booth's high partitions to create an intimate feel. Bamboo shoots and orchids decorated the tables and hostess area, complementing the neutral tones of the walls, furniture, and flooring.

Jackie Shen was behind the hostess counter looking coiffed with her hair wrapped in a bun and a flower clipped to the base of her gathered locks. She was dressed in a beige qipao with a coral flower pattern and coral trim at the collar and on the sleeves. Her matching coral lips turned from a smile into a frown as she realized it was me standing in front of her. "What are you doing here, Lee? Come to steal some recipes?"

I gave her my most elaborate eye roll. "Hardly. I was out this way, and it was too hot to not stop in and grab some food." That was the lamest excuse I'd ever come up with. Shame, shame, Lana.

"Yeah right. I saw your mom in here the other day. You guys are up to something."

"My grandmother wanted to stop in and see what it was like. Don't be so dramatic. Why do you assume that everyone is out to get you?"

"Oh, I don't think that. Just when it comes to your family."

Jackie and I had never gotten along. Not even on our best day. This was partially due to the fact that our parents didn't like each other that much. The rest of the reason she didn't like me was because I was mixed. It's an ugly thing, but there it was.

My mother often told me that Jackie didn't like me because she was jealous of me. But weren't parents always saying stuff like that to make their kids feel better? It's not you, it's them. Blah-blah. Either way, I'd made my peace with it, and to be honest, I wasn't a fan of hers either.

"I'd like a table, please," I said with the fakest smile I could muster.

"Fine, whatever." Right as she said it, two customers were walking up front and gave her a dirty look. She tried to correct this, by giving me a wide smile, but the customers didn't seem convinced.

I followed her to a two-seat table near the window. She slapped the menu down on the table. "You probably think that's funny."

"Only because you deserve it," I said, smiling sweetly at her.

She gnarled her lip at me, and then walked away.

I'm not too proud to say I took some satisfaction in that. Kimmy would be happy.

I reviewed their menu while trying to keep tabs on where Jeffrey was sitting. I finally spotted him seated diagonally from me toward the back by the kitchen. He had his back to me, but I recognized the pastel green polo shirt he was wearing.

The server came by and took my drink order of iced green tea, and I told her I needed time with the menu. Since I was here, I might as well eat. My normal go-to was Hunan beef with white rice, but I was feelin' sassy today, so I decided to go for some kung pao chicken.

When the server returned with my tea, I recited my selections and asked for a check and a box. She gave me an inquisitive glance but didn't ask why and went along her way to place my order.

I wanted to be prepared to leave should the occasion arise. Jeffrey was slightly ahead of me in the ordering process, and though I couldn't see what he was eating, I could tell he had food in front of him by the movements he was making. I only hoped he was a slow eater.

To help pass the time while I waited, I checked some e-mails, sent Peter a text to check in with the restaurant, and fit in a level or two of Wordscapes, a world puzzle game on my phone that I had become too obsessed with in recent weeks. My food arrived about twenty minutes later, and I hated to admit how mouth-watering it looked. It was a perfect mixture of chicken, vegetables, and chili peppers with a sprinkle of peanuts. The thin, chestnut-colored sauce was a delicate blend of soy, hoisin, vinegar, and rice wine with just a touch of chicken stock. The combined scent wafted to

my nose and I eagerly plucked the chopsticks from my cloth napkin.

The deliciousness of their food was another thing I hated to admit. I'd never tell that to Jackie though.

Just as I was really getting into my meal, I noticed some activity at Jeffrey's table. His server was giving him his check and he was settling up.

With a mouthful of rice, I quickly packed up the remainder of my lunch, stuffing kung pao chicken into one takeout container and rice into the other. Jeffrey walked past my table, and I tried not to appear too suspicious as I rushed to leave.

He was already out the door by the time I was all packed up, so I had to hightail it out of the restaurant.

As I passed Jackie at the hostess station, she opened her mouth to make some snide remark, but I held up a dismissive hand and flew out of the door. Looking to my left and then my right, I spotted Jeffrey heading back in the direction of the community center.

I sped up my pace, and right as I passed the center, he whipped around and stared me right in the eye. His gray hair was matted to his head from the heat, and I noticed some sweat at his temples. "Why are you following me, young lady?"

I gasped, completely caught off guard by his accusation. "I wasn't—"

"Are you from the media?" He asked, assessing my outfit. "I'm not speaking with any more reporters about what happened to my sister. If you want any information, you'll have to speak to my lawyer."

"Media?" I asked, pointing at myself. "Talk to a lawyer?" I let out a nervous laugh, which came out sounding like a gurgle. "You must have me confused with someone else."

"Well, who are you then?" he demanded. "I saw you at the community center earlier and then at the House of Shen."

"My name is Lana . . . I work at the Ho-Lee Noodle House in Asia Village."

His eyes narrowed. "Asia Village, huh."

I nodded. "Wait, are you Mildred Mao's brother?"

He grunted his response.

"I'm so sorry for your loss," I said. I didn't have trouble making it sound sincere because I truly was sorry. So at least I had that going for me. As far as my cover story, I had no idea what I was doing or what I was going to say.

"Why were you following me?" he asked again.

"I really wasn't. I was just dropping off some flyers at the community center for an upcoming sidewalk sale, and then decided to have some lunch. It's just a coincidence that we were leaving both places at the same time."

"I don't believe in coincidences," he stated.

I wanted to ask him if that's why he thought June Yi was so guilty—because he didn't believe it could be a coincidence that she was at the salon the same time as his sister. But I felt that it was a little too revealing to ask something like that. So instead I asked, "Do you think it's fate that brought us together?" *Oh my god, Lana . . . what an idiot you are.*

"No, I think you were following me. And I want to know why."

"I really—"

"If you don't tell me why you were following me, then I'm calling the police. Is that what you want? I have your name now . . . not very smart on your part."

I couldn't have him calling the police on me. We

were in Cleveland and though I'd had run-ins with a few of their detectives before, I couldn't say the same for their beat cops. Calling in a favor to Adam at this particular moment didn't seem like the best thing I could do. Giving in, I sighed, "Okay, fine. I was hoping to talk with you about what happened to your sister."

"Were you a friend of hers?" he asked, sounding doubtful as he said it.

"No, I only knew her from a few interactions at Asia Village."

"Then what possible business is it of yours?"

If I wanted this man's help, I probably should come clean with him. I decided to give honesty a try. "I'd like to help figure out what really happened that day, and I thought maybe if I talked with you, I could find out who her enemies were and—"

He scowled. "Did June send you? Is that what this is really about? She's still trying to put on this act that she's innocent. Well, young lady, if you believe she is innocent for one minute, then you are as dumb as she is."

"But don't you think it's strange that June would take a chance like that in front of so many people when she knows that everyone else knows about their relationship?"

"No, I don't think it's strange and I don't really care. Now if you'll excuse me." He started to turn away.

Before I totally lost him, I blurted, "But didn't you used to care for June?"

He whipped back around and glared at me; his hands were balled into fists. "What did you say to me?"

I shrank back a little bit, unsure of what to say next. "Well—"

"That's none of your business. You tell June that

she needs to confess and give this whole thing up. I'm done playing games. And so is my lawyer." He turned around again, and this time he stormed away without giving me a second glance.

So much for that.

CHAPTER
23

When I got back to my car, I blasted the air-conditioning and sat with my face in front of the air vent for about five minutes before I decided to call Donna back. Our conversation was quick since she hadn't heard back from any of her resources yet.

I filled her in on what happened with Jeffrey, and she didn't seem the least bit surprised at his reaction.

Right before we hung up, I said, "Oh, you were in the middle of saying something before and then I had to hang up. What were you going to say?"

Donna took a moment to respond as she tried to recollect our previous conversation. "Oh, it was nothing, dear. I was just going to say that I can find out for you, but really I think that this whole thing is just as simple as it seems. June Yi is guilty."

"Yeah, but what about this new information involving Evelyn meeting with Jeffrey every day? You don't think that's worth looking into either?"

"Lana, that woman has stood by me through thick and thin. When everyone was spreading rumors about

me killing my husband, or that nasty business with my maid, she was the only one who stuck by me. I am returning the favor. She's innocent as far as I'm concerned."

Or until I prove her guilty, I thought.

We hung up, and I made my way back to Asia Village.

I had my carry-out bag with me, and didn't think much of it, until I walked into the restaurant and my mother was there. She and Nancy were chatting away at the hostess station when I waltzed in.

My mother turned around, gave me a once-over, did a double take of my bag and asked, "Where did you go?"

"Just running some errands," I said, trying to pass them and scurry into the back, hoping my mother wouldn't follow.

"Wait a minute. Mommy wants to talk to you," my mother said, following after me.

"I'm doing the sidewalk sale planning for Ian," I told her from over my shoulder. "It's been slow so it's not a big deal."

"I do not care about this," she replied.

We entered the kitchen, and Peter turned when he heard the door swing open. "Hey, Mama Lee, how's it goin'? You lookin' for some lunch?"

"No thank you, Peter," my mother said with a wave. "I am only stopping by for one minute. I have bingo pretty soon."

"Right on." He tipped his hat at my mother and then returned to cleaning the grill.

"Lana, where are you going? Are you in a hurry?"

"To my office." I went through the next door and

kept going hoping she wouldn't mention the bag I had in my hand. "I have some stuff I need to do."

"What about the restaurant?" She was now standing in the doorway of my office with her hands on her hips, looking at me as if I'd just told her I'd gotten a *D* on my report card. "I asked you to do something and you did not do it yet?"

I set my carry-out bag on the corner of my desk. I fully planned to chow down the minute my mother left. I'd only had a few bites and I was seriously hungry. "I'm doing a lot right now, Mom. Can't it wait until after the sidewalk sale is over?"

"This is not a hard job for you to do." My mother eyed the bag. "Where did that come from? Why did you not eat here today?"

"I was over on the East Side—"

"Is that from the House of Shen?" One eye narrowed as if it was going to twitch.

"You were there the other day," was my response. Albeit, not a good one.

"Lana! Do not go there. Why would you do this?"

I couldn't tell her the truth. If she found out I was looking into what happened with Millie Mao, her hair would probably light on fire. "If you must know . . . I was checking out how they had their restaurant decorated."

My mother shook her head disapprovingly. "No, no. We will not copy them."

"Exactly, Mother. I was seeing what they did, so we don't do same thing." I was going to add a "duh" to the end of that statement, but I felt like that was pushing it.

She thought this over and then gave me a thumbs-up.

"Okay, yes. This is a good idea. We want to be better than them. More stylish."

"Don't worry, Mom, I'll make sure of it."

Satisfied, she relaxed her arms and shrugged. "Okay. Then I will go to bingo now." With a wave, she disappeared from my door and I went to reach for my carry-out bag that was now starting to fill the room with its delicious aroma.

Before I could grab it, Peter popped his head in my office. "Hey, man, I wanted to talk to you for a minute."

"Are you going to give me something to do? Or yell at me?" I asked, eyeing him suspiciously. "Because if you are planning to do either, I'll ask that we wait to have that conversation until tomorrow."

"What? No." He shook his head. "I wanted to tell you; I did that thing with Kimmy where I gave her the key in a box just like you said."

"And?"

"It worked like a total charm. So, we're okay again. She also asked me for her own drawer, and I figured what's the harm in that? Then we made up and hopefully now everything can go back to normal."

"Oh Peter, I'm so glad to hear it. I was seriously worried for a minute."

"Yeah, me too. Thanks, Lana, I wouldn't have gone through with it if it wasn't for you."

Smiling as he slipped away, I took a moment to be thankful for at least one thing working out so far. With any luck, it would be a sign of future things to come.

I sank back in my chair and eyeballed my carry-out bag. Alone, finally.

*　*　*

My next plan of action was to find out more about Evelyn Chang and see where that road would lead me. I couldn't ask Donna anything more on Evelyn because she was being supportive of her friend and insisting on her innocence. I'd need another route with someone who wasn't so biased.

Helen might be a good resource, but I'd have to catch her without the other Matrons to be able to level with her. That would have to wait for the morning anyway; I'd deal with it then.

It was just about five o'clock and going home couldn't have seemed like a more appealing thing to do. I watched the clock above the front door, following the second hand trudge along on its continuous journey. The minute hand ticked by, and before I could watch the second hand make another loop, the front door to the restaurant swung open. June Yi stormed in, nostrils flarin' and obviously ready to give someone a piece of her mind. I had a sinking feeling that the person was me.

"Lana Lee!" she yelled. "What did I tell you about minding your own business?"

A hush fell over the noodle house and I turned to see the two tables of customers we had gawking at us from their seats. Nancy came bursting out of the kitchen, presumably to see what the commotion was about.

"Ms. Yi, please," I hissed. "We have customers here."

"I don't care what you have, *Miss Lee*," she replied back, turning up the sarcasm in her tone. "You will not make a fool out of me, do you understand?"

"I don't know what you're talking about. But perhaps we should take this into my office." I stood from

my stool and gestured to the back of the restaurant, trying to hide the fact that my entire body was vibrating with tension.

She folded her arms. "I am not going anywhere with you!"

Nancy scurried up to the hostess station. "June, please keep your voice down. The customers are asking questions."

"Lana should have thought about that before sticking her nose in my business," June spat out.

Nancy pleaded with the angry woman to calm down and to talk somewhere more private. I had a feeling I knew why this was happening, but I couldn't be entirely sure.

Finally, June agreed to talk in my office, and Nancy took over at the hostess station, an expression of concern on her face as I walked away.

Once June and I were in my office, I shut the door, offering her a seat. She gave the chair a dirty look as if it were an extension of me and chose to stand with her arms folded firmly across her chest.

I stood behind my desk, not wanting to sit and have her look down her nose at me. "What seems to be the problem, Ms. Yi?" I kept my body language and tone as neutral as possible, hoping not to rile her up further.

"The *problem* is you think everything is your business around here. Are you trying to get me into more trouble or what?" she asked. "I should tell your mother about this. . . . Maybe she can finally straighten you out."

That statement turned my attitude in a completely different direction. "I need to know what I did before I can answer you," I replied calmly. Beneath it all I was now seething. How dare she threaten me with tattling

to my mother. I was a grown woman. And truth be told, no one was going to "straighten" me out at this age.

"I received a call from Jeffrey Mao just now, telling me that I need to stop sending people to defend my honor. When I asked him what he was talking about, he told me that you were following him and trying to ask him questions about who really killed his sister."

It was as I'd thought. I was worried about that, considering he'd told me to give a message to June for him. Guess he wanted to do it himself.

"Why do you think this is appropriate? I do not need you to help me. Do you think this is some kind of favor?"

I wasn't sure how to go about this because I didn't want to throw her sister, Shirley, under the bus. But it didn't make sense for me to be involved simply out of the goodness of my own heart. After all, we didn't get along. Clearly.

"Lana Lee, give me an answer. What are you up to?"

It was the question of the day, wasn't it? So far, I was mostly successful with my answers. But with June staring at me as if she planned to have my head fitted for a noose, I didn't know what convincing nonsense I could say to smooth this over.

I straightened my back and inhaled deeply, calling on all the powers that be to give me patience. "I think you're innocent, and I'd like to help you prove it."

She stared at me blankly.

"I know we don't get along, and you're not my biggest fan. But it's not about that right now. I'm trying to look beyond that and put our differences aside. You're still someone in need of help, and I've done this sort

of thing before . . . as you know. So, I thought I'd help you out and try to find someone else the police could consider besides you."

She chewed on her bottom lip and diverted her glance to the top of my desk. Her expression seemed to soften, but with June, I couldn't really tell.

Finally, she gave the lip chewing a rest, and in an angry whisper said, "I don't need or want your help. So, mind your own business. I do not want to hear anything more about you and this investigation. Do you understand me?"

"But—"

She held up her index finger. "No. I do not need any help from you or anybody else." She spun on her heel, twisted the doorknob so hard I thought it would break right off, flung the door open, and stormed out before I could say anything else.

It didn't really matter either way because I wasn't planning on giving up at this late stage of the game. I had already aggravated myself enough at this point, and I hadn't done it for nothing. No, I was clearing June Yi of all suspicion whether she liked it or not.

CHAPTER
24

At five o'clock on the dot, I rushed out of the restaurant and hurriedly made my way to the Zodiac. I was through with this day, this week, and maybe even this year. I needed a strong drink and some really unhealthy food to make me feel better.

Megan was not at all surprised to see me, since I usually stopped by on Friday nights to see her and indulge in the happy-hour menu. She acknowledged me with a wink and immediately lifted a bottle of vodka off the shelf to begin concocting some kind of mixed drink, no doubt with a cute astrological name attached. I held up a hand before she could even tip the bottle. "No, nothing frou-frou tonight. I want something strong and bitter. Give me a whiskey, neat."

She put a hand on her hip and cocked her head at me. "Last time you drank whiskey when you were upset, I had to call you an Uber. And, you got so sick that night, I brought your pillow and blanket into the bathroom."

"Never mind that," I said, hopping up onto a stool. "I had a really bad day and I'm being stubborn."

She shrugged. "Fine, suit yourself." She grabbed a bottle of Johnnie Walker from the shelf and poured a small amount into a highball glass.

"More than that," I said.

Megan clucked her tongue and added two fingers' worth to the glass. "Start there. We'll see what happens."

I grunted but accepted the glass. The first sip I took burned my throat and I felt the warmth travel through my body. Some of the tension in my muscles began to disappear.

She leaned against the bar. "Tell me about this horrible day you had."

I started at the beginning and went through the entire fiasco of a day. When I was done, Megan straightened herself, resting her hands on the edge of the bar. "You're not kidding. It's been a rough go so far; I'll give you that. And this Evelyn woman, that's the super-rich one, right?"

"Yup, that's the one."

"You actually think it's a possibility she did this?"

"Honestly, I have no idea. She was definitely at the salon that day and yelled for the women to stop arguing. But what her motive would be, I have no idea. I didn't think she'd had any interactions with Millie. But I also didn't think that she'd be friends with Millie's brother either. The fact that she's been meeting with him on the East Side on a daily basis makes me think I can't possibility leave that stone unturned."

I'd emptied my glass and felt a little lightheaded. When had I eaten that kung pao chicken? It felt like an eternity ago. I told Megan I needed some boneless

wings and French fries, stat. And another round of whiskey to go with it.

When she returned from placing my order, she said, "I did run through all the names on the list you have, and I didn't find anything worth a damn. I mean, absolutely nothing. I tried to find information on the new salon employee, Samantha, and whether or not her family lives here and came up empty. But I'm not sure how accurate or up to date the information is."

"Figures."

"I did notice that another name kept coming up with Samantha's every time I tried a new search phrase: Rochelle Chan. So naturally I got curious and looked her up. I did find a Rochelle Chan who would be in the right age bracket, and she lives over in Cleveland Heights. I tried to find some connection between the two women, but there wasn't anything that I could see. Of course, everyone has their pages on social media set to private now. I couldn't see a friends list or anything that would be helpful."

I committed the new name to memory. "I'll try asking around the community and see if anyone knows who she is. It could be relevant, or it might not be."

While we waited for my food to be done, Megan filled me in on her day and told me about a new speed-dating gimmick that her boss wanted to host in the bar to drum up extra business on a slow weeknight. The whole thing sounded dreadful, and our discussion traveled to our thoughts on the current dating culture until my food arrived.

A few minutes later, Adam showed up.

"I thought I'd find you here," he said, kissing me on the cheek. "I texted you a couple times—didn't you hear your phone?"

"I turned off the ringer," I said through a full mouth of fries.

He sat down on the stool to my left, and picked up my glass, giving it a sniff. He let out a low whistle. "You're drinking whiskey tonight, huh?"

"Bad day," I said. I didn't feel like going through it all again, but Adam was eager to know what brought on a bout of Johnnie Walker.

While I told the story yet again, Megan came by with a beer for Adam, and a glass of ice water for me. After I brought Adam up to speed, he grunted. "Rookie move, Lana. If you're going to tail someone, you have to keep more distance than that. Probably should have stayed in the restaurant a little longer."

"Yeah, thanks, Detective. I know that now."

He smirked. "If it makes you feel any better, we have suspicions about Jeffrey ourselves."

My ears perked up. "You do?" I was shocked that he was sharing this information with me, and a little surprised to hear that Jeffrey was under their scrutiny.

"I'm only doing this because you had such a rotten day. And you have to promise this stays between you and me."

"Of course," I said, holding out my pinky. "I swear."

He laughed and interlocked his pinky with mine. "It seems that they have a considerable family estate through an uncle who has no children of his own, and the inheritance was stacked in Millie's favor. She would get sixty percent and Jeffrey would only get forty."

"And now with her gone, he gets it all, I'm guessing."

"Yes, ma'am. Every dime. So, we're considering that he might have been working with someone who

was at the salon that day. It's very much possible that June was just there coincidentally, but it worked in his favor."

"So, you believe that June may be innocent?"

He sighed. "If we can find some kind of connection between him and one of the women at the salon that day, we may be able to do more digging into that particular angle."

"Evelyn!" I blurted. "You're going to take my information and solve this case without me, aren't you?"

"I do have means to get information that you can't readily access."

I thought about my recent stint with a private detective and how easy it had been for her to retrieve files that I couldn't. Her boss had offered to help get me into the business . . . but . . . I'd dismissed the idea. "I guess it doesn't matter who gets the credit," I said, realizing my petty thinking. "Better you than someone else."

"Well, babe, don't get too excited just yet. It may not go anywhere or mean anything. We're going to interview the uncle on Monday morning and see what comes of that."

"So, what you're saying is that I have until Monday morning to solve this thing by myself?"

He laughed. "No, I'm saying that your job is potentially done. Why don't you try and relax this weekend? You've had a hard week and one of us should at least get a break from all this crime solving."

I sighed into my whiskey glass. "True story."

We stayed for another round. One that I didn't need. But, as I so assuredly told everyone, I was a grown woman, and capable of handling myself. Unfortunately, tonight, I had overestimated my limit.

Adam planned to take me home and spend the night, which made Megan feel a ton better. She packed up my remaining boneless wings and threw in an order of potato wedges for me to eat later on in the evening.

We'd been there so long, day had turned into night, and I was ready for pajamas and my pillow. Adam was going to square away the tab, and in my impatience to get out of the suddenly too loud bar, I took his keys so I could go sit in his car to wait.

I said goodbye to Megan and shuffled myself out the door, searching the darkened parking lot for Adam's car. I finally spotted it on the opposite side of the lot facing the street. With my carry-out box in hand and his car keys in the other, I made my way across the lot, commenting to myself how hot it was even at this late hour.

Suddenly, high beams sprang to life on my left and I heard the sound of peeling tires. My response time was slow, so I turned my head and stared at the bright lights wondering what the heck this person's problem was. It registered too late in my brain that the vehicle in question was coming straight for me.

"Lana!" I heard Adam yell right before I felt his hand grab hold of my shirt and pull me back.

The motion caused me to lose my balance and I fell backward on top of him. He pushed me to the side and ran after the SUV that had just barreled through the parking lot, almost turning me into a Lana pancake.

He came to a halt at the end of the parking lot, screamed some obscenities at the SUV that continued to speed down the road before returning to see if I was okay.

I was flat on my butt, and my tailbone was singing with pain. I winced as I tried to get up. In all the

commotion my takeout box had flown out of my hand and landed on the hood of a blue Ford Focus. Potato wedges and chicken wings were strewn all over the parking spot I was sitting next to.

"Dammit, I was hoping to get the license plate number, but the plate light was out!" Adam was out of breath and as he kneeled down next to me, he rested a hand on my shoulder. "My god, that person almost ran you over. Are you okay?"

"I think I bruised my tailbone," I said, feeling a wave of tears ready to burst at any moment.

"I'm going to call this in. Come on." He stood up and held out a hand for me to grab onto. "Let's get you home and into bed."

I took his hand. "What was that you were saying earlier about a bad week?"

When we got back to my apartment, Adam helped me into my pajamas, and then took Kikko on her evening walk so I didn't have to. I sat upright in bed with my weight shifted to one side to avoid my tailbone, thinking about what had just happened. The alcohol had begun to wear off and the wheels in my brain were turning at a faster pace. My backside was also beginning to hurt a lot more.

Once Adam came back with Kikko, she scurried to my bedroom, and sat down looking up at me with sad puppy eyes and whined. I shimmied myself so I could help her get in the bed with me. She laid down without a fuss, putting her head on my thigh, and let out a long doggy sigh.

Adam was on his cell phone when he came into my bedroom and was apparently talking to someone at the

police station. He gave a description of the vehicle—a black SUV with a burnt-out plate light, license maybe beginning with an *A*, heading west bound on Lorain Avenue. It wasn't much to go on, but he wanted the squad cars to be on the lookout for a potential drunk driver.

He hung up the phone and unbuttoned his dress shirt, draping it over my vanity stool. "I'm beat."

"Do you really think it was a drunk driver?"

"With the way you push people's buttons around this town?" he joked. "No, actually I don't."

"Why do these people always have black SUVs?" I asked. "Even in the movies they have them. Maybe these people should think about adding some spice into their life."

He snorted. "That's what you're worried about? Boring vehicle choices?"

"Should I sit here and panic about how I was almost run over instead?"

With a sigh, he said, "Black SUVs are probably one of the most common vehicles there are. It's just a coincidence."

"Yeah, but still . . . it's weird. I mean, what about a nice shade of blue? Blue would be nice, wouldn't it?"

"You're going to be thinking about this all night, aren't you?"

I nodded. "How can I not? Someone was trying to maybe run me over. If I'm going to overanalyze something, why not focus on the frivolous matter of car-color options?"

"And whoever it was knows that you go to the Zodiac. That's concerning."

"That could be a lot of people though," I said.

"I know. Maybe you shouldn't go there by yourself

while. They may try again, and I might not be re next time . . ." He scrubbed his face with both ands and groaned. "Okay, let's forget about it. You're safe, I'm here, and as far as we know, neither one of us has to get up early tomorrow morning. Let's just veg out with some Netflix and pretend the outside world doesn't exist."

"*Supernatural* marathon?" I asked, sounding hopeful.

"You got it, babe."

CHAPTER
25

Early Saturday morning, before it was even light outside, I woke with a start. My heart was pounding, and
I was gasping for air. But I couldn't remember the
dream that seemingly jarred me awake. All I could remember was a sense of fear and anxiety. I tried falling
back to sleep, but my mind wouldn't let me. Even my
usual fallbacks of counting fuzzy sheep and singing
the alphabet over and over again in my head weren't
working.

I slipped out of bed and stuck my hand under the
mattress. Thankfully I kept my secret notebook on
my side of the bed. Kikko and Adam were still sound
asleep, so I tiptoed out of the bedroom and went into
the dining area, sitting down at my usual seat at the
table. I contemplated making some coffee, but I knew
that as soon as the caffeinated beverage touched my
lips, there would be no chance of going back to sleep.
Instead I opted for some chamomile tea.

I spread my notebook open to a fresh page and
stared at the blank lines that were waiting to be filled.

I was spinning circles around myself, and what I really needed to do was make a list of all the things that needed to be done so I could get on with my life. This wasn't how I thought I'd be spending the remainder of my summer, and I wanted what was left of the season to myself.

I created check boxes on the left side of the page and then wrote down the things I needed to tackle. I was waiting on Donna to see what she drummed up in regard to the person Millie got into an accident with a few months ago. In the meantime, I could dig into Evelyn Chang's life and see if there was anything interesting to be found.

I knew I had to do something about the Mahjong Matrons, but I didn't know what. They usually played mahjong at the community center in Asia Village on Saturdays—maybe I could get Helen by herself at some point. I could even knock out two birds with one stone and see if *she* knew anything about the accident that Millie had been in.

I still had a few items to cross off my to-do list for the sidewalk sale, and even though it was the furthest thing from my mind, I couldn't let it go by the wayside. I'd have to find some time during the weekend to work on it.

And another dreaded avenue was figuring out a way to talk to Jasmine's grandmother, Lynn. I hadn't forgotten about her, but I was stalling on even going forward with it. But now was not the time to be squeamish about hurting people's feelings.

I also wanted to figure out who the heck owned that black SUV, because if they were in fact trying to run me over, they were probably the guilty party in this whole mess.

By the time I finished my tea, my body seemed more ready to cooperate in the sleep department. I went back to bed, telling myself that there was nothing I could do at four in the morning besides try and get some rest. I wasn't going to be good to anyone, including myself, without some decent shut-eye. When I woke up again, the first thing I would do was go to Asia Village and try to sneak Helen away from the other Mahjong Matrons.

The countdown with sheep began again.

The second time I woke up that morning, it was eight o'clock, and frankly too early for a Saturday. But whatever, I had things I needed to do and the fact that I got any sleep at all was a blessing in itself. Adam stirred in the bed, but didn't wake, so I slipped out with Kikko at my heels. After I prepped the coffee to brew, the two of us went on a walk around the apartment complex.

I took my time getting ready, and when Adam woke up about an hour later, he informed me he had some errands to run. We agreed to meet up later in the day. Relief washed over me with the knowledge that I didn't need to explain my whereabouts for that morning. At least not yet.

Right as I was getting ready to head out of the apartment, I heard Megan's bedroom door open. I turned to see my best friend appear in the hallway, her blonde hair swept up in a sloppy bun on the top of her head. She stretched her arms out and yawned. "What are you people doing out here?" She turned in my direction and her bun flopped to the side. "Some of us don't wake up at ungodly times on Saturday mornings, you know."

"Sorry, I tried to be quiet. I need to get to the plaza, so I don't have time to talk."

"Now what are you up to?" She asked, trudging to the couch. She let her body flop carelessly onto the sofa and threw her legs over the armrest.

Hurriedly, I filled her in on what I planned to do.

She nodded with approval and hoisted herself up. "I'm coming with you."

"What?"

"Yeah, I'm coming." She scurried back toward her room.

I followed after her, getting anxious. "I don't have time to wait for you to get ready."

"Says the girl who takes over an hour to get ready when we're running out for waffles."

I groaned. "This is time sensitive. I can't miss my window."

She had her head in her closet and was riffling through the massive amount of clothing she had stuffed in the tiny space. "Okay, fine. I'll just meet you there."

"Fine," I returned, exiting her room in haste. I didn't want to give her the opportunity to convince me otherwise.

Asia Village opened at nine o'clock, and I knew that the Matrons would be at Ho-Lee Noodle House having their breakfast. If I could catch them as they were leaving, maybe I could walk with them to their next stop—the community center—and talk with Helen alone.

I didn't want to step foot in my family's restaurant because I knew that my sister would stop me for a chat-and-bicker session, causing me to miss my chance with Helen. I decided to wait by the koi pond instead,

keeping an eye on the door to the restaurant from an angle where no one could see me. There was a bench adjacent to the entrance to the noodle shop, so I made that my home base, hoping no one would stop me to ask what I was doing. You couldn't do anything around this place without someone snooping into your business.

I pretended to be preoccupied with my cell phone so I could avoid making eye contact with anyone. It worked almost perfectly until Shirley Yi came up from behind me.

"Lana!" she hissed.

I jumped and my phone nearly fell out of my hands. "Shirley! Geez, you nearly gave me a heart attack."

"Sorry, I saw you standing out here, and snuck out of the bakery."

"We probably shouldn't be talking. If June sees you with me, she's going to flip out."

She glanced over her shoulder at the bakery's entrance. "I know, I just wanted to say that I'm sorry. June told me what happened yesterday. She is being very mean to everyone. Even me."

I wanted to comment how that wasn't unusual behavior for June. But the fact that she was being mean to her own sister was a bit on the unheard of side. "It's okay. I expected that to be her response if she were to find out anything. I just didn't think that Jeffrey would be the one to rat me out."

"He is a complicated man," she replied.

"Why didn't you tell me that they were involved with each other?" I asked.

"This was a very long time ago. That does not matter now."

I raised an eyebrow. "I wouldn't exactly say that.

June might not have been over what happened between the two of them, and it created a big problem between her and Millie."

"June does not care about such things."

"I've heard otherwise."

Shirley scowled. "From the Mahjong Matrons, I presume. Well, they are wrong. I am starting to regret asking for your help. You keep making this about June."

My eyes flicked back to the entrance of my restaurant to make sure I didn't miss anything. Still no activity. "Look, I'm not saying that June is guilty. I actually don't think she is. But we have to take everything into consideration. You're too close to this because she's your sister, so naturally you're going to get defensive. Just let me do my thing."

She turned up her nose at this and walked away without saying anything else. Which was just as well because a few moments later, the Mahjong Matrons emerged from the restaurant, chatting away and paying no attention to their surroundings.

I quickly grabbed my purse from the bench and zoomed around the perimeter of the koi pond so I could come up behind them. Helen and Wendy were walking behind Pearl and Opal, so I could easily stop Helen without interrupting the others.

As I neared them, Wendy must have sensed me in her peripheral and turned her head slightly to see who was there. Helen did the same. I maneuvered myself to the left of Helen so as not to get between her and Wendy.

"Good morning," I said, attempting to act casual. "How are you ladies on this beautiful day?"

Now all four women turned to greet me. "Good morning, Lana," they said in unison.

"What brings you to the plaza so early on a Saturday morning?" Helen asked. Her look was pointed, so I knew she understood that I'd come to chat with her.

"Bookstore," I said, using the Modern Scroll as my cover. Everyone who knew me would accept that without second-guessing it.

"It is so nice that young people still like to read," Helen commented. She started to slow her steps, separating herself from the other three.

The ladies nodded in agreement, Helen's slower pace going unnoticed.

Helen leaned in toward me and whispered, "Go into the ladies' bathroom, I will meet you there in five minutes."

I nodded, and then put on a production for the others. "Well, it was nice seeing all of you. I'm off to the bookstore now." With a wave, I swung around the four women and headed in the direction of the bookstore.

I began to slow down in front of my friend Rina Su's store, the Porcelain Doll, as I watched the ladies disappear into the community center. Unfortunately for me, Rina was standing at the entrance of her shop and gave me a quizzical look, her dark chestnut eyes burning holes into the side of my head as I pretended not to see her standing there.

"Lana Lee, what on earth are you up to?"

Acting surprised to see her, I returned her stare with blank eyes. "Oh hey, I didn't see you there."

"Yeah right, 'fess up, Lana." Her raven curls bounced as she shook her head disapprovingly at me.

"I swear, I'm up to nothing whatsoever," I replied. "Just um . . . going to the bathroom. I'll see you later."

She was not convinced. "Uh-huh . . . don't forget to stop by when you're done. I want to talk to you about something."

"Sure, sure," I said as I walked away and headed into the women's public restroom.

Thankfully nobody was in there, so I stood at the sinks and scrutinized myself in the mirror. The lighting was horrible, but my skin appeared to be sallow without the help of fluorescent lights, and these eye bags I was sporting had seemed to become a permanent fixture on my face. Maybe I did need to stop at the Porcelain Doll and at the very least pick up some under-eye cream.

As promised, five minutes later, Helen showed up in the bathroom, glancing nervously over her shoulder. "Okay, we do not have much time. Why are you here to see me? You *are* here to see me, correct?"

"Yes, I am." I gave her a brief rundown of why I needed to talk with her, and that my main focus was finding out information on Evelyn Chang and Jasmine's grandmother, Lynn.

"I see," she said in return. "I do not understand why Evelyn would go see Jeffrey Mao. This makes no sense to me. From what I know, they are not friends. I will try and find something out for you."

"Thanks. Anything you can find out would be helpful. I tried to ask Donna, but they're good friends and Donna wouldn't tell me much. She also didn't think Evelyn and Jeffrey were likely friends either."

"I can tell you about Jasmine's grandmother, Lynn, though. She is a very nice woman and does not have many enemies. But I do know that Lynn often worried

that Millie would give their group a bad name because of all the trouble she would cause."

"Do you think it's possible she would take it this far?"

Helen shrugged. "I am not sure about this. I know she plays mahjong on Saturdays. We all play in the mornings, and then sometimes we will play against each other in the evenings too."

I guess I knew where I was going when I left the plaza. "Okay, I'll see what I can find out about Jasmine's grandmother."

Helen's face brightened. "Oh, Lana, I would be so happy if you found something. Not that I wish for others to be guilty, but it will be good to know that Opal is innocent and did not kill Millie Mao."

"What?" A voice screeched behind us, and both Helen and I turned to face the doorway.

Uh-oh, it was Opal, and the expression on her face told me that she'd heard enough to know what we were accusing her of.

"O-Opal," Helen stuttered. "What are you doing here?"

"I have to use the bathroom," she said. "Why else would I come here?"

"Well, I should be going . . ." I said, feeling like I'd just got caught with my hand in the cookie jar. "Those books aren't buying themselves." I threw in a forced laugh just for good measure.

"Wait a moment," Opal said. "You think that I am guilty of killing Mildred Mao?" She looked between the two of us, her face a mixture of outrage and sadness. She turned to me. "Is that the real reason you dropped food off for me and Pearl? To spy on us?"

"No," I lied. "I would never—" I stopped myself

because I had too much respect for Opal to keep lying about the reason behind my visit.

Helen waved her hands. "No, no, you misunderstand, my friend."

"I know what I heard you say, Helen," Opal replied. "I did not do this. I can promise you that."

"We believe you," I said. But it didn't sound too convincing.

Opal sighed. "I promise and swear to Buddha that I did not do this. But I know who did."

CHAPTER
26

I blanched at the sound of absolute certainty in her voice. "What do you mean you know who did it?"

Opal stepped further into the bathroom, her hands were clasped firmly together, and she refused to make eye contact with me or Helen. "That day, Pearl began acting very strangely at the salon. Then when we saw June there, my sister became very upset. She told me that her stomach hurt and wished to go quickly. My stomach also did not feel right, and I told her I would meet her by the door. I went to use the bathroom and when I came back the beauty parlor was dark, and I did not know what happened. I became very nervous, and I did not know where Pearl had gone. I tried to get back inside Asian Accents, but the door was locked.

"Finally, I saw Pearl had gone to get the car for us and I rushed out to meet her. When I got to the car, I asked her what happened at the beauty parlor. She told me she did not know what I was talking about, but then later that day, we saw on the news what happened, and that is when I knew . . ."

"So, wait," I said before she could say anything further. "You went and used this bathroom instead of the one in the salon?"

She returned my question with a delicate nod. "Yes, that is correct. I wanted some privacy, and the beauty shop's bathroom does not have good walls."

I understood without her needing to say anything further. "So, you really did have the stomach flu?"

"Yes, of course. I would not lie about such a thing."

"But what about Pearl?" Helen asked. "When Wendy and I came to visit at your house, you both seemed okay."

Opal tilted her head. "Pearl told me that she was sick as well, but she did not appear to be so. At home, she did seem normal. That is why I fear I am right, and she is the one who killed Millie Mao!"

"Sister! What did you say?"

Pearl had walked into the restroom and none of us had noticed. This wasn't my best day as far as being aware of my surroundings.

Pearl stormed in and grabbed her sister's arm. "You will accuse me of this when I have been protecting you?"

Opal looked at her sister in confusion. "Protecting me? Why would you need to protect me?"

"Because you are the one who killed Mildred."

As the words came out of Pearl's mouth, all four of us froze and glanced awkwardly at one another.

"Okay, hang on," I said. I began rubbing my temples, feeling the slight touch of a headache coming on. "Helen, you thought Opal killed Mildred; but Opal thought Pearl killed Mildred; and Pearl, you thought Opal killed her?"

"Helen?" Pearl asked, shock in her voice. "You would accuse my sister of such a crime?"

Helen clucked her tongue. "You did as well. Do not blame me as if I'm the only one."

The three women began to bicker.

"For the record," I said, my voice rising about their squabble, "no one in this room killed Mildred Mao, am I correct?"

"We did not," Pearl answered for the group. "I was only protecting my sister from herself. I had left to get the car because neither of us was feeling very good. I knew that Pearl went to the bathroom, but she took a long time, and when we watched the news that evening, I assumed that she was the one who did it. I know that she does not care for Millie, and she had been acting strangely since we left the salon. Then the next day she said she was too sick to leave the house. This surprised me because we never miss a day at Asia Village."

"Because I was worried that you would get in trouble," Opal threw in. "I thought you were acting strangely too."

If I hadn't felt that it was wildly inappropriate, I would have smacked myself in the forehead and followed it with a string of choice words. But I curbed the reaction, and just shook my head in bewilderment. "Okay, well now that we have that all cleared up, I still have to figure out who did this."

Pearl turned to me. "Is this why you have been acting so strangely yourself, Lana?"

"Yeah," I admitted, my chin dropping with embarrassment at the absurdity of the whole thing. "But you have to admit that neither one of you helped convince me otherwise. When I tried to ask questions at

the restaurant, you told me to drop it and that it was most likely June who committed the crime. It sounded like you were all trying to take attention away from any other possibilities. What else was I supposed to think?"

The two sisters looked at each other and started to chuckle. And while I was relieved that it wasn't them and that everyone could have a good laugh about it now, it didn't resolve the fact that I had no good leads. Still.

Helen, who had become quiet, took a step forward. "Perhaps before Wendy becomes alarmed, we should return ourselves to the community center."

"I'm surprised she has not come looking for us already," Pearl commented.

Helen nodded. "Yes, well let's go. Lana, you are welcome to join us, and we may talk further and now more openly."

I checked the time on my phone. "Thanks, but I better get going. I want to try and catch Lynn Ming at the community center on the East Side."

Opal perked up at this information. "Do you suspect her of this?"

"Honestly ladies, I don't know what I think anymore. Maybe this whole thing was just a freak accident after all."

Pearl regarded me before walking out of the restroom. "If this happened to anyone else, I would say yes, this was an accident. But because it is Mildred, I believe it is not. That woman made a lot of trouble for herself. You be careful, Lana. We should hate to see anything happen to you."

* * *

While the exchange had been occurring in the restroom, Megan had texted me to say she'd arrived at the plaza and would be at Rina's shop picking up some eyeliner. By the time I made it to the cosmetics shop, I found Megan with a tiny basket that was more than half full of eye-shadow pallets and what looked to be moisturizers.

She smiled when she saw me. "There you are. I found this eye cream for you," she informed me, plucking a tiny, baby blue box out of her basket.

Geez, was it really that noticeable? I had thought maybe I was being a little harsh with myself in the bathroom earlier. I took the box from her hand and inspected her basket more thoroughly. "Did you even get eyeliner?" I asked.

She clucked her tongue. "Duh. I almost forgot."

While she picked out her eyeliner, I headed to the cash register, where Rina was helping another customer. Once she was finished, she turned her attention to me, her eyes falling to the product I was holding in my hands. "Oh good, I think that will really help. That brand has gotten a lot of great reviews."

My mouth dropped. "Are my eye bags that obviously?"

Megan came up from behind us. "Well, you haven't been sleeping that much. . . . It's starting to show."

"Thanks, guys." I handed the tiny box to Rina. "This is it today. . . . Megan on the other hand has bought half the store."

Rina began ringing me up. "I'm glad you came back. I wanted to talk to you, remember?"

"Oh yeah, what's up?" I pulled my wallet out and grabbed my credit card.

Her eyes slid over in Megan's direction, and then

back at me. "I know you're up to something. You have that look about you."

"I'm not up to anything. We're just shopping."

"Uh-huh," Rina replied. "Well, you can lie to me all you want, but really you need to just stay out of the whole thing. The Yi sisters can handle their own business."

"Yeah, Lana," Megan said, nudging me with her elbow.

I glared at Megan from the corner of my eye. "Don't worry, Rina, I'm not up to anything. And if I were to suddenly be up to something, I promise that I'll be careful."

"Yeah, you say that every time."

I decided not to argue and let her have the last word, which is a really hard thing for me to do.

Rina finalized my purchase and then began ringing up Megan. When she announced the total, Megan and I glanced at each other with wide eyes. With a shrug, Megan swiped her credit card and we said our goodbyes as we headed out the plaza.

When I was sure no one was around, I told Megan, "Man, do I have a story to tell you."

On our way to the East Side, I informed Megan about the ridiculousness of what happened in the bathroom before she arrived at Asia Village. We shared a laugh and then I told her the next part of my plan for talking with Jasmine's grandmother.

"I'm still digging into this Rochelle Chan person," Megan said. "I have to work later tonight of course, but I'll see if I can find anything to help you move that part along."

"Crap, in all the commotion, I completely forgot to ask the Mahjong Matrons if the name sounded familiar to them."

"No worries," my best friend replied. "I'm sure I'll find some slow time at the bar tonight."

I spent the rest of my drive making Megan listen to a podcast with me on positive thinking. Even though she thought it was kind of silly, I really needed all the motivation I could get my hands on right about now.

When we arrived at the community center, I searched the room for Jeffrey Mao, giving Megan a brief description so she could keep an eye out for him too. I needed to avoid him at all costs in case he decided to call the cops on me. I was guessing that he would assume I was there for him. And it's not like I could tell him that I was still snooping around but following someone else now. Maybe I was being overly cautious, but I didn't think he'd care that my attention was focused in a different direction.

I noticed my elderly informant sitting at the same stool as she had been the other day when we'd first met. I grabbed Megan's arm and led her over to meet my new friend.

"Hello there," I said, hopping onto the stool next to her. "It's nice to see you again."

Megan took the seat next to me and smiled, waiting to be introduced.

"Oh, you're that nice girl from the noodle shop. I remember you. Come for more Apple Sidra?"

"I have."

"And who's this cute girl with you?" the woman asked, acknowledging Megan.

"This is my friend, Megan," I said, leaning back

on my stool so they had a clear view to say hello. "I thought I'd show her a little bit of Chinatown today."

The woman smiled with approval. "I'm sure you will enjoy it, young lady," she said to Megan.

"It's a beautiful area," Megan replied.

I signaled the woman who worked the counter and placed an order for two cans of Apple Sidra.

Trying to act casual and like I'd really come to enjoy a late-morning beverage with my friend, we sat in comfortable silence for at least five minutes before I started my interrogation.

"So," I said, twisting my body to face her. "Have you heard of the Mahjong Matrons?"

"Yes, who hasn't?" She laughed. "They are quite popular in this city."

"I was talking with them earlier today, and they mentioned to me that the Tile Tigresses practice here on Saturdays. I heard they're pretty competitive."

The woman nodded. "Yes, very much so. They are sitting back there." She pointed to the back of the room near the Buddhist shrine. "The Mahjong Matrons will come later in the afternoon and play against them. It is very entertaining to watch."

Megan and I turned to observe the four elderly women at the table. It was like an alternate reality version of the Matrons. "Do you know which one of them is Lynn Ming?" I asked.

"Lynn?" The woman craned her neck to look at the table again. "She is the one on the right with the short white hair. Why do you ask about her?"

Lynn was a very stylish and petite woman who wore a full face of makeup and sported a rather sharp pixie cut. You could definitely tell that Jasmine was her granddaughter.

"Oh, she's my friend's grandmother."

"She is a very nice person," the woman said as if confiding a great secret to us.

"Lana, why don't we go over and say hi," Megan suggested in a syrupy sweet tone.

"Yeah, that sounds like a great idea," I said, playing along.

We excused ourselves from the kind elderly lady and made our way toward the back where the Tile Tigresses were seated.

As we passed behind the seat Jasmine's grandmother was sitting in, I turned and slightly nudged the back of her chair with my hip. "Oh, excuse me," I said, attempting to act embarrassed at my clumsiness.

It worked and Lynn Ming turned around to acknowledge me. "That's okay. These are very tight areas to walk around in." Her voice was delicate and her tone good-natured. I could see why Adam would have a hard time believing this woman was guilty of anything.

"Hey, aren't you Jasmine Ming's grandmother?" I asked. "You look so familiar."

Her eyes lit up at the mention of Jasmine's name. "Yes, Jasmine is my granddaughter. Are you a friend of hers?"

"Yes, I am. She also does my hair."

She beamed. "I can always tell. She is a very talented young woman."

"Yes, she is."

Megan poked her head around me. "It looks like someone dropped their cane." She bent down to pick it up.

Lynn twisted awkwardly in her seat. "Oh dear, I'm afraid that's mine."

"It is?" I asked without hiding my surprise.

She took the cane from Megan and propped it next to her against the table. She sighed. "Unfortunately, I fell in my driveway last winter while getting the mail. I slipped on some ice and fell right on my hip." Her hand slid down to the injured hip as she spoke. "I haven't been able to walk without a cane since. I hate it, it makes me feel so old. But Jasmine assures me that I am stylish as ever."

"I'm so sorry to hear that you fell," Megan said.

Lynn responded with a shrug. "These things happen. You can't let them keep you down."

I admired her spirit in the face of adversity, and even without the cane as a hindrance, I knew there was no way she could be guilty. She was too willing to find the good in a situation to do something horrible to Mildred.

We excused ourselves and headed back toward the front of the establishment.

I sighed. This new knowledge totally eliminated Jasmine's grandmother from my suspect pool. I felt like a huge jerk for considering that she was guilty for even a split moment. I owed Jasmine a huge apology.

Megan and I finishing our sodas at our original seats near our informant and thanked her for chatting with us before we headed out.

When we were back outside in the humid August air, and it was just us, I turned to Megan, feeling defeated. "We're beginning to narrow down the possibilities, but I still don't feel productive."

Megan put on her sunglasses and gestured for us to

head to the car. "Yeah, but at least the people we don't want to be guilty aren't."

"True," I replied. "See? That positivity podcast really is starting to help."

Completely unsure of my next moves, I decided to head back to Asia Village and work on the remaining items for the sidewalk sale. I still needed to post the requirements for each shop participating, pass them out to all the owners, and then contact the local newspapers about placing some type of advertisement with them.

Megan had to head back to the apartment to get ready for work, so I dropped her off at her car and we said our goodbyes.

The restaurant was a little busy, and it kept Anna May preoccupied while I snuck into my office. I even managed to bypass our alternate cook, Lou, since he was too busy grilling shrimp to notice me slip by.

Once in my office, I turned on my computer and got to work on the requirements and the official informational page that needed to go to the shop owners.

Donna's phone number lit up my cell, and I was relieved for a distraction. "Hi, Donna, how are you?"

"Oh, just fine, dear, thank you for asking. And how are you on this dreadfully hot Saturday afternoon? Staying cool, I hope."

"For the time being," I said. "I'm at Ho-Lee Noodle House getting some work done on the sidewalk sale."

"The sidewalk sale? Why are *you* working on that? Did Ian pass that off to you? He did, didn't he?" Her voice betrayed a little anger at this news.

"Um . . . I offered to help since he has so many

other projects going on," I lied. I didn't know what Ian's angle was with this, but I was going to strangle him for fibbing to me.

"You really are a dear, aren't you? But never mind that right now, I have some news that you will most definitely find interesting."

"Oh good, because I'm ready to rip out my hair any minute."

"I managed to find out some information about the accident that Millie was in. Apparently, it never officially went to court and was settled between the lawyers in private."

"Great, so who was it then?"

"Well, I'm afraid that's where things get a bit unsavory. At least for me. Now you must understand, this is extremely delicate."

"Who was it?" I could hardly contain myself from leaping out of my seat.

"The accident occurred with a young woman by the name of Rochelle Chan."

"Rochelle Chan?!" I practically screamed into the phone. It was the same name that Megan had found during her search for Samantha Hui and who she was planning to dig up dirt on later this very evening. Whoever this Rochelle person was had a tie to Samantha and now maybe we'd figure out why.

"Do you know of her?" Donna asked.

"I've heard the name before in passing . . ."

"Well, you can see why I'm upset then, can't you?"

I furrowed my brows. "Actually no, I don't. Do you know her personally?" I asked.

"Oh, I thought you knew the association. I'm sad to say that she's Evelyn Chang's niece."

CHAPTER
27

When people call Cleveland a small city, I cringe. It doesn't get the credit that it deserves, and I'll be the first to tell you that every time the topic should arise. But when you take the intimate nature of the inner communities and the circles that run together into consideration, it's kind of an unavoidable stereotype.

Donna's clear disappointment in Rochelle's tie to Evelyn made my heart ache because she had been so confident that her good friend had no reason to go after Mildred Mao. So, it was near impossible for me to go into further speculation about the wealthy woman's involvement with Donna of all people.

What I couldn't quite understand was the connection between Evelyn, Millie's brother Jeffrey, and Evelyn's niece Rochelle, and then what it all had to do with Samantha Hui from the salon.

We hung up and I promised her that I would at least hear Evelyn's side of the story before taking any action. In turn, I made Donna swear that she would not

alert Evelyn to the fact that I was heading straight for her house to get more information.

I pulled up for the third time to the stately home and found my sense of awe had not been diminished by what I knew. As I got out of the car, I wondered if it was true that money corrupted even the best of people. After a certain point, many believed the wealthy played by their own rules, knowing that money would often make all their worries go away.

Of course, that was a wild generalization because I did know many good people who were swimming in money and seemed to do just fine in the moral compass department. This situation, however, wasn't supporting that fact in my favor.

This time it was Evelyn's housekeeper, Susan, who answered the door. She smiled at me as recognition set in. "Lana, right?" She was dressed in a short-sleeved knit set and a plaid skirt. Like the first time I met her, I couldn't help but notice her conservative ways and compare them to Anna May's own reserved wardrobe.

"Yes, hi Susan, long time no see," I joked.

She laughed. "What's it been? About a whole three weeks?"

"Give or take," I replied. "Hey, is Ms. Chang home? I'd really like to speak with her if she's available."

"Yeah, she's home. She's in her library, actually. The kids are away at a summer camp, so you've come at a good time. The house is extremely quiet today, which is a rare occurrence. Follow me."

I followed Susan to the home's lavish library and tried to remind myself to not get distracted. I was here on a rather grim manner and would be sitting across from someone who wasn't going to take kindly to what I had to say.

Susan gave a soft knock on the door, and announced that she was coming in. When Ms. Chang noticed that I was behind her maid, shock passed over her face. "Lana, what a nice surprise. Come in, please. Susan, would you mind getting us a service of tea?"

"Yes, ma'am," Susan said as she excused herself from the room.

"Come have a seat with me, I was just enjoying one of my Nora Roberts trilogies." She held up the book for me to see. It was a copy of *Key of Light*. "Fascinating read, really. Are you familiar with it?"

"I am actually," I replied. "I've read all three in the set. I really enjoyed them."

"Well, don't tell me what happens. I am just dying to find out. I can't read it fast enough. If I don't read these while the kids are away, I'll never get the chance."

I'd chosen the chair across from her and squirmed in my seat while we went on about the business of small talk. Normally I would be thrilled to talk to someone about books we had in common, but today was not the day for that.

While we chatted about her favorite romance and romantic suspense authors, Susan returned with a tray of tea. She poured each of us a cup and then excused herself again.

"Now, Lana, what brings you by? I have a feeling it wasn't to discuss fiction novels."

I let out an anxious laugh. "You caught me."

"Is this something to do with what we spoke about the other day?"

"It is," I said, taking a sip of tea. My mouth suddenly felt like sandpaper. I was incredibly nervous and had no idea how to go about saying anything without

outright accusing her. And my current track record wasn't giving me much confidence.

"Lana . . ."

"Last time I was here, I asked you if you happened to know who Millie had gotten into an accident with, and you told me you didn't have any idea." I let the statement hang in the air while she processed what I was saying.

"I was afraid you might find out," she said, setting her teacup down.

My stomach sank. "Is that why you sent me on a wild goose chase in the opposite direction?"

"Not entirely, but talking to Rochelle wasn't going to get you anywhere, and there was no reason to drag my niece into this whole mess. She didn't do anything wrong."

"I know. But you did, and I can understand why you did what you did—"

"What?" Her hand flew up to her chest, and she leaned back in her seat. "How is protecting my niece considered wrongdoing?"

"Protecting your niece isn't the problem, it's how you chose to do it."

"I got her the help she needed after the fact. Honestly, Lana, does the girl deserve massive punishment because she made *one* bad decision in all of her life? She was an honor student, for heaven's sake."

That made me pause. "Hold on, let's back up a minute. What exactly are you talking about?"

"I should ask you the same question," she spat, her voice taking on a defensive tone.

I couldn't say the words, but the longer I was silent, Evelyn seemed to catch on to my train of thought.

"You think that *I'm* the one who killed Millie, don't you?" She rose from her chair and started to pace.

"Didn't you?" I whispered. "To get back at her for going after your niece?"

An abrupt laugh escaped, and she covered her mouth with her hand. "I will say, you do have a wild imagination. And if you weren't a dear friend of Donna's, I might likely throw you out right this minute. But, seeing as I know you and that you're only trying to help, I will entertain this. No, that is not at all what transpired. I thought you were talking about the fact that I covered up what happened with my niece and the car accident."

"No. . . . There was a cover-up?" This was news to me, and probably explained why it was settled out of court and there was so little information to be found about it.

Evelyn's amusement disappeared and her lips curved into a frown. "Rochelle was driving drunk when she rear-ended Millie. I'm ashamed to say, she was well past the legal limit. Apparently, she had just gotten in a huge fight with her stepsister and drank herself silly. Her good judgment had clearly disappeared, and she took off in her car, just wanting to get home. Mildred was at a stop sign, and Rochelle didn't see it. She slammed right into the back of her car. Not knowing what to do because of her *condition*, my niece called me right away. Thankfully Millie had yet to call the authorities, and I managed to smooth the whole thing over with her."

My breath caught, and I tried to clear my throat. "I had no idea."

"Yes, well, it was rather awful, I can tell you that. Millie planned to sue the pants off my niece who doesn't have a dime to her name, by the way. And I couldn't imagine what would happen to her with a DUI. I knew

she wasn't this type of girl. And frankly, my sister—her mother—is no help. So, I paid off Millie quite handsomely to keep the whole ordeal from going any further."

"Your niece got away with it scot-free then?" I asked.

"Don't be so judgmental, Lana. We all make our mistakes. I made sure she went to AA meetings when it was over. I wanted her to understand the severity of what she did, but I don't think she is the repeat-offender type. Nor do I think she has a drinking problem, if you must know my personal feelings on the subject."

"She doesn't happen to own a black SUV, does she?"

"No, why would you ask that?" Evelyn asked, appearing stupefied.

"Just wondering is all."

"Anyhow, I had nothing to do with Millie's untimely demise. The whole situation was taken care of, and I had no further dealings with her after that. A little of the information did spread because Millie couldn't help but brag to everyone about how she received such a generous sum, but thankfully she kept mine and Rochelle's name out of it. How did you find out, by the way?"

"I'd rather not say." I didn't know how Donna had obtained the information, and I didn't want to rat her out either. I'd done enough damage already.

"Well, I hope they're happy with themselves, whoever they are." She folded her arms over her chest.

I opted to switch gears with my questioning before she tried to get more out of me about my source. "Okay, that clears up a lot, but then why have you been

going to see Mildred's brother, Jeffrey, every day?" I asked. I was still confused by that whole aspect. Originally, I thought they were working together, but now I didn't know what to think with this new information coming to the surface concerning her niece.

"Oh that?" Evelyn chuckled to herself. "I can see how someone might find that odd. I've been trying to persuade him to drop any type of lawsuits against Asian Accents. He plans to make a big stink about how unsafe it is at Asia Village, what with the recent history of the place. And the last thing Donna needs is any more problems. I think we can both agree she's been through her fair share as of late."

Knowing the nature of her relationship with Donna, I found myself believing Evelyn completely. I shook my head, disappointed with myself. "Wow, I am so sorry, Ms. Chang. You must think I'm an awful person to come accuse you of anything when you were just trying to help."

Taking her seat again, she leaned forward and picked up her teacup. "Not at all. However, as I said before, if Donna didn't speak so highly of you, I might have a few reservations. But we are ultimately all working toward the same outcome. I'm just relieved you came to me first before sharing this information with your boyfriend."

I winced. "About that . . ." I admitted to her that I thought she might be working with Jeffrey Mao in some way, and though she found it slightly amusing considering the circumstances, she was a little perplexed with Adam's decision to investigate her background. And rightfully so.

"It will all get handled somehow," she resolved. "I would appreciate you leaving out the part about

my niece Rochelle being drunk during the accident. It would go a long way in putting things right in my book. You are welcome, however, to update your boyfriend with the rest of the information we discussed today. I'll let my lawyer know it's okay to confirm the surrounding details of what happened and how things were settled out of court. My hope is that will be enough for them to go on without further questioning anything about the cause of the accident itself."

"I'll do what I can to help since I clearly made it worse." I blushed. "You really are handling this gracefully. As you said, someone else would have thrown me out of their house already."

"If there's one thing I've learned in my years, Lana, it's that everything can be handled with a touch of class." She crossed her legs and leaned against the back of her chair. "Now that you've eliminated me as your prime suspect, what will you do next?"

With a sigh, I confessed, "I have just one more real lead outside of June, and I'm stumped on that one too. Actually, maybe you could help me with it. It might have something to do with Rochelle, but I'm not sure how it all fits together just yet."

"Do tell," she replied. "I can guarantee you though, Rochelle is innocent of anything."

"That might be so, but what is her connection with Samantha Hui? I can't figure it out."

"Sam?" Evelyn sat up straight in her chair. Disapproval spread over her features, and her lip turned up in a snarl. "Samantha is Rochelle's stepsister. She's the one who caused my niece to get in that damnable accident in the first place. Sam is the daughter of my sister's second husband, and what a nightmare of a little girl she used to be. Always causing trouble . . . always get-

ting Rochelle into trouble. Well, the accident was Rochelle's last straw. She told Sam that she would never speak to her again."

"Do you know what the original fight was about?"

"What, dear?"

"The original fight that made Rochelle start drinking to begin with."

"Oh, that. From what I understood, it had something to do with Rochelle wanting to move out of state for some type of medical program. Like I said, she's a bright girl. I don't think Sam took to the news that well. She claimed that she moved back here just to be close to her sister. Well, you know what I say to that? Rochelle doesn't owe her a thing. No one asked her to come back. She should have just stayed in Pennsylvania."

"I see." My brain was sorting information while Evelyn continued on with her explanation.

"Here she is, putting this big guilt trip on Rochelle, and telling her she's never going to succeed with medical school. Sam actually said that she changed her plans just to come back here. Supposedly, she had an opportunity to start her own salon somewhere else but turned it down because the girl wanted to start her business in Atlanta. Well, I ask you, how is that Rochelle's fault?"

Before I could respond, she answered herself. "It's not, plain and simple. So, then the poor girl ends up drinking herself stupid and well, you know the rest."

"So, she hasn't spoken to Sam at all since this whole car accident thing happened?"

"No. She has totally shut her out of her life. Rightfully so, if you ask me. The girl is nothing but trouble."

"She sounds a little abrasive, that's for sure."

"The little brat even tried to offer paying me back, thinking it was going to help get her out of trouble with her sister. She pleaded with both me and Rochelle to make up some sort of payment plan to pay me back, but Rochelle wouldn't have it. Not that I expected anything in return. I'm certainly not going to put my niece in a position to pay me back when her future is so bright. I'd rather take the loss instead of leaving her to worry about being in debt to me. Besides, Rochelle is better off without her, so if the two don't ever make amends, I'm not going to lose sleep over it." Evelyn paused, and squinted at me. "Lana, are you all right?"

I'd begun to zone off to la-la land. I was pretty sure I'd just hit pay dirt.

CHAPTER
28

I told Evelyn that I needed to be on my way, thanked her profusely for her time, and then rushed to called Megan for a quick update as soon as I got back to my car. When she answered, I rattled off the story to her, barely stopping to take a breath, and triumphantly told her that I was going to track down Samantha Hui. "It's gotta be her," I said.

"Whoa, slow down, Lana," Megan replied. "First of all, you're really lucky that Evelyn Chang was so understanding of your accusations, but from what you've told me so far about this Samantha girl, it doesn't seem like she'll be quite as forgiving if you're wrong. You don't actually have any evidence against her."

"But it's all so clear now. Samantha is the reason that Rochelle got into the accident with Millie to begin with. And then Evelyn tells me Rochelle won't talk to Samantha anymore because of it. Samantha probably blamed Millie's actions instead of her own for the real reason why Rochelle won't talk to her anymore. So, to get back at her for ruining their relationship, she decides

to kill Millie when she gets the perfect opportunity. It may not solve the problem between her and her sister, but maybe she'd feel like she'd gotten revenge, and a little bit of satisfaction. I mean, think how mad this girl must be, thinking she gave up a huge opportunity to start her dream business for someone who isn't even talking to her anymore. Meanwhile, June takes the hot seat because she can't keep her mouth shut and sounds like the perfect suspect to everyone she comes in contact with."

"It's possible, but I still think you need to be careful. You sound a little hyper and you know how easy it is to slip up when you're like that. Don't do anything today. You should take some time to process and re-evaluate before you make your next move. We covered good ground today, let's not get ahead of ourselves."

"I'm not hyper, I'm motivated," I replied, dismissing her concern. "And I'm already heading back to the plaza now. I'm going to see if Samantha is working at the salon. Then I'll come up with something depending on if she's there or not."

"I still don't think it's a good idea. You don't have a solid plan. Can't you just wait until tomorrow, Lana? I finally have the day off and we can do something about this together. Let me look into Samantha a little more like we originally planned and then go from there."

"But I don't want to wait anymore. I want this whole thing to be over and done with. So I can go back to my normal life."

"I get that, but what's another day? Please?" Megan whined.

I huffed. She knew I had a soft spot when she pleaded with me. "Okay, fine. I won't do anything drastic today.

But I'm still going back to the plaza to scope things out."

"Alright, check in with me when you leave though. If you stop by the bar, I'll give you some boneless wings on the house."

It did sound tempting, and it reminded me that I'd lost my leftovers in the parking lot. "Deal. I'll stop by when I leave the plaza. But I want potato wedges too."

"As if I'd leave them out."

We hung up and I made my way to Asia Village feeling an itch to take some kind of action. Samantha was right under my nose this whole time, and I hadn't given her much thought because I'd had no luck finding anything significant. But my first instinct about her had been right. There was something definitely off about her story.

Fifteen minutes later, I was at the plaza and I could feel a headache starting to form at the base of my skull. I hadn't eaten since waking up and had done so much running around I didn't even realize it. Once I got in the restaurant, I'd have Lou make something for me.

Still in the parking lot, I felt my brain hiccup and I realized I should check the parking lot for a black SUV. Even though there wasn't much to go on, and plenty of people had them, I had the urge to check just to be on the safe side.

Of course, to my dismay, there were a handful of them sprinkled around the lot. But only two in the employee section. It was a long shot, but what could being thorough really hurt? Attempting to be inconspicuous, I checked both license plates. One of them had an *A* in it, and I distinctly remembered Adam saying he thought there was an *A* in the plate number of the SUV

that came at me. I made a mental note of where the vehicle was parked and headed into the plaza.

My first stop would be the hair salon. Not just to see if Samantha was working, but also to officially apologize to Jasmine. She'd had time to cool down, so with any luck, I could make things right with her.

Upon entering the salon, I saw that both Samantha and Jasmine were there because they were behind the hostess station chatting with each other. The two women turned their heads toward the entrance as I walked in.

"Hi, Lana," Jasmine said. Her voice was rigid, and I could tell that she was still upset with me from our last interaction. "What brings you in today? I didn't see you in the appointment book."

Samantha regarded me with a head nod before walking away to give us privacy. As she disappeared into the back, I said something smarmy in my head like, *"I'll deal with you later, you murderous she-devil."*

With the front of the salon completely empty, it seemed as good a time as any to talk with Jasmine. If I put it off any longer, I was going to drive myself insane with guilt. Then it dawned on me that Yuna was nowhere to be found, which was just as unusual as the Matrons being separate from one another. "Where's Yuna?" I asked.

"Oh, she has really terrible allergies, so I sent her home. She was sneezing all over the place and I couldn't have her around the customers like that. Anyway, what's up?"

I shifted my attention to my hands, noticing my chipped nail polish. "I just came by to say that I'm sorry. I should have never insinuated your grandmother

would do anything like that. I hope that you can forgive me for insulting your family. And if not, I completely understand."

"Lana . . ."

"I'll find another hair salon to go to and everything. I would absolutely get it."

"Lana!"

I looked up at her. "Yeah?"

"I forgive you."

"Oh."

"I get a little protective over my family sometimes, and I know you didn't really mean anything by it. What happened here is pretty strange and I know you were just grasping at straws."

I sighed with relief. I didn't bother to tell her that I only truly eliminated her grandmother because I found her physically incapable of committing the crime. "Thank you for forgiving me. I know I would go completely bonkers if someone accused my grandmother of murdering someone."

She laughed. "Well, if I ever do that, then I get a free pass."

We talked for a few minutes and I booked my next hair appointment. Not sure if I was inspired by the boldness of Yuna's unicorn-esque hair, but I wanted to try something similar on my next salon adventure.

Leaving the salon in better spirits, I decided to hang out at the restaurant, grab an early dinner, and work on the remainder of the sidewalk sale items until my brain decided to cooperate with a plan for what to do next in regard to Samantha. I had to be careful, and since she was an employee of Jasmine's and we had finally made amends, I didn't want to go messing that up so quickly with inaccurate accusations.

In the meantime, I gorged myself on shrimp dumplings, half a plate of watercress, and two bowls of spicy noodles with bok choy, then polished it all off with an almond cookie. I'd stuffed myself so thoroughly I didn't think I'd have room for the boneless wings and potato wedges that Megan had promised me.

The food coma caused my eyes to close and I drifted into a nap at my desk. No clue what time it was or how much time had passed, I woke up to my sister yelling my name. When I lifted my head, I realized I'd been drooling on the calendar blotter that covered the top of my desk. "What's up?" I asked, trying to act like I hadn't been sound asleep.

"I could hear you snoring through the door," Anna May complained. "What are you still doing here anyway?"

I stretched my arms and straightened my back. There was a crick in my neck from the way I'd been sprawled on my desktop. "I didn't sleep well last night. I guess the day finally caught up with me."

"It's probably because you ate all that food."

"I was hungry," I replied defensively. "I hadn't eaten all day."

"Henry says if we gorge ourselves—"

"Oh, will you shut up with the 'Henry says' stuff. Can't you find the inspiration to annoy me on your own behalf?" I flopped backward in my chair.

Anna May stuck her tongue out at me. "Whatever, grumpy."

"And what's the deal with you guys anyways?" I asked. "What exactly are you hiding?"

My sister blushed. "I'm not hiding anything."

"You're hiding something, and if you don't tell me,

I'll just end up finding out anyway. You know I always do."

"Just mind your own business, okay? My romantic life isn't up for discussion." She crossed her arms over her chest. "Mom is always telling you to worry about yourself, and that's exactly what you should do."

"Ha! You *are* hiding something, Anna May Lee, and the more you deny it, the more obvious it is. I'll figure it out eventually." I said it so assuredly that I actually believed myself. My sister didn't usually do things that weren't one hundred percent aboveboard, but in this instance, that fluttery sensation in my gut told me that I was on to something. I just needed more time to do some extra snooping.

She shook her head at me and turned to leave. "You're delusional. Maybe you better go home and sleep off whatever your problem seems to be. It's time to go anyways. The plaza just closed."

I sprang out of my chair. "What? It's closing time already?"

"Yeah, Lou just left, and I was ready to leave myself when I realized you were still back here."

I collected my things and followed my sister out of the restaurant. I was still trying to fully wake up, contemplating if it was too late in the day to drink some coffee. I'd fall asleep at the bar for sure if I didn't do something to get my energy back up.

As we began to leave the plaza, I noticed there were still people inside Asian Accents. One of them was Samantha. I needed to ditch Anna May, but I didn't see what excuse I could come up with, so I decided I'd just have to wait in my car.

Anna May and I said goodbye and talked briefly

about seeing each other at dim sum the next morning. I took my time getting to my car, noting that the black SUV was still there, and waited for Anna May to pull away.

It was a little muggy, so I turned my car on and ran the A/C. Ten minutes later, I watched Samantha and Jasmine exit the plaza together. They stood for a while chatting in the parking lot and I became increasingly impatient with each passing moment. Not just because I wanted to physically watch Samantha get into that black SUV, but because I had to pee. My sister had ushered me out in such a hurry that I didn't get a chance to go to the bathroom.

Another ten minutes went by. Now I saw the Yi sisters exiting the plaza. They seemed to be bickering about something and they also stopped to have a conversation in the parking lot. My annoyance level had reached its maximum . . . and so had my bladder.

I shut off my car and got out. I couldn't wait anymore. The last thing I needed to do was pee my pants at twenty-eight years of age. Trying to rush and keep it together at the same time, I shuffled back toward the entrance of the plaza. Jasmine noticed me and waved, and I strained a wave back, not wanting to relax any of the muscles in my body.

Just as I was about to enter the plaza, I heard Jasmine yell, "I'll see you tomorrow." I halted and spun around to watch Samantha get into that black SUV with the *A* in the license plate.

But it wasn't her who got in. It was June Yi. And she was staring right at me through the windshield.

CHAPTER
29

I didn't have time to stick around after witnessing June get into the SUV. My bladder wasn't going to hold out much longer. I scuttled to the public restrooms as fast as I could without unclenching my thighs and barreled into the first stall. Once I had answered nature's call, I called Adam from my cell. I was still in the stall, trying to catch my breath.

He answered on the second ring. "Hey, babe, where have you been all day? I've tried texting and calling a few times."

"It's June!" I yelled. "I saw her in the black SUV; the license plate had an *A* in it. June is the one who tried to run me over."

"Calm down," he replied. "Where are you? Why is your voice echoing?"

"I'm in the bathroom at Asia Village. I fell asleep in my office and didn't know how late it was. Anna May woke me up when it was time to close up."

"Is June still there now?" he asked.

"No, she was leaving for the day. But she saw me

see her. What if she knows that I know? I bet you it's a rental car or something. She tried to mow me down with a rental car. I have to get out of here."

"Okay, first what you need to do is calm down, you can hardly breathe."

"Everyone kept saying it was her the whole time, and I just refused to believe it. It just seemed so trite. I've blamed everyone else under the sun, made a complete ass out of myself in front of several people . . . and—"

"Lana!" Adam yelled into the phone. "Calm down, take a deep breath. There's no way you could have known any of this. If June hadn't slipped up with the SUV, we couldn't have put anything together. Plus, we're not entirely sure it's the same one. So just calm down and breathe for me, okay babe?"

I took some exaggerated breaths for his sake so he would know I was trying to breathe. But really, I couldn't control myself. I saw this woman every day. I'd just spoken with her and admitted to her that I was trying to help clear her name. And then she tried to run me over. How was I supposed to calm down?

"Are you too rattled to drive? Do you want me to come pick you up?"

"No, I'll be okay," I said. "I don't want to stay here alone. Everyone's already gone, and this place gives me the creeps at night. Can you meet me at the Zodiac? I told Megan I would be there hours ago."

"Yeah sure, but first I have to call Higgins and talk to him about this and the rental car. It's a little thin to go on, but maybe he and I can come up with a way to work this to our advantage."

"Okay, you do that. I'm going to head back out to my car. Megan is never going to believe this."

We hung up with the promise of seeing each other soon. I knew once I got to the bar, I'd be fine. A crowded place and a stiff drink were exactly what would settle my nerves. I'd have to be careful in the parking lot though, just in case June was waiting to try and run me over a second time.

No need to worry about that though because when I exited the stall, she was standing at the sinks staring at me. My eyes slid down to her hands, and my brain took some time to process the fact that she was holding on to a tire iron.

Before I could speak, she said, "I heard your conversation with your police boyfriend. I was hoping you wouldn't tell him anything."

"You tried to run me over the other night," I spat. "What did you think was going to happen?"

"I was only trying to scare you into being quiet. I knew that you wouldn't give up so easily. I could see it in your face when I yelled at you the other day. You never listen to anybody, do you?"

"So, it was you. This whole time, and I went around blaming everyone else." I tried to ignore the fact she had this weapon in her hand. Would she really try and hit me with that thing? Adam knew where I was, and he knew she was the one with the black SUV. She couldn't really think she'd get away with anything now, could she? My only hope was that she actually cared. If she knew she was going to be found guilty of a crime, she may not care what else happened at this point.

"Yes, this whole matter of you trying to prove I'm not guilty is confusing to me. Why, Lana Lee, would you help me? I am not your friend. I don't even like you."

I was done protecting her sister. At this point, all bets were off. "Shirley came to me and asked me to help find you innocent. She really believed that you didn't do it."

June chuckled. "My poor sister is so innocent sometimes. She will always defend me. I gave up much of my life to take care of her so she will always trust me."

"No one asked you to give up your life," I said, not feeling one ounce of pity for this woman. "You chose to do that, and you have no one to blame but yourself."

"Ha! Is that what you think?" She shook her head with disgust. "Our mother and father died very young. No one would take care of us but me. Shirley was always sick, and I could not leave her. Yes, maybe no one asked me, but I have much honor and would never leave my family. I guess you do not know anything about this type of sacrifice."

While she talked, I concluded my best option would be to try and lock myself in a stall and call 911. I thought about trying to run past her, but the entrance into the restroom was narrow and it was likely she'd strike me on the back with that iron rod before I could make my getaway.

I slowly started to back up, sliding one foot behind the other.

She noticed immediately. "You can leave if you'd like, but it won't help you."

This confused me and I stopped moving. "You're going to let me leave?"

She glanced at the tire iron in her hand as if she'd forgotten all about it. "Why yes. I don't plan to do you any harm with this. This is for me."

"Huh?"

She snickered and waved the iron in the air. "I be-

lieve that your generation calls it taking one for the team. Yes?"

"I don't understand," I confessed. Or maybe I did but didn't want to admit it.

"It's very easy to understand. I will use this to harm myself and then blame it on you."

The calmness of her statement unnerved me, and a chill ran down my spine at the very thought of it. "That's not going to work," I said, with a little too much confidence. "I already talked to Adam, and he'll put everything together."

"Yes, he will, won't he? You were trying to defend yourself against a poor, older woman. You became obsessed with finding the killer, as you always do, and this time you went a little bit crazy. I think that he will believe it. You did sound crazy on the phone."

"He'll believe me. He knows I'd never hurt anybody."

"That's okay too. People will think he is protecting you because he's your boyfriend. I win either way." She smiled innocently at me, raised the tire iron above her head, and swung it in a downward motion straight at me.

I dropped my phone and my purse, thrusting my hand up and grabbing hold of the thin rod of iron right before it smacked me in the head. "What are you doing?" I screeched. Had she given me a false sense of security by telling me she wasn't planning to use it on me?

We wrestled with it for a minute, then she abruptly released her hands and held them up in the air, showing me her palms. "You really are simple, Lana. Now your fingerprints are on the weapon." She started to laugh again. "This was too easy. I thought you were smarter than this."

I dropped the tire iron on the floor and wiped my hands on my jeans as if that were going to help. "You're demented. I've never liked you, June. Not a day in my life, but I really didn't think you were like *this*."

"It's about time you learn life's most important lesson," she said with venom. "Trust no one."

Very carefully, I picked my phone up, keeping my eyes on her. I planned to call 911 from right here. I just needed to unlock the screen with the emergency button on it. But my fingers were sweaty, and the phone wasn't recognizing my thumbprint. "You really feel that way? You really feel there's no hope for anyone? Even though, I of all people, was willing to help you?"

She bent down and picked up the tire iron. Immediately I felt stupid for not having taken it away from her. If she went through with her plan, I would need to explain to more than just Adam about what really happened. Panic set in when I considered the fact that someone else might think I was capable of doing what June planned to make up. "I'm sure there was something in it for you. Money, recognition, or maybe you wanted to think you are better than me because you are willing to help someone you don't even like."

I took some time to think about that statement. Was she right? I couldn't see any reason I would benefit from any of this. It's not as though I was accepting any money from her sister. And did I even want the recognition for having helped? Firmly I decided no, it had never been about that for me. Ideally, I'd prefer that no one ever knew what I was up to.

"It doesn't matter!" she shouted, perhaps agitated by my silence. "I don't regret what I did. That woman was going to take everything I had left away from me with her stupid lawsuit. I wanted to marry Jeffrey, but she

sure that wouldn't happen. She claimed I wanted
for his money. Ha! I have taken care of myself
d Shirley almost our whole lives. I didn't need his
money. I don't need anybody."

"So, killing her was the answer?" I asked. I tried
wiping my hands on my jeans again, hoping that my
thumbprint would work this time.

"It shut her up, didn't it?" June retorted. "That
woman had it coming. All she's done her entire life is
try to take from other people. But she made her final
mistake when she threatened to sue me for everything
I had left. All I have is that stupid bakery and my sister.
And now what? Now she wanted that, too? I've worked
too hard to let someone like her ruin my life anymore."

As I pressed my thumb to the digital button, I saw
my phone screen change and it began dialing 911. I
shielded my phone behind me but kept the speaker
in an upright position so the dispatcher could hear
our conversation. All I had to do was leave it on long
enough for them to trace the location of my call. Hopefully I could stall June long enough for the cops to arrive.

"But what will you do now?" I asked. "Now that
you've killed Millie, you're going to lose everything
anyway. Including your sister."

June regarded me with confusion because I'd raised
my voice. But it wasn't enough to stop her from saying,
"The cops are stupid, and they'll never figure out that
it was really me. What evidence do they have?"

"How did you pull it off anyways?"

"What?"

"It's impossible for you to have done what you did
and then return to your seat without tripping over
something or running into somebody along the way.

And how did nobody see you?" My disbelief in this whole thing was beginning to resurface. Even though she had admitted it to me just minutes before, I still didn't see how it was plausible.

June smiled to herself. "Not as smart as you once thought you were?"

"Unless . . ." I quickly replayed a conversation that I'd had with Jasmine about what we'd seen that day. "You didn't go back to your seat . . . at least not right away. The bathroom right there. You went in there and hid until the lights came back on. Then, knowing that no one was paying any attention to you, you slipped back to your seat during all the commotion of finding Millie's body."

Her smile wavered for the briefest of moments, but she did not confirm or deny my theory.

I took that as my answer. "I'm right, aren't I?"

"Suppose I say that you are correct, will anybody believe that I truly did this?"

I silently prayed that this was all being recorded, and the dispatcher had heard everything—including her insinuated confession—loud and clear.

June seemed to catch on to what I was doing and tried leaning sideways to see behind my back. I twisted just in time, but I gathered that she already knew what was going on because she then dramatically yelled, "Ow! Lana! What are you doing? Please don't hurt me!"

I gaped, completely outraged. But I didn't have a lot of time to be offended because she rose her arm, positioning the tire iron, ready to strike herself.

Dropping my phone again, I dove toward her to stop her disgusting plan before she could get away with it. We struggled for a little bit, and then she kicked me

in the shin, which caused me to crumble forward. In doing so, I involuntarily pushed her back, and we both fell to the ground, the tire iron clattering to the floor as she tried to catch herself.

She landed on her butt and I fell on my side with a hard thud. She struggled to regain her footing and I grabbed hold of her ankle, pulling her toward me so she couldn't get up or reach the iron.

While each of us attempted to stop the other, loud footfalls could be heard echoing outside of the restroom. I heard a few shoes squeak on the bathroom's linoleum tile, but I didn't want to divert my attention.

Then I heard a familiar voice yell, "Freeze, nobody move!"

We did as we were told, and when I craned my neck upward to see who it was, I saw Adam staring down at me.

CHAPTER
30

Adam, his partner, Detective Higgins, and two uniformed police officers were surrounding us in the women's bathroom. Adam holstered his gun and helped me up. Higgins grabbed hold of June's forearm, and hoisted her up while one of the officers reached for his cuffs and began reading her rights. She glared at me as they escorted her away.

"Lana, are you okay?" Adam asked, giving me a once-over. His glance slid over to the tire iron that was now under the bathroom sinks.

"Yeah, I'm fine," I said, rubbing my hip. "My tailbone isn't the only thing bruised anymore."

"My god, what a psycho."

"How'd you know to come here?" I asked, bending down to pick up my phone and purse. Thankfully—one small favor—my phone screen hadn't cracked. Now that would have made me really mad.

"When I got to the Zodiac and didn't see your car in the parking lot, I figured that something must be wrong. You should have beaten me there because I

didn't leave the house until I'd gotten off the phone with Higgins. I didn't even bother going in, I just drove straight here and called him on the way. The uniforms were already on their way here from your 911 call. They briefed us on our way in. I told them to check the bathrooms first since that's the last place I heard from you."

"Well, you guys have amazing timing. I didn't know how much longer I was going to be able to hold her off. She's deceivingly strong for her stature."

He eyed the tire iron. "If she had used that thing on you, I would have had to shoot her myself." He wrapped a protective arm around my shoulder and squeezed. "I still can't believe this whole thing."

"Oh, she wasn't going to use it on *me*," I told him, sinking further into his strong embrace. For a split moment the world slipped away, and I took comfort in knowing that I was once again safe.

"Huh?"

I looked up at him and smirked. "Yeah that's what I said."

"She was planning to use it on herself?" he questioned.

I removed myself from the safety of his arms and grabbed his hand. "Come on, you can listen in while I give my statement to your partner."

After I gave my statement to Higgins, Adam and I made our way to the Zodiac where we filled Megan in on everything that had gone down at Asia Village. That night, all my drinks and appetizers were on the house.

I ate with a ravenous appetite, forgetting how full

I'd been earlier that evening from gorging myself on Chinese food.

When we got home, I promised Adam that I would try and stay out of my trouble for at least another month.

As far as clichéd sayings go, I knew a lot of people said that promises were meant to be broken, but I still fell asleep with a clear conscience that night.

EPILOGUE

Two weeks had passed since my ill-fated confrontation with June Yi. Asia Village had been abuzz ever since the news broke that she was Millie Mao's killer. Several interviews had been requested of both families' siblings and close friends. The lawyer handling the Yi family's side of things made a public apology during the six o'clock news on behalf of June and Shirley. Millie's brother, however, refused all reporters and sent them for a statement directly to his lawyer, who promptly replied, "No comment." There was word that Jeffrey had been in contact with Shirley, but everyone was unclear as to what they'd spoken about. Most thought Shirley was apologizing for her sister's actions. I, of course, found out that little tidbit from the Mahjong Matrons.

And not to be left out of the mix, a few reporters came my way as well. I also declined comment as I'd had enough stints in the paper myself. It didn't stop them from printing my name in the front-page story though. My parents were none too happy to find out

that I had been involved in yet another murder investigation, but I did get some nice text messages of praise from my favorite P.I., Lydia Shepard, who had read all about me in the *Plain Dealer*.

Thankfully, I'd been able to preoccupy my mother with talk of the restaurant updates that I was planning to begin once the sidewalk sale was through, so she got over the news pretty quickly.

My sister had finished her internship at the law firm and was now back to helping out at the restaurant on a more regular basis. She was still being hush-hush about the relationship she was having with Henry. I didn't bring it up to her anymore because I wanted her to think I'd forgotten about the conversations we'd had. But, I hadn't, and as soon as the opportunity arose, I was going to find out one way or another what Anna May was up to.

As far as sightings of Shirley went, there were none. She had been more than devastated to find out her sister was in fact a murderer, obviously, and Yi's Tea & Bakery had been closed ever since June's arrest. The Matrons had tried reaching out to Shirley for support several times, but to no avail.

That's why I was shocked and amazed when she showed up at the noodle house's doors the first day of the sidewalk sale. "Shirley!" I rushed around the hostess station and gave the woman a hug. It was something I'd never imagine myself doing with her of all people, but I felt the situation called for it.

She returned the hug, and there was a look of bewilderment on her face. I guessed that neither one of us had thought the interaction possible. "Hello, Lana. It is nice to see a friendly face."

"How are you holding up? We've all been very worried about you."

She took a step back and nodded. "Yes, I thought it might be best to hide myself for a while. It is difficult to share a face with someone who is a killer."

The thought hadn't occurred to me, and now that she mentioned it, I realized that Shirley had changed her appearance considerably. Her hair was now much longer, and she had it curled loosely, instead of wearing it pin-straight like she always had in the past. She was also wearing makeup that seemed a little too dark for her complexion, and the clothes she had on were bright, happy colors versus the usual bland outfits she and June were accustomed to wearing.

"You look very nice," I said awkwardly. It seemed like an unusual situation to compliment someone in, but I didn't know what else to say.

"Thank you," she said, color rising to her cheeks. "I won't keep you; I know today is a big day. I was only stopping by to thank you again for your kindness and for believing in my sister even though she didn't deserve it."

"You're welcome, Shirley. I'm really sorry that things turned out the way they did."

"You and me both," she returned. "I also wanted to apologize for involving you in this terrible mess." She shook her head. "It is still hard for me to believe. I had no idea my sister was capable of such evil actions."

"I think that's normal," I said with reassurance. "You can't always know what's going on inside someone else's head, no matter how close you are to them."

"Yes, perhaps you are correct about this." She gave me a resolute nod and turned to leave. "I don't know

when I will return to the shop. Maybe I will sell it . . ." She sighed. "Goodbye, Lana. Take care of yourself."

I said goodbye and watched her leave. I wondered what their future held for them, not just as individuals, but as family.

Kimmy came barreling through the restaurant doors, jerking her thumb over her shoulder repeatedly. "Holy geez, was that Shirley Yi that just came through here?"

"Yeah, she doesn't look like herself, does she?"

"You're not kidding. Someone went a little heavy on the Lancôme if you ask me," Kimmy snorted, folding her arms over her chest. "How's the old girl doing?"

I shrugged. "As good as she can, I suppose. She's taking some time off, might even close the tea shop."

"Wow." She let out a low whistle. "That shop's been around since the beginning. As much as I never cared for the old biddies, it's hard to think of it not being there."

"I know. The whole thing is so weird."

The two of us stood in front of the doors, gazing out into the plaza, our attention focused on the darkened bakery.

Kimmy shifted, and I could feel her studying me from the corner of my eye. She nudged me with her elbow. "The sidewalk sale looks like it's going to be a success though. Good job, Lee."

I let my eyes drift over the length of the indoor plaza and watched as people starting to arrive bustled to and from the many beloved shops of Asia Village. Each storefront had folding tables in front of their entrances covered with sale items and bargains too good to pass up.

"I think I need to get some fresh air," I said to my friend.

We stepped out into the noisy plaza and passed Vanessa at our own table filled with chafing dishes containing various appetizers like steamed dumplings, pork buns, and teriyaki sticks, along with General Tso's chicken, vegetable lo mein, and other various lunch menu specials. My teenage helper was more than happy to come in for some extra cash in her paycheck, and I was relieved for the help.

I signaled to her that I was stepping out for a minute, and Kimmy walked with me, stopping in front of her shop. "The drama is over, Lana. You can take a deep breath now, okay? Things can go back to normal and you can find a new wacky color to dye your hair."

I smirked. "How are things with Peter?"

She bobbed her head back and forth. "Better. He gave me a key to his place. It was kinda cute because he put it in a box like it was a gift."

Smiling at the news, I decided to keep the fact that it was my idea a secret. "That's great. I'm so happy for you guys. You're really a great couple"

"Yeah, well, just don't tell him I said it was cute." She grinned.

"Deal."

"He just moves slower than I do, and this whole girlfriend thing is new to him. I have to respect his feelings."

I nodded in return and we said goodbye after I wished her luck on an eventful sale day.

Right as I was about to head out the main entrance, I almost ran right into Samantha Hui, who was probably

hurrying along to the salon. I know the Asian Accents ladies were anticipating a lot of business from the side-walk sale.

"Watch yourself," Samantha spat at me as she passed me.

"Oh, excuse me," I replied, almost losing my bal-ance as I moved to get out of her way. As I straight-ened myself, her tone settled on my nerves, causing me to pause and turn back around. "Wait a minute," I said, moving in her direction.

She whipped around. "Yeah?"

"What's your problem with me? Did I do something to offend you?" I asked. I couldn't understand why she seemed to only be mean to me. It made no sense.

Now that I knew she wasn't guilty of anything, I tried to view her in a different light, but all I could see was her nasty disposition, and her attitude with me just now wasn't helping. I thought back on my conversation with Evelyn and wondered if she had been correct in that Samantha was just bad news.

Samantha let out a snicker. "You're actually asking me that? What, are we in fourth grade?"

I furrowed a brow at her. "Huh? I'm asking you like a grown woman."

"Whatever," she replied, shaking her head. "Okay, fine. There's just something about you I don't like." She sized me up again just like she had that day at the salon. "Either it's because you're a busybody and it's written all over you, or you're a goody-goody. Any way you spin it, I just don't like you. Can't be friends with everyone, right? Now, if you'll excuse me, I'm late to work, so thanks for that."

I stood there watching after her, stupefied and

slack-jawed. Guess we had our new version of June Yi on site, at least when it came to me. It would be interesting to see how this would pan out in the future. That was, if she even decided to stay in town.

Doing the best to brush off the idea of a new arch-nemesis, I made my way outside and opened the doors, thankful for the light breeze. As I took a deep breath and tried to relax my mind, my attention couldn't help but shift over to the spot where the fateful car accident had occurred.

A feeling of sadness came over me and my mind filtered through all the events that had taken place, and then cycled back through all my interactions with June Yi since I'd first begun working at the plaza.

As much as I hadn't liked her, I would have never seen it coming. Sure, I'd felt often enough that it might be plausible given her unpleasant nature. But when push really came to shove, I didn't want to believe it was real. I couldn't imagine what that would have been like for her own sister. For a moment, I appreciated the fact that *my* own sister's greatest flaw was her ability to nag me to death.

The whole ordeal made me think of something my mother had said to me not too long ago about people surprising you and being so hurt by something they'd willingly blame anybody for anything. In this instance, that seemed true. June took issue with everyone ruining her life, except for herself. In the end, we create our own outcomes, and whether they be good or bad is completely up to us.

And you can call me crazy all day long, but even after all I'd seen, I wasn't ready to give up on the human race like June had. There was still good in this

world, and positivity podcasts or not, I would always strive to keep seeing it wherever it would flourish.

Besides, I still had two whole weeks left to uphold my promise of staying out of trouble with Adam. So, if my little world could just behave itself for the time being . . . that'd be great.

Read on for a look ahead to

Fatal Fried Rice . . .

The next installment of the Number One Noodle Shop Mystery series by Vivien Chien . . .

Now available from St. Martin's Paperbacks!

Read on for a look ahead to

Fatal Fried Rice . . .

The next installment of the Kung...One Noodle Shop Mystery series by Vivien Chien.

Now available from St. Martin's Paperbacks!

CHAPTER
1

"If you tell anyone about this, I'm gonna have to kill you," I said, staring my best friend squarely in the eye.

"Okay, geez, Lana. I won't tell anyone. No need to be so dramatic." Megan rolled her eyes as theatrically as possible.

"No one can know what I'm doing or where I'm going. Not even Adam. If they were to find out . . ." I paused. "Well, I don't even want to think about what would happen."

"I said okay, Lana Lee. Now will you get going? If you don't leave right now, you're going to be late."

I checked the time on my cell phone. I hated it when she was right. "Fine, I'm leaving. If anyone comes looking for me—"

"No one is going to come looking for you. Would you relax?" Megan stood from her seat at the kitchen table and waved her hands at me, shooing me out of our apartment.

I patted my black pug, Kikkoman, on the head and made my way out the door.

As I hurried through the parking lot, I debated on whether or not I was being dramatic. Perhaps. But if my mother found out that her youngest daughter, and manager to the family restaurant, Ho-Lee Noodle House, was taking a Chinese cooking class—with strangers—her hair would probably light on fire.

A few weeks ago, my older sister, Anna May, who can be an absolute thorn in my side, had begun giving me an extra hard time and teasing me relentlessly on my lack of cooking skills in the Asian cuisine department. Did I love Chinese food? Yes. Did I want to cook it myself? Not really.

Aside from making rice, the whole thing was an ordeal that I'd rather not get mixed up in. But, with me now in charge of the family business, it was a little odd that I didn't know how to make eighty-five percent of the items on our menu. Not that there was really a need for me to do much cooking at the noodle house. Our head cook, and one of my very best friends, Peter Huang, was miraculously never sick, and didn't request many days off. In the instances where he was out for the day, our evening chef and backup, Lou, would pick up the slack. My sister and mother were then next in line for kitchen duty. So, really, was any of this necessary? It was still a question I couldn't answer.

But, man, did it really eat at me that my sister was being this relentless. So here I was on a Tuesday evening, driving out to the city of Parma, a large suburb of Cleveland, Ohio, for an adult course in ethnic cooking. I'd been nonchalantly watching the course listings at a local learning center as each quarter provided the community with a different ethnicity. The last class had been for Mexican food, but oddly enough I can wrap a burrito like nobody's business, so I figured I

was okay in that department. When I saw that they were featuring Chinese food for the next eight weeks, I signed up for the class posthaste.

September in Northeast Ohio can be an interesting time. Things either get cold really fast and we're forced into an early winter, or we're blessed with random spurts of eighty-degree days that go all the way into December. Right now, we were experiencing a warmer than usual beginning to the fall season. And that was perfectly fine with me since I was not a huge fan of chilly weather.

I took 480 eastbound toward the Brookpark area, blasting my stereo and singing along to the Artic Monkeys. It's the only time you'll catch me testing my vocal abilities. All things considered, I was in pretty high spirits. It had been a rough summer at Asia Village, the plaza that houses our family's restaurant, and it was nice to look forward to doing something regular and mundane. I honed in on the fact that eight weeks from now, I was going to have some impressive Asian culinary skills and would wow my sister and my mom. Of course, my boyfriend, Adam Trudeau, would be amazed too, but he didn't really care either way if I could cook Chinese food. I think the man would be happy if we had chicken wings and curly fries every night of the week.

I merged off the freeway at the Tiedeman Road exit, and turned right heading toward Barton's Adult Learning Center that was on York right across from a local community college. Within ten minutes, I was turning into the parking lot of the two-story, glass building and feeling the excitement of my secret jump around in my belly.

When I got out of the car, I turned toward the street

to look across the way at Cuyahoga Community College. It had been a long time since I'd been on this side of town. Memories of times past flooded my mind as my eyes swept over the length of the Tri-C campus. Though Megan and I had graduated from Cleveland State University, I spent a little time at the local college. Aside from the community events they held, like music festivals and Fourth of July celebrations, I'd taken a few courses there back in my college days.

My line of sight travelled over to the southern entrance of the school, and I visualized a younger, more innocent version of myself scurrying to the doors, rushing to get to class. A laugh escaped at the thought of how naïve I had been at the time, and though I'd mostly held on to my idealistic ways, there were parts of me that had changed. I was now more aware of the darkness that hid in society, and for a brief moment I wished for those careless days of thinking that nothing horrible could touch you. Though I am only twenty-eight years old, the times of thinking that I'm invincible are long gone.

Some of that is partially due to the things I've experienced in the past year, a few murders, a boatload of deceptions, and, of course, working with the public.

I shook the thoughts away and turned to head toward the main entrance of Barton's. They'd provided a map in their course book, and I pulled it out of my tote bag to find my way. The adult learning center wasn't very big and looked like a repurposed office building. The lobby led into an open common area covered in neutral tones with couches, chairs and dark wooden tables sprinkled throughout. Artwork by local talent adorned the walls and I vaguely remembered reading in the course book that everything was for sale. I thought

that was nice of the school to support local artists, and I made a mental note to check out what was for sale.

I found my class at the end of the hall, and watched a variety of people walk into the room, noting that so far, I was the only one of Asian descent. Even though I'm only half Taiwanese, you wouldn't know it by looking at me. A little bit of insecurity slipped in at the idea of what people would think of someone like me taking a class like this. Shouldn't I already know how to cook Chinese food? Didn't I have a family member that could teach me these sorts of things? Should I tell people that I was adopted?

I shook my head at that last thought. *Nonsense, Lana, no one is even going to be thinking about you because they are too concerned with themselves.* I squared my shoulders, took a deep breath, and continued on into the room, repeating positive affirmations in my head. This was going to be the best cooking class ever.

CHAPTER 2

I walked into the classroom with my chin up, attempting not to recreate the sensations of insecurity and doubt that come along with something like your first day in high school. Legend has it that some people actually looked forward to their first day, and rumors from past generations often said those were the best years of your life. If you're asking me specifically, that still remains to be seen. I have never actually met anyone in my age bracket that can confirm that supposed truth.

The room was almost full, and I found myself staring into a gathering of faces that well represented the American melting pot minus the Asian demographic. A mixture of ethnicities and ages sprinkled the eight cooking stations lined up neatly in two rows. A larger, more elaborate cooking island stood at the front of the class.

While I assessed the room, I hadn't realized that I'd frozen in place near the door and was staring blankly at everyone in front of me. Suddenly, I was sixteen

years old all over again and wondering if I'd forgotten to do something crucial like zip my pants.

A thin, blonde woman in her mid-fifties who sat at the table closest to the door smiled brightly at me. "Hello, are you the class instructor?"

A nervous laugh bubbled out at the insinuation and it took me a minute to put two and two together as to why she would assume that *I* was the teacher. "Oh, no . . . I'm here to take the class too."

She tilted her head in confusion, but did not say anything else.

I smiled awkwardly and headed to the last empty cooking island all the way in the back of the room. Some things never change, I guess. While my mother had always firmly believed that I should be front and center in any class I was taking, so that my teacher would notice me, truth be told, I didn't like the attention. Never in my life have I been the person who raises their hand to answer or ask questions. Funny considering that now all I seem to do in my spare time is ask people things.

I settled my purse on the stainless-steel countertop, and placed my Asia Village tote bag on the available stool next to me. A few people turned to look my way, but I pretended to be preoccupied with putting my phone on silent and avoided making eye contact.

A few minutes later, a middle-aged Asian woman walked into the room carrying a box of supplies in her arms and a few tote bags slung over her shoulder. She was pretty in a simple sort of way with shoulder-length, black hair that was smooth, straight and lacked definition. Her eyeliner and eyebrows were tattooed on, a fad that was extremely popular with their gen-

eration. Aside from that, she had no actual makeup on except for a neutral gloss that was barely visible.

A kind smile spread over her lips as she acknowledged the room. "Hello, I'm Margo Han, and I'll be your cooking teacher for the next eight weeks." She set the box down on the counter and removed the tote bags from her shoulder.

Scattered "hellos" floated around the room as we watched her unpack the box of utensils and bags of supplies she'd brought in. When she was finished, she turned to the large, dry erase board behind her and wrote her name in red marker in the top right corner.

Capping the marker, she turned around to address the group. "The way this class will be structured is one week of demonstration rotated with one week of hands-on learning. We will learn four popular Chinese dishes to prepare in the next eight weeks. Since I'll spend the first hour of tonight's class going over the basics of utensils, equipment and popular ingredients used to prepare Asian meals, we'll be learning how to make a simple recipe of fried rice for our first dish. It's the least time consuming of what I have prepared for you to learn. I'll start with roll call and then we'll get right into it."

The class attendees all nodded along as the teacher spoke, and I found myself relieved that we would be starting out with something easy like fried rice. I basically knew most of the steps for that as I'd watched my mother make it quite a few times in my life. I wasn't a huge fan of fried rice and preferred white over it any day, but this was a good way to get my feet wet and build some confidence.

After she finished calling names, Margo began

talking about cooking utensils and popular Asian ingredients. Within five minutes my mind and thoughts started to drift over to people watching mode. I will be the first to admit that my attention span is not the greatest. And when left to my own devices, I tend to phase off into la-la land.

The majority of people in the class were women, but there were a handful of men too. Most of the women were older than me, but there were two who seemed to be close in age to myself. I took some time evaluating each person and what their purposes behind taking this class might be, wondering if I was the only one doing this to show up a family member.

At the front of the class, I noticed a rather irate-looking woman sitting next to the blonde who questioned me earlier. Maybe it was just her face, but she appeared to be scowling at our instructor. Her body language also seemed rigid and her hands were clenching the edge of the cooking island. I couldn't imagine what her issue would be. Margo was explaining Chinese Five Spice powder, a popular blend of seasonings that is used for a lot of Asian meat dishes.

The mixture traditionally includes cinnamon, fennel seeds, anise, ground cloves, and Szechuan pepper, but different variations existed, some substituting licorice root over anise, for example. But this wasn't anything to get worked up over.

I decided to pay attention to Margo for a few minutes, and realized she was making eye contact with everyone in the room except for the angry woman. The speculative side of me couldn't help but wonder what that was all about. Maybe this woman had taken a class instructed by Margo in the past and didn't like

her methods. Or maybe she thought she knew more than the teacher. There was always at least one know-it-all in every class.

At the end of our explanatory hour, Margo gave us a fifteen-minute bathroom break and the opportunity to stretch our legs. She intended to set up her station while we were gone and when we returned, the actual cooking lesson would begin.

On my way back from the restroom, I ran into one of the younger women in my class. She was considerably taller than me, and I put her at a solid 5'11" compared to my meager 5'4". If I had to guess, I'd say she was either my age or slightly younger.

Dazzling a sparkling white smile, she approached me as I neared the brick pillar she'd been leaning against outside our classroom. "Hi, you're Lana, aren't you?"

I returned her smile and stepped to the side, getting out of the way of others returning to the room. "Yes, that's me."

"I'm Bridget. I absolutely love your hair and wanted to ask where you get it done." Her hand lifted to her own chestnut brown hair, and she ran her fingers through the loose curls. "I am so bored with mine and I really want to do something drastically different. You know . . . make a statement." Her eyes widened with excitement as if she were sharing a conspiracy theory with me. "But I'll be honest, I'm kind of afraid to have it done."

"Oh, well, thank you," I replied. My hair was currently recovering from a bout of attempts to dye my bleached peek-a-boo highlights with a metallic gray that didn't go over so well. Frustrated with the results,

my stylist and I were now adding in a cobalt blue color to help bring out the appearance of tinted silver. "I go to a place called Asian Accents."

Her eyes lit up and she gasped. "I knew you seemed familiar. I thought I saw you in the newspaper a while back. There was that article with you and that P.I. lady . . . Lydia something?"

I blushed. My hopes of not being recognized by anyone in the class were shot down. Although I hadn't thought it would be from the newspaper. I was more worried about running into a Ho-Lee Noodle House customer. "Yeah, that was me." She was referring to when I'd teamed up with Lydia Shepard, a local private investigator, who helped me handle a tricky situation for Donna Feng, the property owner of Asia Village.

"So, wait . . . that means you're the manager of that noodle restaurant, right? The one that's over there in Fairview Park?"

"Yeah . . ." My face continued to warm; the redness of my cheeks was going to start producing heat waves any minute now. "That's where the salon is located, in that same plaza."

"Oh ok. Then how come you're in this class?" she asked, pointing toward the classroom door. "I'd think if anything you'd be able to teach it yourself."

"You'd think," was my reply.

Laughing, she nudged my arm. "Don't worry, I won't judge. I'm a disaster in the kitchen. Before I started taking cooking classes, I was lucky I could even boil an egg. A few months ago, I started dating this guy and he totally made fun of me because I didn't know how to make French toast. So, I started taking all these courses to impress him with my newly found culinary skills."

I laugh good-naturedly remembering the first time

I'd cooked for Adam. He'd been quite surprised that I'd known how to do anything in the kitchen at all. "I can relate. How many classes have you taken so far?"

"This will be my third course at Barton's. I took one on general cooking basics, and then a Mexican food class."

"That's great, I hope it's working out for you. You must really like him to go through all this."

"Well, everyone always talks about how the way to a man's heart is through his stomach. I didn't think I'd care about that sort of thing, but here I am." She ended the sentence with a shrug.

Noticing that most of our classmates had returned, I jerked a thumb over at the entrance. "Wanna get back in there? Looks like she's going to start soon."

Bridget nodded in agreement. "Yeah, we better get back so we don't miss anything important. It was really nice chatting with you. Maybe in the next class we can sit together. It would be nice to have a partner who actually has a personality. The guy who's sitting next to me has zero social skills."

I chuckled. "I'd like that."

As we headed back into the room, Bridget turned around and whispered, "Oh, and don't worry, I won't tell anyone who you are. It'll be our little secret."

Praise for the

"Will appeal to fans
mysteries."
—*Booklist*

"Funny, warm, and terrifying at times, *Wonton Terror* adds yet another delicious dish to Vivien Chien's growing menu of enticing, cozy mysteries."
—*Suspense* magazine

"Provides plenty of twists and turns and a perky, albeit conflicted, sleuth."
—*Kirkus Reviews* on *Dim Sum of All Fears*

"Vivien Chien serves up a delicious mystery with a side order of soy sauce and sass."
—Kylie Logan, bestselling author of *Gone with the Twins*

"Thoroughly entertaining . . . fun and delicious."
—*RT Book Reviews*

"*Death by Dumpling* is a fun and sassy debut with unique flavor, local flair, and heart."
—Amanda Flower, Agatha Award–winning author of *Lethal Licorice*